Changing Lara

Changing Lara

ANNA JACOBS

Allison & Busby Limited
11 Wardour Mews
London W1F 8AN
allisonandbusby.com

First published in Great Britain by Allison & Busby in 2019.

A CIP catalogue record for this book is available from
the British Library.

First Edition

ISBN 978-0-7490-2365-2

Typeset in 11/16 pt Sabon by
Allison & Busby Ltd

Chapter One

Lara looked her boss in the eye and said it slowly and firmly, hoping her feeling of relief didn't show. 'I'm afraid I can't accept that posting. I'm about to retire.'

'*You!* But you're only fifty-two, in your prime.'

'Gunther, I'm fed up of moving all over the world for the company, more than ready to settle down.'

He chuckled. 'Good tactical move. OK, we'll increase your salary.'

That was his answer to everything: throw money at it. 'Sorry, but the answer is still no.'

He frowned. 'I should have explained it better. Mal Porter has just dropped dead in Australia and we desperately need you to take over there.'

She was startled. 'Mal? The fitness freak?'

'The same. Just goes to show that nothing in this life is foolproof, eh?'

Nothing and no one, she thought, and that only made her more certain she was doing the right thing in retiring early.

'Mal was in the middle of a big project and you're the only one with the skills and experience to take over mid-stream. The financial penalties will be huge if we don't bring it in on time.'

She felt more concerned about the people involved. 'Poor Mal. His wife must be feeling gutted. They were such a close couple.'

'Yes. Yes, of course.' With barely a pause, Gunther added, 'So will you at least consider it?'

She spoke without thinking it through, wanting only to get out of this easily. 'You'd have to double my salary to get me out to Australia. My family are all living in England now and my first grandchild is about to enter the world.'

'*Double it!*'

'Yes.' She didn't let him outstare her. 'I'm not at all keen to do this, Gunther.'

'I'll, um, see what the powers that be say.'

She didn't expect them to agree to *that*, but when they did offer to double her present salary, plus supply totally subsidised accommodation, if she'd take over the project, she had to rethink.

After doing some sums and deciding she could face a few more months of working, she agreed.

That meant she missed the birth of her granddaughter, which she regretted deeply, but she told her daughter about the amount of money involved and after the first stiff reaction, Darcie said she understood.

'I won't take on anything else after this.'

'You said that last time, Mum.'

'Well, this time I mean it with all my heart.'

She really did mean it. She'd changed in the past year or

two, didn't exactly understand what was going on inside her head now but she definitely *felt* different.

As for her son, well, Lara doubted she'd see much of Joel even if she was living in England because he sounded to be busier than ever. All he said when she told him about her new job was, 'Good for you, Ma!'

'It's my last project.'

He chuckled. 'Oh yeah? You said that last time. Hang on. Ah. Have to go. There's someone I need to speak to on the other line. Keep in touch.'

And he was gone.

Joel was as bad as she used to be about work, Lara decided. No point in telling him to slow down and smell the roses. He liked the smell of money far more. It was no wonder he'd left several broken relationships behind him. Who'd want to settle down with a man who was never there, however personable he was?

Or with a woman who was never there.

Lara had moved on far enough from her divorce by now to acknowledge that Guy had been right about one thing: she had been away too often to maintain a worthwhile marriage. He was the sort of man who enjoyed company and he'd told her bluntly that he wanted a wife who shared his bed regularly.

It had been a relatively amicable split, compared to some, with regret on both sides but no quarrels over finances. Their relationship had been cooling for a while and she hadn't been willing to give up her job just when she was on the cusp of a big step upwards.

She'd taken that step, but done it alone.

As for Guy, he'd soon started dating again and after

a while he'd found someone else to share his life with.

Lara hadn't. Who did you date when you were the boss? And when most of your staff were younger than you?

There were times when Lara regretted choosing what she now thought of ironically as her 'brilliant career'; there were other times when she was very proud of what she'd achieved.

Had it all been worth it? Mostly she thought it had, but sometimes, in the middle of yet another dark, lonely night in a bland, beige hotel room, well, she couldn't help wondering.

Lara had worked in Australia before and once again she enjoyed many things about living down under. Who wouldn't? Great climate, friendly people, excellent food.

To her surprise, however, this time she didn't enjoy the job itself. Been there, done that. She was bored by the minutiae of revamping the Australian branch. She couldn't raise any enthusiasm for sales figures or customer communication programs, let alone selection procedures for new staff. She was missing her family more than she'd expected to, far more than she'd ever done before.

She had only 'met' her tiny granddaughter online and longed to hold her. She heard from Darcie regularly about how adorable little Minnie was and what a wonderful grandfather Guy was.

The latter hurt more than Lara had expected.

She soon stopped showing baby photos to her colleagues, most of whom only pretended an interest, but in private she regularly studied the photos of the baby she'd never touched, the baby who was her flesh and blood. She even shed tears over them. She must be getting soft in her old age.

Old? She wasn't old. Well, not very.

The day she turned fifty-three, she bought herself a bottle of champagne but didn't open it. She scolded herself for getting upset. She should be used to having no one to celebrate her birthday with by now. But the tears took a while to stop.

A few weeks before she planned to retire for real, there was a business downturn and the company began shedding jobs, something it did periodically. Brilliant! She applied for voluntary redundancy.

Morris Turner, current CEO of the whole Australasian region, visited Sydney and called Lara into his office for a private meeting. 'I'd like you to withdraw your application for redundancy, Lara. We need you to move to Singapore and—'

'I'd rather not.'

'We'll make it up to you financially, of course.'

'No, thank you.'

His voice became persuasive. 'Just give us a few more months, Lara. Come on, you know you enjoy managing these projects. You've handled this last one brilliantly.'

She stared at his elegant figure: stylish business suit, modern hairstyle and all. What stood out to her were the gleaming white teeth parted in a slight smile. He'd spent a lot of money on having his teeth fixed. She was suddenly annoyed by the falseness of that smile, which he could don so easily. It was very different from the real smile he occasionally wore when he was with his wife.

'Lara? Are you with me?'

'What? Oh, sorry. You're wrong, Morris. I no longer enjoy managing these projects.'

He continued to try to persuade her to accept and when she didn't give in, the discussion turned nasty.

'I'll make sure you don't get that redundancy,' he said suddenly.

'If you do that, I'll make sure it tarnishes your reputation as a manager. It could even be seen as discrimination against a woman because Harley Black has been granted redundancy and he's at my level.'

'Be very careful that you can live on your savings, then, Lara, because if you don't do this for me, I'll make sure you never find work in the company again, possibly even in the industry.'

Her voice was as sharp as his. 'I'll never *want* to find work like this again, Morris. I have my next occupation all planned. It's part-time and will be far more enjoyable.'

She started towards the door without waiting for him to say anything else. And he must have believed her because he let her go.

Back in her own office, she sat down, covering her face with her hands for a few moments and using a breathing exercise to calm herself down. She'd suspected for a while that she was in danger of burning out if she didn't take care, but she hadn't told anyone that.

Retirement day came at last, and to her amusement her last working day was 1st April. It seemed appropriate, she thought as she got ready for the obligatory party and fuss.

Inevitably, Morris Turner was there and at one stage, he cornered her. 'I meant what I said, Lara. You won't easily find another job. No one messes with me.' His smile never faltered as he spoke.

'For heaven's sake, Morris. I didn't do it to mess with you. I need some downtime.'

'You've never needed it before. And smile, damn you. Do you want everyone to know we're at odds?'

'Doesn't matter to me now.'

She turned and walked away from him, nodding and saying suitable goodbyes to people as she pushed steadily through the crowd.

Done, she thought as she left the ugly modern office building. *Over and done with*.

She didn't look back.

It was a huge relief to board her flight to the UK that evening. The flight seemed to go on for ever but at last they landed at Heathrow.

After she'd retrieved her suitcases from the carousel, she joined the shorter queue of British citizens returning to the UK, passing quickly through the various checks to the airport exit. She was home to stay.

Only, was this her home now? She hadn't lived in the UK continuously for years.

Yes, of course it was home! She'd grown up here, married here and her children were here. There was nowhere else she would want to go.

She'd even found herself somewhere to live, couldn't wait to see the house she'd bought online. It was in a new housing development in Wiltshire, called Penny Lake. The name had caught her eye first, then the fact that it was a small development of the sort often called leisure villages, on the same campus as a golf club and hotel.

As long as she wasn't extravagant, from today onwards

she wouldn't need to work at all unless she chose to.

Why wasn't she bouncing with joy, then?

Why did she feel so off-balance?

It was mid-morning local time when she wheeled her luggage trolley towards the meeting point and looked for the driver of the limo her financial adviser, John Crichton, had volunteered to organise to take her to Wiltshire. She scanned the signs various drivers were holding up to collect their passengers but there was no 'Lara Perryman' on any of them. Strange, that. Perhaps her car had been held up by traffic.

She waited impatiently for a few minutes but no driver looking for her joined the group. Most of them collected their passengers and left within minutes.

Taking out her phone, she rang John's office to find out what was happening but there was no answer. His receptionist was usually there at this time of day, even if he was out. Lara had never really taken to Sandra, but the woman was super-efficient, you had to grant her that. However, there wasn't even his usual 'sorry to miss you' answerphone message today.

Almost half an hour crawled past and still there was no sign of Lara's vehicle – nor had she managed to get through to John's office.

Feeling more than a little frustrated, she decided she'd waited long enough. What had gone wrong? Could he have mistaken the day? It seemed unlikely. And even if the car he'd hired for her had been in an accident, someone would have phoned John and he'd have got in touch with her. Only they'd have got no answer from the office either.

In the end she decided to hire a car and drive herself to Wiltshire. The delay made her wish she hadn't given in to John's insistence on arranging transport for her, but he was usually more efficient than this. He'd managed her finances ever since her divorce and done it well, too.

She intended to organise her own finances from now on and was looking forward to doing that.

She glanced round for car hire companies, not looking forward to driving along the crowded M4 motorway. It wasn't pleasant at the best of times and today she was exhausted before she even began. However, needs must. She'd probably go straight to bed when she got to the hotel on the same site as her as yet unfurnished house.

After going through the necessary formalities, she was driven out to the depot where you picked up your vehicle.

They had coffee or tea available for customers. The tea was ghastly stuff but she downed a plastic cup of it quickly to help keep herself awake, then was taken outside and given a gabbled run-through of how the controls worked.

Once the young guy had gone back inside, she settled into the driver's seat, following the signs to the M4 and easing into the heavy traffic. Thank goodness she was on the very last stage of her journey.

She didn't bother with the radio because her mind was on her new house. It had been ready for several months now, but her diversion to the Australian project had stopped her even checking it out. She'd bought it while working in America from the online plans, an impulsive act very unlike her.

She'd only been half-heartedly looking through houses for sale in England at the time, just to start getting the feel of property prices in Wiltshire, where she'd decided to settle.

Of course she'd contacted the builder and asked a lot of questions before she signed up for a house. She wasn't *that* rash.

A sign read 'Slough'. She nodded at it, then went back to her thoughts.

John Crichton had counselled her against buying a house like that but for once she'd ignored his advice. She was good at reading house plans and could use them to mentally walk through the place. The design she'd chosen would suit her needs perfectly and the fact that it was in a leisure village would bring her a way of life as well as a home. There would be neighbours to meet, things to do. She might even take up golf. No, perhaps not. She'd never been in to sport. But walking, yes. She would enjoy walking in the English countryside.

Her daughter, Darcie, and her son-in-law had gone to check out the development and later checked her finished house. They'd said it had been well built.

In spite of that, her accountant had said it would be risky to make the final payment till she'd seen it herself. She'd ignored that advice too. Her daughter wasn't a fool, nor was her son-in-law.

Besides, this developer wasn't a big, faceless international company but one where you were in direct contact with the people who owned the business. She didn't know why but she instinctively liked and trusted Molly Santiago, who took care of sales and customer relations at Penny Lake while her husband supervised the building side of things.

It was like that sometimes, even online: you felt an instant rapport with some people and not with others.

The redundancy payment Lara had received added a nice extra chunk to her savings. It was sitting in her personal bank account right now. It would more than cover furnishing her new home and buying a car.

John had also said he could get a better day rate than she could for placing the money temporarily, but she'd wanted to have it to hand so she'd refused his offer.

When she stopped at a motorway services near Reading for a comfort break, she tried again to reach John with the same result: no answer.

She was beginning to feel uneasy about this. He hadn't had a heart attack or something, had he? But even if he had, the answering service would still be operating, surely?

She'd soon be passing Swindon. Living round there would be convenient for visits to her daughter and her son, because Joel worked in Bristol and Darcie lived in nearby Gloucestershire. Lara's mother had died a few years ago and her father had found a new partner and moved to live with her in Portugal. Lara would drop him an email once she was settled in, maybe go and spend a few days with him and whatshername, as he'd invited her to do. Or maybe not.

She'd felt a tinge of envy at the thought of how quickly both her ex and her father had found new partners, though Guy's second marriage hadn't lasted, had it?

She'd have liked to find someone too but it just hadn't happened. So all right, she would remain Ms Independent and cope on her own with whatever life threw at her. She was used to that.

Not long now to her turn-off. She couldn't wait to get there.

Chapter Two

Ross Welby stared across the table at his soon-to-be ex, who was putting on a 'poor me' act and doing it brilliantly, as usual. He hoped the arbitrator wasn't easily fooled by pretty women like her and that his own feelings of annoyance hadn't shown too clearly in his face.

He and Nonie Jayne were here to decide the fairest way to settle matters financially so that they could finalise their divorce. Arbitration was the only thing they'd agreed about so far, because neither of them wanted to spend a fortune on lawyers and court cases.

He'd refused to give her what she wanted because she'd been ridiculously greedy in her demands. He couldn't afford to pay that much and keep the home that had been in his family for nearly two hundred years, could he?

And why should he anyway? They'd only been married a short time and she wasn't dependent on him for living expenses.

Talk about a mismatch. She was still the most beautiful

woman he'd ever met, but once they'd married and started living together full-time, he'd found out that they had nothing whatsoever in common except for physical attraction.

There was a tap on the door and a young man peered in. 'Sorry to disturb you, Mr Smyth, but there's an urgent message for Mr Welby and the caller said it was some last-minute information relevant to this meeting.'

Smyth waved one hand in a gesture of permission to pass on the message.

Nonie Jayne folded her arms and let out a huff of annoyance.

'Mrs Morgan says please could you phone her ASAP, Mr Welby.'

Ross looked sideways at Smyth. 'She's my cousin and she's keeping an eye on my house. I could phone her from the corridor outside, if that's all right with you? I'll be quick, I promise.'

Smyth looked at his watch. 'Why don't you take it in here, then I can decide immediately whether it's relevant to our meeting or not? We do need to get on with this.'

So Ross took out his phone and switched it back on. Fiona wouldn't be phoning him for no reason.

She answered immediately. 'Ah, Ross. Thank goodness I caught you. There's been another incident here today, as you suspected there might be, but we repelled the would-be invaders.'

'Thanks, Fiona. I owe you for that.'

'There's more. The private investigator phoned. He said your ex was definitely behind the other attempt to get into your house and he found out something else. I've sent you an email with a summary and an attachment containing the details.'

'Good.'

'How's it going?'

'Slowly.'

He ended the call and switched over to his emails, reading the summary and attachment. Surely this would make a difference to the final payment? He didn't want to lose his long-time family home. He turned to the arbitrator. 'This is definitely relevant to our conversation today, Mr Smyth. See for yourself.'

Nonie Jayne cast a suspicious glance across the table and said in a sharp voice, which was in great contrast to her usual soft tone, 'Surely what we're doing is more important than him picking up his emails!'

Ross ignored her and held out the phone to the arbitrator. 'Here.'

Smyth glanced quickly at the summary, then looked at Ross. 'May I see the attachment as well?'

'Yes, of course.'

A couple of minutes later, Smyth asked, 'Why is your cousin involved?'

'I asked her to look after my house while I was at this hearing because there has already been an attempt to enter it unlawfully. I also hired a security guard to stay with her, not only for her protection but as an independent witness.'

Nonie Jayne pushed her chair back and stood up, her American accent stronger than usual. 'This is *not* why we're here today. I won't stay to—'

The arbitrator looked at her. 'I think you'd better stay, Ms Larson. Unless you're not interested in having any input into my final decision.'

All hung in the balance for a moment, then she sat

down, scowling at them. 'I should have been allowed my own attorney today.'

She'd said that several times and Smyth ignored her remark. 'This appears to be proof that you've been married four times, not two.'

'That isn't a crime!'

'But you stated in your deposition that Ross was your second husband.'

She shrugged.

'And you apparently received large settlements when your former marriages broke up, so you're not as short of money as you claimed.'

Another shrug and a scowl in Ross's direction.

He was still trying to get his head round the idea that he'd been her fourth husband.

'Finally, you seem to have hired people to remove certain objects from Mr Welby's house. You gave them front door keys, so they must have assumed that you had right of entry.'

Nonie Jayne's face twisted with anger and the glance she threw at Ross would have curdled milk. 'Well, it's my house too and I had possessions to retrieve. *He* wouldn't let me in.'

'What possessions?'

'Some ornaments that I'm particularly fond of.'

Ross leant forward. 'Every single item of yours has been returned to you, Nonie Jayne, as you well know. You not only signed a statement to that effect but gave me back the house keys. Which means you must have kept a set.'

She smirked at him briefly, then turned back to the arbitrator and put on her big-eyed, mournful face. 'I hadn't remembered everything when I made the first list, Mr Smyth, I was so upset about him throwing me out. These sentimental items are still missing and he won't let me in to find them.'

Smyth spoke again and this time his voice sounded much more forceful. 'Let me remind you once again that it isn't your house any longer, Ms Larson. We established that at the beginning of today's session and you should take it on board. Mr Welby has offered you a sum of money in full quittance of any further financial obligations, to help you reorganise your life. Since The Gatehouse has been his family's home for over two hundred years, it's perfectly reasonable for him to keep it and for you to move on.'

She blinked her eyes and a couple of tears rolled down her cheeks. Ross knew she could do that at the drop of a hat.

'That's *sooo* unfair! I loved living there and it quickly became *my* home as well! We don't have such beautiful old places in the States.'

Ross snorted in disgust. 'If you loved it so much, why were you looking into selling it just before we split up?'

'I didn't!'

He pulled some papers out of his document case. 'I have statements here from two estate agents about being invited to look round and value the house. I was away on business on the dates they gave me, Mr Smyth. Luckily for me, one of the agents was a friend's son, who asked me why I was selling, or I might not have known about that.'

'I only wanted to know how much it was worth.'

There was a pregnant silence, then she began to sob, doing it as prettily as she did everything when she was on display. She looked very different when indulging in a private quarrel, not nearly as pretty then.

Ross leant forward, raising his voice. 'And the people you sent to the house to retrieve things were trying to take away my most valuable silver, Nonie Jayne. Family treasures.'

'You *gave* them to me after we got married.'

'I'd never do that. They're family heirlooms to be passed on to the next generation.' Ross turned to Smyth. 'The items she's talking about are described and listed in the prenuptial agreement.' He pulled out his copy of it from his folder and showed them, highlighted in bright yellow, offering it to the arbitrator.

'I have a copy, Mr Welby, thank you.' Smyth turned back to Nonie Jayne. 'Ms Larson, you both signed this to say that in case of a break-up you'd each keep what you brought to the marriage.'

The sobs stopped abruptly. 'A prenup isn't legally binding in the UK. Everyone knows that.'

Smyth leant forward, speaking slowly and clearly. 'As I said earlier, it may not be *legally* binding, but most people consider it *morally* binding these days. You should view the one you signed in that way, especially given the brevity of your marriage, Ms Larson. And actually, the British courts have been increasingly taking note of prenups during the past few years, as long as they've been drawn up and signed in a proper legal fashion. Which yours was. The contents of The Gatehouse were checked and the valuable items photographed by an independent valuer as part of that process.'

Ross didn't say anything. His cousin Fiona was the one who'd nudged him to make a prenuptial agreement and he was extremely grateful to her for that.

When Nonie Jayne moved out, after only a few months of marriage, she'd taken a valuable figurine and several pieces of family silver with her. The latter had been traced by the police to London and CCTV had shown the seller to be his ex. He'd threatened to accuse her of theft if she didn't return the rest of the things she'd taken and he'd found them one day on his doorstep. He hadn't had her charged because he'd got the items back.

All he wanted now was to get his divorce finalised and never speak to her again.

Unfortunately, around the time they broke up, his health had begun to deteriorate and then his great aunt Iris had fallen ill. He'd had to supervise the old lady being moved into a hospice until she'd died, which had distracted him more than a little.

After one very stiff visit, Nonie Jayne hadn't gone near his aunt – he could see now that she'd been making sure Iris wasn't wealthy and had lost interest at the mere sight of the small house. He doubted she'd even remember now where his aunt had lived.

He missed Iris greatly and was finding it hard to get down to clearing her house. He would inherit everything from her once they got probate, and it might be mercenary, but thank goodness Iris had died after he and Nonie Jayne had separated, so that his ex had no claim to a share of the inheritance.

His aunt hadn't been rich but she'd left him a small house, which would bring in enough to more than make up for this expensive mess.

The arbitrator looked at Ross. 'All right if I download this document from your private investigator? It'll be relevant to keep a copy of it in our records.'

'Yes, of course. I'll send it to you as an email attachment, shall I? No, how about you do that yourself? Then you'll be certain that what you get won't have been tampered with.'

'Thank you. I will, if you don't mind. But please watch me do it. I don't want to make a mistake or for there to be any doubt in your mind – or Ms Larson's – about exactly what I've done.'

Ross leant closer, nodding as the correct file was forwarded.

Nonie Jayne didn't attempt to check, just drummed her fingers on the tabletop and muttered something to herself.

When he'd finished forwarding the files, Smyth stood up. 'Excuse me for a moment.'

After he'd left the room, Nonie Jayne said in a low voice, 'You'll regret cheating me like this, Ross Welby.'

'No, I won't, because I'm *not* cheating you. You should let your attempt to get more money out of me drop right now. You're leaving our farce of a marriage with a good profit, far more than you could have earned in a year working as a model. Be content with that.'

'You could've afforded to be a lot more generous, you cheapskate. My other husbands were.'

'You must have way overestimated my wealth or I doubt you'd have married me in the first place. I think you were also dazzled by the idea of living in a historical house, however small. I've had to make serious economies to buy you off and you're not getting another penny beyond that if I can help it.'

'Just watch me!'

He'd never seen her so angry or heard her talk so wildly.

'Excuse me.' Smyth had returned and was standing in

the doorway listening unashamedly. 'I wonder if you could confirm that you have a copy of the settlement suggested by Mr Welby, Ms Larson?'

'Of course I do.' She tapped the papers in front of her. 'It's pitiful. How can he cry poverty with all those valuable items in the house?'

He came in and closed the door, sitting down before he continued. 'Please listen carefully: my finding, in view of what has happened today at The Gatehouse and your previous marital situation, and also in view of the very specific prenuptial agreement, is that this list be applied to your situation.'

Nonie Jayne looked older and not nearly as pretty when she gave in to her temper, Ross thought as she stood up and thumped the table.

'He's cheating me!'

'No, he isn't.'

'I shall definitely appeal!' She grabbed her papers and stamped out of the room like a child throwing a tantrum.

Smyth switched off the recording device and looked at Ross. 'You expected something like this to happen today, didn't you?'

'Yes. As far as I can work out, she's been using her beauty to make serial marriages and build herself a fortune and she's furious that I'm not as rich as she thought.'

'Worried about her making an appeal?'

'Yes.'

'Off the record, I doubt she'll succeed, though of course I can't guarantee anything. But this is England and she seems to be judging everything by American precedents. I think you've been very reasonable, given the circumstances.' He paused and frowned. 'Have you any idea of what *she* is worth financially?'

'I know what she *says* she's worth.'

He grinned. 'Maybe if your PI can find that out, you could ask her for financial support.'

Ross rolled his eyes. He didn't want anything from her.

Picking up his document case, he stuffed the papers back into it. This mess was his own fault. If he hadn't stupidly rushed into marriage, it would never have got to this stage. Only, his first marriage had been so happy he'd somehow expected a second one to be the same. He rubbed his forehead, which had started to ache again.

'Are you all right, Mr Welby? You've gone rather pale.'

'I think I'm coming down with the flu.' He didn't tell people he had been diagnosed with chronic fatigue syndrome. Some folk still thought it was an imaginary illness. He wished! Perhaps he should take a holiday or something.

And leave his house unoccupied? No way! He wouldn't feel safe until Nonie Jayne found another fool to marry, hopefully one who lived in Timbuktu!

Chapter Three

Lara slowed down as she left the motorway and drove through the village of Marlbury, which was the closest place to her destination. It was as picturesque as its online photos. She'd take the time to explore it one day.

With the satnav guiding her, she easily found Penny Lake, just to the south. Pushing her tiredness aside, she parked and went into the hotel before she did anything else, smiling at the woman in reception. 'I'd like a room for a night or two, please.'

'I'm so sorry but we're fully booked tonight. We have a big wedding on, you see. They've taken every single room and even so, some of their guests have had to stay elsewhere.'

'Oh dear.'

'We've rooms free from tomorrow onwards, if that's any use, and I can direct you to somewhere nearby for tonight.'

'Thank you. That'd be helpful. I'd better book a room for tomorrow while I can.'

She took the business card of a B&B and walked out to her car, feeling leaden with fatigue and disappointment. As she glanced to her right she could see the village, looking just like its most recent online photos. She drove the couple of hundred yards to the sales office, which was still open, thank goodness.

A woman of about her own age looked up from the desk.

'I'm Lara Perryman. I'm supposed to be taking possession of my house today.'

'Ah, yes! Welcome back to England! I'm Molly Santiago. We've been emailing each other for months, so I feel I know you. It's great to meet in person.'

They shook hands.

'Want to look round your house?'

'I'd love to. I can't do an inspection or anything today, though. I've just got back from Australia and I haven't slept for about thirty hours.'

'You must be exhausted!'

'Way beyond that but I'd still like a quick peek at the house.'

Molly pulled out a sign that indicated she'd be back soon, took some keys out of a drawer and stood up. 'Let's go.'

They walked down a gentle slope and past a few neat houses at various stages of being built. There was a large, completed house beyond the short terrace of houses, with a car in the parking bay. One of the 'detached residences', as the brochure had called them, but it was the small terrace of six houses that Molly headed for.

She flourished one hand at the left-hand house. 'This one is yours.'

As if Lara hadn't devoured the online photos till she knew every pixel by heart!

Unlocking the door, Molly gestured to Lara to go inside first. 'I'll have to come round with you until we officially hand it over and sign the forms. Sorry to intrude on this special moment but we have to be so careful with insurance requirements.'

Lara had been walking round the house mentally for months and as she did it for real, she was thrilled to find it had turned out just as she'd hoped: clean, bright spaces and polished wooden floors. Not a big house, but with decent-sized rooms – there was only her to live in it, after all. A quick look round thrilled her. Her daughter was right. It had been beautifully finished.

She was so looking forward to moving in and furnishing it to her exact taste after the years of rented, characterless 'executive accommodation', mostly in serviced apartments.

She went outside onto the back patio, from which she could see part of the lake itself to the right. It was only about three hundred yards away and she could see herself strolling round it regularly.

Then a huge yawn caught her unawares. 'Sorry. I'd better go and find somewhere to stay. I gather there are a couple of bed and breakfasts nearby.'

'Aren't you staying at the hotel?'

'Unfortunately they've no vacancies.'

'Oh yes, it's the Callander wedding tonight. Big affair.' Molly stopped walking to frown, then said, 'You look exhausted.'

'Tell me about it.' Another yawn fought its way out.

'Um, should you be driving?'

'I shall drive like a careful snail.'

'Look, you're welcome to say no, but you could stay in that caravan for tonight, if you like.' She pointed to a small, rather battered-looking caravan next to the sales office. 'There'd be no charge. It's very basic, but it's clean and has an attached bathroom. I stayed there myself for a while when I first came to work here.'

Lara didn't have to think twice. 'That'd be lovely and I accept happily. I'll still have to drive out to buy some food so perhaps you can tell me the closest place to do that?'

'You could get a full meal or bar snack tonight at the hotel, or buy something to take away from them. You can also get breakfast there tomorrow, however full the hotel is.'

Lara had to struggle not to weep in sheer relief. 'That's *wonderful*! I'm so grateful for your help, Molly.'

'Better come and look inside the caravan first. You may hate the feel of it. It's very small.'

'I doubt I'll pay much attention to my surroundings. I'll be asleep within minutes, I'm sure, because I never sleep much on planes.'

'Let me get the key, then.' She hurried back to the estate office.

Lara walked across to the caravan to wait.

Molly joined her and opened the door. '*Voilà!*'

Lara peered inside. 'It'll be fine.'

'You don't want to check out the amenities?'

'Not as long as you guarantee there is a bathroom, Molly.'

'You poor thing. You really are beyond exhaustion.'

'Yes. Not to mention jetlagged. You're being very kind.'

'I arrived here on my own a few months ago and people

were kind to me. I'm just passing it on. You can do the same one day, pass it forward.'

Lara had heard other people say that sort of thing and thought it, well, a bit New Age, even soppy, but something about Molly said she was being sincere and really meant it. That was a charming attitude to the world.

With her companion's help, Lara took everything she'd brought with her out of the car and into the caravan, then listened to instructions on how the various mechanisms worked. All she really wanted was to be alone so that she could fall into bed and sleep for a million years.

But Molly was frowning at her. 'Don't go to sleep quite yet. I'll bring you some tea-making stuff and a packet of biscuits. You really should have something to eat and drink before you sleep. We keep a supply of that sort of thing in the sales office, so it won't take me a minute.'

It would have been rude to reject this further kindness and now Lara came to think of it, she was rather hungry. She opened her case and got out her nightdress and dressing gown, then her toiletries. The bathroom was tiny but hey, it had everything she needed.

She considered making one last attempt to contact John, but Molly returned just then and the sight of food made Lara set her phone aside.

After consuming a fruit juice and two biscuits, Lara visited the bathroom, kicked off her shoes and wriggled out of her clothes as fast as she could. She couldn't be bothered to set up the double bed, so slipped into the lower of the two bunk beds.

Groaning in delight, she let the world fade away.

*   *   *

When Lara woke, it was daylight and for a few moments she couldn't figure out where she was. Then she remembered and eased herself out of the bunk to visit the amenities, which were in a sort of annexe to which the caravan was connected by a narrow tunnel. She hadn't noticed such details last night.

Staring at her face and tousled hair in the mirror, she grimaced. She still looked deep-down weary.

'Jetlag rules,' she said aloud and took a wonderfully hot shower.

Holding a cup of coffee in her hand, she sat on the steps of the caravan, turning up her face to let the morning light bathe her skin. That always helped banish jetlag, people said, though she wasn't the sort to waste time sunbathing otherwise.

She wondered briefly what had happened to the car that was supposed to pick her up, then shrugged. Water under the bridge. No doubt there would be someone in John Crichton's office today and they'd explain what had happened.

It was still only just after six o'clock and she wondered whether the hotel coffee shop would be open yet. She was absolutely ravenous and no wonder. She'd hardly eaten a thing for the past twenty hours.

On that thought she drained her coffee and went inside, grabbing her shoulder bag and locking up the caravan before following the path across to the hotel.

To her relief, the coffee shop was open and, better still, she was able to go through into the hotel dining room and order a full English breakfast, even this early.

When she came out, full of good food, she paused to watch a group of women making their way past the hotel to the golf course. She'd never been able to understand why people chased little white balls so avidly, but there you were; it took all sorts.

She glanced at her watch again. Still too early to phone John. Too early to do anything really. As she'd found out after her first stint of working in Australia, English people were much later starters in the mornings and it took time to adjust. Down under, her local supermarket had opened at seven and done good business at that time too.

No use trying to do anything till she could sort out her house.

She'd take a brisk walk round the lake, then.

The sales office had a sign in the window saying it opened at ten o'clock. At nine o'clock Lara was on the point of phoning her accountant's office when she saw Molly's car draw up. She put the phone away and went across to say good morning.

Molly waited for her. 'Did you sleep well, Lara?'

'Brilliantly. I was too tired to do otherwise. I'd better return the caravan key.'

'What about your luggage? You won't be able to get into your hotel room until two o'clock. You won't want to cart it around with you all day. Why don't you keep the key and the caravan till then?'

'Thanks. But if we can do the inspection of my house, I can leave everything there.'

'All right. I'll just get the checklist.'

This time Lara felt as if her brain had come alive as she walked round. She checked every single cupboard door and drawer, every tap, everything she could think about which might not function properly, even though Darcie and Carter had come and done the same thing. It was all in working order, thank goodness.

Molly smiled tolerantly. 'I don't blame you for checking but my husband is very particular that his houses are built properly and finished in every detail. Shall we go back to the office and sign off, then the house will really belong to you? There will be a chance to do some snagging later on, of course, if you find anything not working properly.'

'Yes, good.' Lara beamed round, reluctant to leave. She absolutely loved the feel of her new home.

By the time they'd finished the paperwork of the handover, it was ten-thirty in the morning. Lara transferred her suitcases into her new home and took out her phone, sitting down on the stairs for lack of any furniture.

When she clicked on John's name, the number appeared on her phone screen but it didn't ring. There was just a message saying that this number was no longer in service. That message hadn't been there yesterday, so she'd just thought the answerphone had been switched off.

She tried to email him but the message bounced.

One possible explanation crept into her mind and she tried hard to push it away. No, it couldn't be! Surely not? She tried his website, with the same result. The web page had vanished.

Then she sat and stared at her phone, her stomach churning as she faced the worst-case scenario.

Could John have run off with his clients' money?

Surely not? He had come highly recommended, had been helping her with her investment portfolio for years, building its value up steadily, had always seemed such a kind, charming man.

But why else would his office and email have stopped working, when last week everything had been normal? There had definitely been no notification of any changes about to be made.

It suddenly occurred to her to ring the concierge's office in the same building. They'd got her a taxi two years ago and given her a card in case she needed their help in future. She'd entered their number into her phone automatically. Frantically she searched through the list, trying to remember what name she'd used for it, sighing with relief when she found it under 'John's concierge'.

The man who answered the phone was very polite. 'I'm afraid Mr Crichton closed down his office the day before yesterday, or rather his secretary did. He left last week. I don't know where she is now. She said she had another job to go to.'

Oh no!

'Do you have any forwarding address or number?'

'No, sorry. I'm afraid not. Mr Crichton said he was retiring and everyone who needed to know about it had already been sent the necessary information.'

'He didn't tell me he was retiring and I'm one of his clients.' She closed her eyes, couldn't believe what the concierge had just said.

'Oh dear. You're the third client to say that.'

Her heart sank. She didn't know what to say.

'We could take your number and if he gets in touch, we'll tell him you called.'

'Yes. Thanks.' She reeled it off.

'Is there anything else I can do for you, madam?'

She tried to pull herself together. 'No. No, thank you.'

She sat there, phone in hand, seeking frantically for another explanation, but could only return to her earlier conclusion, the only one that made sense now.

John Crichton must have run off with his clients' money.

What other explanation could there be for his sudden disappearance? Businesses didn't simply close their doors when they had clients still listed with them.

She couldn't move, couldn't think what to do.

Chapter Four

Nonie Jayne stormed out of the building where the arbitration conference had been held and went round the corner towards the car park. She was so angry she didn't look where she was going and bumped into someone just inside its entrance. When the man kept hold of her arm, she opened her mouth to scream for help.

He let go quickly. 'I'm not a mugger.'

She took a step backwards, still sizzling with fury, more angry than she could ever remember since she'd been a helpless child.

'Would you like a drink? You look so upset I don't like to leave you. You might walk under a bus next.'

So she looked at him more carefully. Not a wealthy man but strong-looking, and the admiration in his eyes as he stared at her was comforting.

'There's a nice bar just round the corner.'

'Very well.' She didn't drink but he was right: she was too angry to drive safely, especially when she had to do it on the wrong side of the road. Why had the Brits chosen that side? Because they were stupid fuddy-duddies, that's why.

He bought her a drink, seeming surprised when she chose only fizzy water. How did he think she kept her figure if she dived into alcoholic drinks like his huge glass of beer?

But he was a good listener and she found herself telling him about her English husband, who had treated her so meanly.

'I could help you.'

'Come again?'

'I might be able to help you get those ornaments back that he gave you.'

'How?'

He paused, then added softly, 'I may be able to help you retrieve them . . . unofficially.'

She frowned at him. What did he mean by 'unofficially'? Was he talking about stealing things?

She didn't do crimes, but really, Ross deserved to pay properly for how he'd treated her.

'Look, let's carry on talking somewhere else. Where you're parked is out of sight of CCTV cameras but this place has got two of them. It might be better to part company and meet again in the car park.'

'Oh? Why?'

'So that no one can tie us together if you take me up on what I'm going to suggest.'

The way he was looking at her said he found her attractive. She relaxed a little. Men who eyed you like that weren't as likely to attack you, she had always found.

The outer door opened and a woman loaded with shopping came in. The man had bent to pretend to tie his shoelace as soon as the door began to open. Nonie watched as the woman passed them without a second glance, her attention on her shopping.

'All right. I'll meet you there.'

'Better still, there's a children's playground at the back of the car park. Go straight past your car, then past the swings and sit on the bench near the rose garden. You can't miss it.'

She eyed him assessingly, then nodded. She'd be safe enough in public areas and he had definitely caught her interest. After all, Ross hadn't prosecuted her last time. He was too soft for his own good, that one. People like him *deserved* to be taken advantage of. She'd given up two of her best years, and for what? For a measly sum of money.

'All right. But I hope this is worth it.'

'I'm hoping the same thing.'

'What's your name?'

'Gil. And yours?'

'Nonie Jayne.'

She wondered if that was really his name, but who cared? At least this encounter promised to be interesting. She'd been so *bored* lately. And he was an attractive guy, in a rough sort of way. She'd had enough of solemn English men with pale faces, who were as boring as they looked.

She might have a little holiday, take a little pleasure for herself before she found another target.

Gil studied the surroundings as he walked through the park, not seeing any signs that anyone was following him. He'd done nothing but try to pick up the most beautiful woman he'd ever met, a woman who was too angry to think straight. She looked expensively dressed. Maybe there might be something in this for him. His finances were certainly at a low ebb.

He stopped by the wooden bench and sat down beside her, but not too close. He didn't want to frighten her off, but he wanted to know more about her. It didn't take him long to get her talking.

'I'm not staying here long,' she announced, shivering. 'So you'd better be quick about telling me what you think you can do to help me.'

'From what you tell me, you'd still like to get your things back, but perhaps not quite as openly. I could definitely help you there.'

Nonie Jayne sat quietly as this sank in. More than getting the silver, she'd like to get back at Ross. 'Why would you want to help me?'

'For the money. You'd be generous, not keep all that I retrieved for yourself, I'm sure.'

Gil covered her hand with his and a shiver of excitement ran through her, the sort of excitement that she hadn't felt for a man in a good while. This guy was dangerous and exciting. Ross had been utterly predictable. And boring.

'I'll have to . . . um, think about it.'

'Why don't you have dinner with me tonight while you're thinking? I can answer any questions then.'

She'd seen a pirate film once with a man like this as the hero. Should she accept his invitation? Dare she?

Then the thought of Ross and his stingy ways swept through her like a firestorm. The thought of her own stupidity, too. She was angry with the whole world today.

'All right. I'll have dinner with you. It's boring eating alone. The rest I'll have to think about rather carefully.'

'But you're not saying no.'

'I'm not saying anything yet. I'm staying at Cashton Towers.'

'I've got a room nearby.'

It didn't surprise her that he wasn't staying in the hotel itself. He didn't look as if he could afford it. 'Let's get one thing straight. Even if I see you tonight, I don't leap into bed with strangers.'

'Nor do I. I value my health too much.' He stood up. 'I'll find somewhere nice to eat and leave a message for you at the desk.'

'All right.'

'We'd better not walk back to the car park together.'

He was being very careful. She liked that. You could get away with quite a lot if you were careful how you went about it.

She watched him go. She'd never met a man quite like him, kept thinking about him as she walked slowly back to the big car park.

Most of all, though, she kept thinking how good it would feel to upset Ross, who cared more about his stupid old ornaments than about the modern world. It might be worth finding out more about Gil.

She probably wouldn't go any further with his suggestion. She wasn't a *thief*, after all. Just . . . opportunistic about men and their money. And money was far more important than men.

When Ross got home, he thanked the security guard for his help in keeping an eye on the house, then sat for a few minutes in the kitchen with his cousin, sipping a cup of coffee.

Fiona looked at him shrewdly, as if she could read what had happened by the expression on his face. 'No need to ask how it went. That woman is poisonous. I could never understand what you saw in her.'

'Nor can I – now.' He went through the details of what had happened at the hearing.

'Will she abide by the arbitrator's decision?'

'Who knows?'

Fiona hesitated. 'Has she taken you for a lot of money, Ross?'

He told her the amount.

'Oh no! That's ridiculous. Why are you paying it?'

'Act like a fool and you pay the price. I wanted to get rid of her quickly, but this is more than I'd expected the arbitrator to suggest, I will admit.'

'If you need a loan, I can help.'

'Thanks, but no. I have the house and contents from my aunt.'

'We should all have an aunt who leaves us money!' She shrugged. 'Well, until you get probate and sell that house, my offer is there. Perhaps you can tend to your health now, for a while.'

He looked at her wearily.

'What did the latest specialist say, Ross?'

'Same as the one before him: I appear to have chronic fatigue syndrome, also known as ME. It's a syndrome, not a single-cause illness and there's no easy treatment. He wanted me to take anti-depressants. I refused.'

'Is this because of the divorce, of you being stressed out?'

'The specialist said that stress makes things worse. Ha! As if I hadn't noticed that.'

'And the prognosis?'

'No one knows for certain with ME. Some people recover; some don't.'

'Well, now that you've sorted out your financial details, you can get your decree absolute and be rid of her for ever. Then you can have a good, long rest.'

'She may appeal, though the arbitrator said she wasn't likely to win.'

'There you are then. Get rid of her, have a rest and don't take on any more projects for a while.'

'What? Sit around and do nothing all day? I'd go mad.' He hesitated, then added, 'The strange thing is, I didn't believe in this chronic fatigue syndrome stuff until it hit me. I considered it psychological. Snap out of it, I used to think when I saw people on TV talking about it. Stop wallowing. Mind over matter. Ha!'

He tried to laugh at himself, but didn't manage a convincing sound. Why couldn't he have come down with a more straightforward illness, something you could tackle and win? Or not win, but at least you'd know where you stood.

Fiona frowned. 'I heard about a guy who treats it differently, with a nutritional approach. I think he calls it orthomolecular medicine. He cured a friend of mine who'd suffered for years with it.'

Ross held up one hand. 'No, thanks. I've seen enough real doctors to last me the rest of my life. If *they* didn't know how to cure it, no quack will.'

'This guy trained as a GP – what does that take? Seven

or eight years, isn't it? He might know a thing or two, even if it only improves matters. Worth a try, surely?'

When Ross only shook his head, she shrugged and started to leave, turning at the door to say in her usual quiet way, 'Let me know if you change your mind. I've got his phone number. This isn't a time to put on your stubborn hat.'

'I've had enough of doctors.'

He let her show herself out and went for a stroll round the rather neglected kitchen garden, intending to do a little hoeing and weeding, which usually calmed him down. But he got tired and went back inside within the half hour, feeling utterly boneless and weary, needing to rest.

As he sat down in his favourite armchair, he asked himself yet again what he would do if he didn't get better. He still hadn't found an answer to that. All he knew was, he didn't intend to bounce about from one medical snake-oil salesman to another. He'd seen the specialists his GP had recommended and that was it.

His first wife had tried various quacks in sheer desperation as her cancer progressed. It hadn't helped. Poor Diana. She hadn't deserved to die so young.

He leant back in the armchair, fell asleep and woke with cramp in one leg.

There were various indoor jobs that needed doing. He really ought to start on them. You had to keep up with things in an old house. This one was Grade II listed, the oldest part having been built in the early eighteenth century. It wasn't all that big, just a comfortable home with four bedrooms, two small bathrooms squeezed into corners when the house was modernised, plus attics and a few outhouses.

But the structure and fittings needed regular maintenance and he usually did the minor jobs himself to save money. He *had* to get better, had to.

Surely once this divorce was over and done with, the lack of stress would be reflected in his health?

In the meantime, he had his great aunt's house to dispose of, not to mention the contents. She'd owned more ornaments and tea sets than a china shop, plus mirrors, glassware, gleaming old furniture that made you want to stroke it – you name it. He'd had a quick check and none of it looked to be of very great value, so he'd got a quote from a company which specialised in clearing out the houses of people who'd died.

They'd agreed with his analysis of the house's contents: nothing really valuable. But the amount they'd offered had been so low, Ross had rejected it instinctively. He could do better himself by selling things piece by piece on the Internet. If he could work up the energy to organise it, that was.

He walked up and down until the cramp had gone, thought about going over to his aunt's house to start making a detailed list of the contents, but couldn't drum up the energy.

He'd think about it tomorrow. Make some plans. Definitely.

Switching on the television, he sat in front of it for most of the evening, grabbing a bowl of cereal when he realised he hadn't eaten lunch.

As he went up to bed, he couldn't say what he'd watched, but the sound of voices had been comforting in a weird sort of way.

*   *   *

Nonie Jayne picked up the slip of paper from the tray the lad was holding out and shut the door of her room on him. She was paying enough for this hotel without tipping anyone till she left.

The paper simply said: *The Arbour restaurant 7 p.m.*

She wasn't going. Definitely not. She went and poured herself a fizzy water from the mini-bar in her room, then switched on the television. There was the usual load of rubbish being shown. She'd go mad staying in this place on her own for another evening.

She turned her head to stare at the piece of paper and sighed. Should she?

It wasn't till she was dressed that she accepted that she was going to meet Gil.

The taxi arrived at the restaurant at five past seven, as she'd planned. She got out, paid the driver and said, 'Can you wait a minute? I'm supposed to be meeting someone here, but if he's not arrived, I'm going back to the hotel.'

'OK.'

But Gil was there and the restaurant seemed a classy place, so she hesitated only briefly, then waved the taxi away and walked across the room.

A waiter came and held the chair as she sat down opposite Gil.

'I'm glad you came, Nonie. What would you like to drink?'

She looked round the room before she answered him. 'A fizzy water. And my name's Nonie Jayne. I *never* shorten it.'

'Nonie Jayne, then. Quite a mouthful.'

'I like it.'

'Is that why you chose it?'

She sucked in her breath. How could he know that she'd picked out this name for herself? He couldn't know. Of course he couldn't.

'You're on edge. Perhaps we shouldn't talk business tonight, just get to know one another better.'

'I'm here to talk business. If you meant what you said, that is, about getting me what that rat owes me.'

'I did. But it's not the sort of thing we should discuss here.'

'You're not coming back to my room! I don't pay in kind.'

'Nor do I need to force women into my bed. I chose to help you because you are, quite simply, the most beautiful woman I've ever seen – and it doesn't seem fair that you can't get what is due to you from your ex.'

'That's . . . an interesting reason. If you mean it.'

'We'll discuss it later, eh?'

The waiter came up then and Nonie Jayne ordered a starter of prawns and salad. 'That's instead of a main course,' she told the waiter.

As they chatted, she found herself warming to Gil. He was very good at poking fun at the world.

To her surprise, she enjoyed the evening.

But she didn't invite Gil into her hotel room, nor did she let him see that she was disappointed when he didn't suggest even escorting her back to the hotel, just saw her into a taxi outside the restaurant, saying, 'I'll be in touch, Nonie Jayne.'

She shrugged. 'Thank you for the meal.'

She didn't think he'd meant it when he said he'd help her get some things from Ross. Or had he?

Oh, who knew anything? She was getting more and more frustrated with her situation. She ought to cut her losses and go looking for another old fool to charm out of his money.

Chapter Five

Eventually Lara put the phone in her handbag and stood up, trying to pull herself together. But her thoughts were in a tangle. Surely she'd made a mistake? Oh, she must have done . . . mustn't she? John Crichton wasn't the sort to steal from his clients.

What sort of person did steal from clients, though? You'd have to be very personable to win people's trust so that you could steal their money, wouldn't you? And John was very personable, a real father figure. She'd always thought that reassuring.

It took a while for her to realise that she hadn't checked her own bank accounts. It must be the jetlag making her so stupid. In theory, he didn't have access to them, but he knew her account numbers, so she'd feel a lot better if she checked.

'I'm an idiot!' she muttered as she got out her laptop and set it up on the kitchen surface. Then she hit the side of her head with one hand because she still wasn't thinking straight. She hadn't got a service provider here. She'd have to use her phone and was old enough to have a few problems with her eyes and small screens. She probably needed reading and computer glasses.

There was a knock on the front door before she could do anything and she opened it to see Molly holding out a bouquet of flowers.

Her smile faded as she looked at Lara. 'Have you had some bad news?'

She nodded, swallowed hard and felt the world spin round, so clutched the door frame.

'I'll just put these flowers on the surface.' Molly did that quickly, then came back. 'You'd better sit down for a few moments, Lara.'

'On what?' The room no longer looked bright and spacious, but empty, seeming to echo her worries back at her and offer no comfort.

'Do you want to come across to the sales office?'

Lara could see that there was a car parked outside it. 'No, thanks. I don't want to face other people yet. What I need is to get online and check my bank account. It may have been – hacked. Only, how do I do that?'

'Why not come up to the caravan? You can sit down there and be as private as you like. You can use the hotel's server from there.' She nodded to the laptop.

'Would you mind?'

'Not at all. I'll give you the visitors' password and the caravan's close enough to the modem in the sales office for everything to connect. I used to work in the caravan sometimes when I first came here. There's a table you can use as a desk. And if you need to print anything out, you can come next door into the sales office and do it there.'

Lara's thoughts seemed slow and muddy. 'You're very kind. I will come up to the caravan to do that, if you don't mind.'

'Of course we don't mind. It's a service we provide for our customers.'

When they got there, Molly hesitated. 'I'm a good listener if you need some moral support.'

Lara didn't usually pour her heart out, but this situation was potentially so horrendous, she desperately needed someone else's input. 'Are you sure you don't mind? I'd really appreciate a second opinion on my situation.'

Molly came in and sat down. 'Go on.'

'I think my accountant may have run off with all my savings and superannuation money. His office has been closed down, his phone number is no longer in use and his email address bounces.'

'That does sound suspicious. I'm so sorry!'

Lara gestured to the laptop. 'I need to check that my personal bank accounts are all right.'

'Do you want me to wait?'

'Please.' Lara gestured to the seat opposite before opening her laptop.

Molly waited quietly as she got online and tried her main account. It was untouched, with her redundancy payment sitting in it, waiting for some of it to be added to her superannuation account, or so she'd planned. Thank goodness she hadn't had time to transfer the money to John! It wasn't much to live on, compared to her savings, but it was something.

Had all her years of hard work gone for nothing?

She shuddered and covered her eyes with one hand for a moment, fighting for control. 'What do I do?'

Molly's voice was gentle. 'I think the first thing will be to report this to the police. It's quite a major fraud, don't you think?'

'Oh yes. I should have thought of that. Only I can't seem to think clearly.'

'Shock. Look, one thing I can do to help is let you have the caravan without charging you till you've sorted something out and can buy furniture and equipment for your house.'

'I couldn't take advantage of you like that!'

'Why not? The caravan is just sitting here doing nothing.'

'Well then, thank you.'

'And didn't you say you'd booked a room at the hotel? I can cancel that for you.'

'Please.' The less she had to spend on accommodation the better . . . now.

'What about your family? Do you want to contact them?'

Should she ring Joel and Darcie? Lara wondered. No, not yet. What could they do that she couldn't? And anyway, she hated the thought of telling people she'd been robbed, felt such a credulous fool.

Besides, her children would tell their father and Guy would be very scornful, she was sure.

She turned to Molly. 'All payments have been made on the house, haven't they?'

'Yes. That happened a while ago.'

'I just needed to be absolutely sure. Thank goodness for that!'

Now that Lara thought about it, she'd had to press John

to attend to that. He'd wanted to delay payment till she was ready for the handover, had tried to persuade her that the money would gain interest if she kept it in the bank. Oh, thank goodness she'd expected to finish her project earlier and had wanted the house to be ready!

She had to keep saying it aloud to take it in and accept that horrible truth. 'So I have an unfurnished house, a little money but no income and no car except the one I hired.'

'Did you leave any clothes or possessions in England?'

'Yes, a few. How strange that I'd forgotten them. They're in my daughter's shed in packing boxes. There's no furniture, though, just books, photos, odd ornaments and mementoes, as well as a few family antiques. Oh, and some sheets, towels and clothes.'

'I see. Well, if you want to move into your house, we can lend you a bed and a few chairs, some odds and ends of crockery too. These were things left over when Euan and I got married last year and combined our goods and chattels. It's only the shabbier things. We've not got round to taking them to the charity shop.'

For some reason the word 'charity' hit Lara hard and she began weeping. How was she going to manage? Would she have to apply for unemployment benefits? How humiliating!

Could she get a job back with the company? No. The memory of Morris's vicious expression as he swore she'd never get another job with them was still all too clear. And if she applied, he'd spread the word not to employ her to other companies, she was sure.

And anyway, the company had been shedding staff lately, not hiring.

Where could she find work, though?

There would be nothing at management level, she suspected, but you could live on a lot less money than that. But now wasn't the time to consider her options. She sighed and looked at Molly. 'Thank you. I'd better go and report it to the police before I do anything else.'

'I'll tell you where to go in Marlbury. It's only a small police station but the people there will know what to do next.'

Lara nodded and wiped away the tears. She had to stop weeping. It didn't help.

This wasn't like her, anyway. She was usually in control of her emotions. In fact, that had been one of the things Guy often complained about. He didn't like being married to an iron woman.

Molly patted her shoulder. 'I'm sorry I can't come with you. Euan has a meeting this afternoon for one of his other business interests and I need to be here to look after the sales office.'

The other woman's kind touch helped Lara straighten her spine. 'I can manage. I was just – shocked.'

'Who wouldn't be?'

The police station was small, with a young officer behind the counter. Lara took a deep breath and explained her situation.

The woman blinked. 'I'd better fetch the sergeant. I've never had to deal with anything this major, but he'll know what to do.'

Lara had expected a fatherly figure, but Sergeant Gorton was a smart fellow, younger than her. He looked strong and fit, would make a good hero in a TV series.

He took her into a small office to one side, looked at her warily but, thank goodness, she no longer felt like weeping.

After bringing in the female officer he asked her to tell them everything she could think of.

When she'd finished he sat frowning down at his notes. 'This is major fraud squad stuff, I think. If you're right, it's well over a million pounds that's been taken. I wonder where this chap's gone?' He pushed his chair back and stood up. 'Can you please wait here while I ring the inspector?'

She nodded.

It was a while before Gorton returned, frowning.

'You're the third person to complain about Crichton in the past couple of days. And it seems his secretary has vanished too. The officer in charge of the investigation is Donald Metcalf. He's out following up a lead but he'll get in touch with you later. Have you got somewhere to stay, enough money to manage on?'

'Yes. For the time being, anyway.'

'We, um, can't guarantee to retrieve anything, I'm afraid.'

She knew that, of course she did, but it hurt all over again nonetheless. Oh, how it hurt! She'd been so proud of being able to retire early, had worked and saved so *hard*.

She gave the officer her address and phone number, then walked outside. The day was bright and sunny. She'd have preferred clouds or even rain, to match her bleak mood. The sunlight felt to be mocking her.

Oh, she was being utterly stupid!

She drove to the small supermarket she'd seen as she came into town and bought a few groceries to tide her over.

When she'd unloaded them from the trolley into her car boot, she stood staring into space till an elderly woman stopped to ask, 'Are you all right, dear?'

'What? Oh. Sorry. Yes, of course, but thanks for asking. I was just thinking about something.' She returned the trolley to its pen and drove back to the leisure village.

What a pity the fraud squad officer had been out. She needed action, not waiting around.

What was she going to do with herself? She couldn't even furnish her house until she was sure of her financial situation. It'd have to be second-hand stuff, the sort of pieces she'd grown up with, used when she was first married, the sort she'd vowed never to use again. And Molly's old furniture.

She still missed the beautiful big house she'd lived in with Guy, only he'd sold that years ago. She'd been planning to buy only furniture she loved for the new place. Ha! Beggars couldn't be choosers. She'd take anything she could get.

Maybe she should ring Darcie now and tell her what had happened?

She looked at her watch. No, her daughter had gone back to work, leaving the baby in a daily childcare centre. She couldn't contact Darcie until the evening.

It wasn't the sort of news you dumped on someone at work, wasn't the sort of news you wanted to share with anyone.

And she was *not* going to cry again.

When she got back, Lara put her groceries away in the caravan's tiny fridge but was unable to settle, so she went across to her house. She walked round it slowly, relieved that the fridge and cooker had been included in the price.

How few items of furniture could she get away with? A bed, a sofa, a table and a couple of upright chairs?

Slowly, determination grew in her about one thing at least: she wasn't giving this place up. It had taken too much effort to buy the house and be mortgage free. She'd take any sort of job, live frugally, manage somehow, but she wasn't giving up her new home. And she wasn't going on social security, except as a very last resort. She never had done and never would do willingly!

On that thought, she sealed her vow with a nod of the head and went across to the sales office. Molly was there, chatting to a couple. Lara saw a rack of tourist brochures for the area and went to look through them. She even put a few into her shoulder bag.

When the couple had gone to look round one of the show houses for a second time, Lara looked at Molly and managed a half-smile and a shrug. 'I've reported it to the police. I'm not the only one Crichton's stolen from, apparently. Someone from the fraud squad is going to get in touch with me.'

'I hope they catch him, and quickly. I hate cheats and thieves!'

Lara took a deep breath and did something she loathed, something she'd tried not to do since her divorce: she asked for help. 'Can I take you up on your offer of some furniture, please? I can manage with very little for the time being, just stuff you were going to chuck out. I'm going to move into my house and once I've spoken to the police again, I'll go round the charity shops and see what I can find.'

Molly looked thoughtful. 'Look, Marlbury makes a big thing of its half-yearly Pass It On Day and people put all sorts of things they no longer need outside their houses, including furniture. The council boasts that it acts responsibly about waste, so it offers support for the initiative. Call me cynical, but I think it's also a lot cheaper for them to let people take things away at no cost to the town than it is to dispose of them.'

She patted Lara's shoulder. 'You're in luck with one thing at least, because this is the weekend of the spring recycling appeal. You might find it cheaper to drive round the nearby suburbs this weekend and simply pick up some of the things people have put outside their houses. Some of them are free, some have a price on them. They're never expensive, though. If you go early, like about seven o'clock in the morning, you'll probably have a better choice.'

'Good idea. I'll do that.'

'I'll find a map and mark on it where I'd go first.' Molly came across to the rack of brochures.

'I'm really grateful for your help.' Lara heard how quavery her voice sounded and was annoyed with herself.

'I wish I could do more to help. I'll introduce you to my husband later. We'll bring the bed and stuff round tomorrow morning early on our way to work. If you'll be all right in the caravan tonight, that is? Only, we're going round to some friends' for dinner tonight.'

'That'll be fine. And thank you. I think I'll feel better in my own home after tonight, though.'

'I would too.'

Lara went back to the caravan, sat down and stared at her minimalist possessions. Two suitcases, her carry-on bag and a few food items.

She couldn't bear it, so went out to get a breath of fresh

air, ending up following a well-marked trail round the small lake. It was peaceful but getting chilly as the sun had now started to go down.

She sat on a bench and watched some ducks.

How on earth was she going to fill the time till things were sorted out about John Crichton? She'd expected to be happily busy making a home, getting to know people.

Hunger drove her back to the house and she made a sandwich, but could only eat half of it. She was about to throw the rest away when she realised she couldn't afford to waste a mouthful of food, so she wrapped it up again and put it in the fridge. She'd been super-careful after her divorce and it had paid off. And later an unexpected inheritance from her godmother had made a big difference to her retirement fund as well. She'd been lucky – until now.

When her phone rang she nearly jumped out of her skin. 'Yes?'

'Lara Perryman? Donald Metcalf here, from the fraud squad. Would it be convenient for my partner and I to come round and speak to you now?'

'Yes, of course.' She told them where she was living at the moment.

'We'll be about ten minutes.'

'Fine,' she said as she hurried back to the house.

The doorbell rang shortly afterwards and she looked round in despair as she answered it.

They immediately showed her their ID cards and she nodded. 'Come in. I'm afraid I don't have any furniture yet. I'm staying in the caravan till I can find something.' She indicated it through the window.

'Wiped you clean, has he?'

'Of my superannuation money and most of my savings, yes.' She gave them the details of what had happened and answered their questions.

When they'd finished, she couldn't resist asking if they had any idea yet where John Crichton had gone.

'I'm afraid not. I think he must have set up another identity. These people often do. If so, he's done it more skilfully than usual. But we'll keep going until we've exhausted all avenues. This is my number if you find anything out. Even the smallest detail can help.' He handed her a card and his companion did the same.

Then he hesitated. 'You don't have a clear photo of him, do you? We've not managed to get hold of one that's any use. His driving licence photo is rubbish and he's left no photographs behind in his flat.'

She had to think hard, then said slowly, 'I don't have one but my daughter might, if she's still kept it, that is. He didn't like having his photo taken, but I think one of the first times I went to see him I took Darcie with me and she had a new mobile phone with some sort of special camera on it. She kept taking photos of everything all day or asking me to take photos of her. Nearly drove me mad. What do people *do* with all these photos?'

'Who knows? Could you ask her if she still has his photo? We can't find a decent one of him anywhere and since this is the first time he's committed a crime, he's not on our books.'

'I'll do that and get back to you, probably tomorrow evening. I need to see her and tell her what's happened. I can't do that on the phone.'

She said goodbye to them, went across to the caravan and ate the rest of the sandwich, and an apple.

Afterwards she phoned Darcie and asked if she could call and see her tomorrow. 'I have something to tell you.'

'From the tone of your voice that sounds ominous, Mum.'

'It is bad news, I'm afraid.'

The words were sharp. 'You're not ill?'

'No, no. It's nothing like that. I'll tell you tomorrow.' She tried to divert Darcie's attention and succeeded. 'I'm so looking forward to meeting Minnie in person. She looks gorgeous in the photos.'

'She is gorgeous. Carter's besotted with her. Talk about the proud papa. Look, I've got the afternoon off tomorrow. They let us do some flexing at work and I built up a few hours. You could come mid-afternoon. I'll have finished all my shopping and washing by then. We'll have a good old natter and then we'll all go out to the local pub for tea. They do a good meal at a reasonable price.'

'What will you do with Minnie?'

'Take her with us. She's a most obliging baby. She loves going to places full of people and when she's tired she falls asleep, even if it's noisy.'

'Lovely. I'll be there about three.'

So that was another step organised. She wondered what Darcie and Carter would say to her news, whether they'd think her a fool for trusting Crichton.

Was she a fool? How could she have known, though? He'd been so charming, the pig.

Molly and Euan were bringing some furniture round tomorrow morning, so she'd be able to move into her own house. It'd be a rush to get everything done before she saw

Darcie, so that was the day nicely filled. Then on Saturday morning she'd go hunting for furniture to fill the gaps.

She might have a preliminary look at second-hand cars on Sunday. Only what did she know about the best sort of vehicle to buy? She'd had company cars since she and Guy split up and he'd been the one to sort out their personal cars while they were married, because he'd started out as a car salesman. He had his own car dealership these days, a big lucrative one, but she wasn't going to run to him for help.

He'd probably sneer at her for getting into trouble. He'd prophesied that she wouldn't manage her money well when they split up.

He was right. She'd thought she was so clever, finding a financial adviser to handle things. And look at what had happened.

She was so jetlagged she went to bed early, expecting to lie awake, but instead she fell straight asleep.

Chapter Six

In the morning, Lara felt somewhat better physically and more in control of her emotions, thank goodness. She made herself a cup of tea and since there was a bench in front of the caravan and it was a beautiful morning, she sat outside to drink it. Maybe she could find a bench to put outside her own house.

She held her face up to the sun, trying to will her body to respond. She needed to shake off the dopiness of jetlag and fit into this time pattern as quickly as possible if she was to pull herself out of this mess. Surely the police would catch Crichton and get her money back? She had to hold on to that hope.

By eight o'clock she'd had breakfast, cleared up and was ready to move all her possessions into her own home.

As she chased another fly out of the caravan, she felt glad she'd had insect screens fitted to the house, as they did in Australia. She didn't want to share her house with wasps or bees, to whose stings she reacted badly, not to mention bluebottles and – ugh! – daddy-long-legs. The latter were her weakness. She hated the horrid fluttery things, had done ever since one of them had got tangled in her hair when she was a child.

To her relief, Molly and Euan turned up pulling a trailer soon after she'd unpacked her clothes and hung them in the built-in wardrobe in her new bedroom. She hurried outside to join them, eager to see what they'd brought.

'*Voilà!*' Molly gestured towards the trailer, which was heavily loaded with a jumble of furniture.

'Are you sure you can spare them?'

Euan chuckled. 'I'm delighted. It saves me a trip to the council tip and a payment to them for taking these off my hands, so you're doing us a favour. Just one thing, though!'

'Oh?'

'We don't want them back.'

Lara relaxed a little at the thought she was actually giving something in return. 'Well, then, thank you very much.'

'They're all rather old and worn,' Molly said apologetically. 'And nothing matches.'

'Appearance is the least of my worries. If I have a bed, I can move in.'

'Do you have any bedding?'

'I will have by this evening. I'm going to pick my stuff up from my daughter's this afternoon. She lives near Cirencester.'

'Not too far away, then.'

'No, not too far.'

When they left, Molly to open the sales office and Euan to work in his office at the hotel, Lara walked round the house. She was now the owner of a single bed. It was a cheap one and bounced about when you turned over on it, but who cared? Maybe she could do something about the legs to steady it or put the mattress base on the floor.

There was an old chest which could be used as a bedside table, she decided. It was so heavy she and Euan had had difficulty lugging it upstairs. Thank goodness the wardrobes and a few sets of drawers were built in for both the larger bedrooms. She'd paid extra for that when the house was being constructed.

Downstairs there were now an old armchair and an equally elderly sofa. They were different in style, one maroon and one fawn, but who cared? She was also now the proud owner of seven assorted garden chairs, five of which were white plastic that had faded to a sort of grotty ivory colour. Two were made of bare wooden slats and much less comfortable. One of the plastic ones had paint splashes on it, to add to the elegance!

There was a garden table too, also of white plastic, which she'd use indoors with a tablecloth covering the stains. And finally there were two boxes of assorted crockery and odd items like vases and mixing bowls.

She unpacked them, glad of every single one because she had nothing in her kitchen cupboards at the moment, except for the few tins and packets she'd bought yesterday.

The last item was an old radio and she pounced on that in delight, plugging it in and feeling better to have human voices and occasional music to keep her company.

She'd have to do a big shopping trip to stock up her pantry because it was cheaper to cook for yourself and anyway, she had to watch her weight. It was a continuous battle to keep down to a size 14 because her body seemed eager to gain weight if she so much as blinked at a bar of chocolate.

She spent the rest of the morning sorting everything out. Then she began making lists and prioritising what she absolutely had to buy, like a kettle.

At one point she phoned the car company asking whether she could have a refund if she returned the car early and they said yes, but they'd have to ask for one extra day's payment as penalty. So buying a car went higher on her list.

She was dreading doing that, though, absolutely dreading it. Guy had always said you could hear whether an engine was working smoothly or not. Well, *he* might be able to, but she couldn't.

She forced herself to go for another walk round the lake. Daylight and exercise, that was the trick to shake off jetlag and to fight off depression.

It was a relief when it was time to leave for her daughter's in the afternoon.

She decided to buy or rent a TV quite soon or she'd go mad in the evenings. And find a few books from a charity shop or the cheap tray in a newsagent's.

All the time she kept expecting a phone call, disappointed when the police didn't get back in touch. How could a person just disappear? It made her furiously angry to think that John Crichton might get away with his thefts.

When Lara drew up at Darcie's house, she took a deep breath before getting out of the car. She wasn't looking forward to telling her tale.

Her daughter opened the front door before she got there, holding a chubby baby in her arms. Little Minnie was beaming at the world and waving her arms around, and was even more adorable in person than when you FaceTimed her.

'She's lovely!' Lara automatically held out her arms and the baby reached out to her. With tears in her eyes, she held the rosy infant close as she followed Darcie inside. Then her daughter took Minnie out of her arms and put her on a blanket on the floor.

'My turn for a cuddle now, Mum, if you're in the mood for it. You aren't always.'

'I am today.'

So they rocked to and fro, and Lara managed not to cry.

'What is it?' Darcie asked softly. 'I can't remember seeing you this upset, except when you and Dad were breaking up. Sit down and tell me what's wrong before we do anything else.'

So Lara did that, unable to stop herself shedding a few tears as she explained the situation. 'I'll have to get a job, of course. But first I have to buy a car and some furniture, and – you know – settle in a bit. At least I have a mortgage-free house.' She shrugged helplessly.

Darcie was wiping her eyes too. 'It's horrible, just horrible. How could that man do this to you?'

'How could I be so stupid as to be taken in by him?'

'I met him once, didn't I? He seemed charming, if he's the one I'm thinking of.'

That reminded Lara about the police wanting a better photo of him and she explained about it to Darcie.

'I'll look through my files tonight and let you know. It may take me a couple of evenings to find it, but I rarely destroy anything. If I remember correctly, you were in the shot too. I'm not likely to have destroyed the photo, then.'

'Good. I'd do anything to help the police catch him. I read in the paper before I left Australia about a facial recognition system picking a wanted criminal out of a crowd. Crichton's a wanted criminal now, only they haven't got a good enough photo of him.'

'Let's hope we can help! Now, shall I make us some tea?'

'That'd be nice. Have you seen Joel?'

'Not for a while. He's rushing up and down the country, organising things at the moment. He's got tunnel vision about making money.'

'I'll email him, then.'

'Shall I do that for you?'

'No, darling. It's my bad news, my job to cope.'

Which brought her another hug.

After that they settled down for a quiet natter until Carter came home from work and then they talked about what to do for tea. They didn't go out to the pub, because Lara didn't feel like facing happy crowds, so Carter nipped down to the fish and chip shop.

Before they ate, Lara helped give Minnie her bath. It had been a long time since she'd held a baby. She'd forgotten how soft and cuddly they were, how innocently they looked at the world.

She didn't leave it too late to set off home because her body still wasn't on UK time and she didn't want to drive in the dark till she knew the area better. The car was now filled with her old possessions and there were still a few more boxes to come. It'd be good to see some of them again. Ludicrous too. A house full of ratty old furniture and a few pieces of really elegant old silver from her aunt's estate.

As she started the motor, Darcie ran forward to tap on the window.

'Carter says you mustn't be afraid to ask if you're short of money. I know you've been ferociously independent since the divorce, but I *am* family.'

'I've got enough to manage on for a while with that redundancy payment, but thanks for the offer. It means a lot. I might ask his help about choosing a car, though.'

'He'll be happy to do whatever you need. He is such a kind darling!'

That kindness brought tears to Lara's eyes as she drove off.

What had got into her today? She just about never cried, prided herself on coping stoically with whatever life threw at her.

Well, disasters were bound to affect you, weren't they? She just had to make sure that they changed her for the better and that she didn't let herself get bitter. She wanted her family to still enjoy her company.

When her mother had left, Darcie phoned her father and told him about the situation.

'I'm surprised that Mrs Capable let herself be taken in like that,' he said in that snarky voice she hated.

'I met that investment guy. He seemed really nice, so I'm not surprised she was taken in by him. I was too. Don't be mean, Dad!'

'Hmm.'

'Look, I know you two haven't really got over the divorce angst, but if you won't do this for Mum, I want you to do it for me.'

'Do what?'

'Find her a car, a real bargain, and don't charge her too much for it.'

A short silence, then, 'Do you think she'd take one from me? I don't.'

'You'll have to make her, then. Come on, Dad, you could persuade a worm to turn purple if you set your mind to it! We can't leave her in this mess, we just can't. I've never seen her cry so easily before. She's shattered by it.'

As he still didn't speak, she added, 'Mum hasn't even got any furniture, you know. She'd have nowhere to sit, no bed to sleep on if the owners of the leisure village hadn't given her some ratty old stuff they were throwing out – yes, and brought it round to her the very next day. If a stranger can do that for her, you can do something, surely?'

Silence, then, 'OK. I'll see what I can do. But it's for you, princess, not her.'

When she put the phone down, Carter looked across at her. 'Are you sure this is the right thing to do, love? They've been divorced for a long time now.'

'Yes, I am. Mum needs a car. Dad can easily find her one. It's not like I'm asking them to get back together again. Or asking him to *give* her a car.'

'Good. Because I don't think they ever could get back together.'

'Who knows? I've seen it happen to others.'

He stared at her, eyes narrowed. 'Don't get your hopes up, darling. Your mother is one of the most stubborn people I've ever met and she was badly hurt by Guy ditching her.'

'I know. And she's badly affected by this, too.' Darcie reached out and snapped her fingers close to his face. 'My mother is that far from a breakdown, Carter.' Another snap. 'That far.'

He sighed. 'Yeah. I could tell. But you can't do much about that.'

'I'm not sure yet, but there must be some way we can help her. She won't *ask* for help unless she's desperate, but I'll think of something once I've visited her and seen what she's got.'

'It's a job she needs now.'

'She didn't sound very optimistic about finding one in her old area after offending the big chief in Australia.'

'Well, it might do her good to work on something else. It's early days yet. Come here.' He pulled her into his arms. 'We'll be here for her if she needs help.'

'You're a lovely man.'

'Thank you, lovely lady. I'm rather fond of you too. And if you ever try to leave me, be warned, I'm coming with you.'

It was an old joke between them, but they both meant it.

When Guy Marsham put down the phone, he whistled softly. You read about this sort of thing, con artists stealing hard-won nest eggs from their victims, but he'd never encountered it in a person he knew, and would never in a million years have expected it to happen to someone as capable as Lara.

His ex had said she hated him when they split up. He hadn't hated her, but he'd hated the travesty of their marriage because after the kids grew old enough to leave home, she'd spent so much time working away and climbing the corporate ladder, as she called it, that he'd not seen much of her. She was, she said, taking advantage of affirmative action initiatives. He hoped it had made her happy.

All *he* had wanted was a proper married life, with a partner who wasn't always rushing off to the other side of the world to manage a project. He hadn't found a good life with Julie either, though, had he? What did a second break-up say about someone? Perhaps he just wasn't good at relationships. Some people weren't.

To his surprise, he found himself planning to help Lara and hoping she would accept it. It wouldn't take much to find her a second-hand car. He could afford to *give* her one, because his business was thriving, but she wouldn't take that from him. Or would she? How desperate was she? Had she any money left?

He hadn't been happy about his second break-up. That's what you got for hooking up with someone so much younger than yourself who suddenly grew desperate to have children before it was too late, someone who'd said she never wanted children when they first got together. He hadn't wanted to go through the child-rearing years again, especially the teenage traumas. No way.

He was just glad he and Julie had handled the financial side of the separation amicably. Well, both his wives had. They were strong women, able to stand on their own feet and earn a living for themselves. Except that Julie had remarried rather quickly and was now pregnant.

To his surprise he couldn't get the thought of Lara's predicament out of his mind and found himself determined to give her a car. Surely she'd accept the gift if it was a cheap trade-in? Who knew?

The older he got, the only thing he was sure about was that no one could ever understand another human being completely, inside marriage or out. It was hard enough understanding yourself.

That same morning Ross woke after a poor night's sleep. To his dismay it was nearly ten o'clock and sunny. He must have fallen hard asleep just after dawn turned the world outside grey.

He'd meant to make an early start on clearing his aunt's house. The sooner he could clear it out, the sooner he could put it up for sale or rent it out. He wasn't sure which to do yet, would have to work out the costs and benefits.

He didn't enjoy the accounting side of business, but it was necessary and he'd become reasonable at it, if he said so himself. He'd need to build up his reserve fund again for the ongoing repairs on this historic house. He'd have to use most of his current funds to pay out Nonie Jayne, damn her.

He paused for a moment or two to beg the fates not to let her appeal against him. Surely the arbitrator was right and she couldn't win it, even if she did try?

On that thought he decided to contact the PI again and ask him to look further into her finances. If she was as comfortable as Ross suspected, maybe he didn't even need to pay her so much. In that case, *he* would be the one making an appeal.

He got ready to go out, switching on the new security system at The Gatehouse which had cost him an arm and a leg, and then driving over to Penny Lake Leisure Village by the scenic route. That always lifted his spirits. Wiltshire was such a beautiful county and spring was the best time of year.

As usual, he felt sad at the sight of the house where his aunt had been so happy for the last ten months of her life. It was near some of her friends and she'd made new ones, including that charming American woman. What was she called? Cindy something or other. She'd been one of the first people to move into the village.

He'd let her know when Iris died and received a charming letter of condolence. Cindy hadn't been able to come to the funeral, however, because she'd been in America just then.

He'd been having tea with his aunt regularly on the first Monday of the month for several years even before she moved to this house. He was surprised at how much he missed that. Iris had been such a lively woman, not at all old in the head.

The house smelled musty so he opened all the windows and the doors that led out of the living area on to the back patio. Then he looked round in despair. Where did he start? There were so many ornaments and mementoes! Every windowsill, table and shelf was loaded with them. He couldn't simply throw them away, because whether they were valuable or not, the old lady had had exquisite taste and nearly all of the ornaments, dishes and vases were pretty.

Some were made by names he recognised and some weren't. He'd had a quick trawl round the Internet and come to the conclusion many of them could be called 'art pottery', and some of the silver was well worth selling carefully. Why had he considered handing over the disposal of all this to a man who'd have cheated him? Iris would have thrown a fit.

He started the day by checking through the kitchen cupboards, something he should have done before now, finding some unopened packets of food that were still usable and some opened ones that needed throwing away. He got out a bin liner and made a start, half filling it with risky food items.

He piled the usable goods on a surface. He'd take those home with him. He could almost hear Iris saying, 'Waste not, want not.' Like most of her generation, she had despised waste of any sort. The current generations were coming round to the same view these days, only they called it 'recycling' or 'repurposing' and seemed to think they'd invented the concept.

Smiling at that thought, he went upstairs to his aunt's bedroom, feeling like an intruder. He shuddered when he was faced for a second time with those drawers full of old-fashioned underwear. He opened them briefly, slamming them quickly shut one by one, not wanting even to touch the contents. It still seemed wrong for a man to paw through an old lady's most intimate garments. And if he was being oversensitive about the knickers and bras and whatever the other stuff was, too bad. It was how he felt.

His initial look round the house weeks ago had shown him that the drawers in the spare bedroom contained bedding and spare towels. Those should be safe to go through today. He smiled wryly at himself for being so stupid and sensitive, but there you were. Your emotions didn't always make the best sense. He'd have to ask a woman friend to go through the underwear for him, perhaps his cousin Fiona. She wasn't related to Iris, came from his mother's side. If there was anything decent, it could go to a charity shop.

He went across to the big chest of drawers to the right of the spare bedroom window. What did they call these things? Tallboys. This one came up to his shoulder, six drawers in all with a small cupboard across the top whose doors had carving and oval mirrors on them. He'd never really studied it before and was surprised at how pretty it was. Was it worth something too?

The top drawer contained pillow cases, more than his aunt would have ever needed. Some were still in their original packets and looked quite old. Where did they all come from? he wondered. Had she kept on buying them right till the end? And were things like this worth selling individually, maybe at a pop-up market stall? Who knew?

The second drawer contained a layer of towels, underneath which he found rows of little boxes containing what he assumed was costume jewellery. He hunted for hallmarks on the various pieces but found none, so they couldn't be real gold and silver, let alone real jewels. Not valuable, then. Pretty, though. Far too pretty to throw away.

But what was he going to do with them? Why had she bought them anyway? He'd never seen her wearing brooches and necklaces, apart from a couple that had belonged to her mother.

And why hadn't he noticed these the first time round? Pete Bromhill didn't seem to have noticed them, either, when he quoted for clearing out the whole house. Ross paused to frown. No, Pete was too shrewd not to have opened drawers and cupboards. Perhaps he had seen them and kept that secret because they might be moderately valuable? There were so many that even at ten or twenty pounds each, the money would mount up nicely, Ross was sure.

All the lower drawers were the same; towels or sheets covered the contents of each, and underneath were ornaments, boxes – bigger ones in the bottom two drawers. Were the coverings meant to be a precaution against theft? He smiled wryly at the thought. *Wouldn't have worked these days, Iris, my old love.*

He turned and went across to the wardrobe, where clothes hung, old-fashioned garments smelling faintly of something spicy – not mothballs, thank goodness, whose stink he loathed. He sniffed again. Possibly sandalwood.

This spare wardrobe was chock-full of clothes. She hadn't worn any of these, as far as he could remember. Had she kept all her discarded clothes from decades ago? He frowned. They didn't look at all worn. He was no fashion expert but he knew a bit about history from his work, and these were surely from before Iris was born or at least from when she was a small child, the twenties or thirties perhaps. He'd have to look them up somewhere.

By then his head was aching and he went outside to get a breath of fresh air, waving to Molly Santiago, who'd married the owner last year and now ran the sales office. He knew her and her husband slightly since he'd helped his aunt buy the house. They'd been kind to the old lady, even doing some shopping for her, he'd found out afterwards.

He should have noticed that his aunt needed more help, felt guilty about that, but he'd been trying to deal with the divorce and his increasing feeling of being unwell.

In the end he gave in to the fatigue, closed up the house and went home. He picked up a pizza on the way, realising as he stood in the queue that he hadn't brought the usable food from his aunt's house with him. Well, he could pick it up tomorrow.

He ate a couple of slices of pizza before he fell asleep in front of the television.

His last thought was that at least he'd done something useful today.

But not much. He got tired so damned easily.

He'd taken three months' leave from his work with a heritage architecture practice to deal with everything that was going pear-shaped in his life. No one would wonder at his absence because the group of partners were only loosely tied together for business purposes. They came and went according to the commissions they were working on, specialising in extending period properties. The practice acted as a clearing house and provided secretarial services for them all as needed.

You couldn't be money-hungry to work like that, but there was immense satisfaction in helping to preserve old buildings or modernise their interiors in a way that didn't destroy the structures. He loved what he did.

Chapter Seven

The following morning, which was Saturday, Lara took Molly's advice and went out early, having set her alarm to be sure of waking up. She intended to scour the streets for discarded furniture of all sorts. No use being proud. She had a house to furnish.

Anyway, it felt a lot better to be doing something other than sitting around waiting for the police to get back to her. She could answer a phone call wherever she was.

She was amazed to see that the street verges were littered with furniture already, more than she'd expected by a long chalk. Much of it looked broken or no longer fit for purpose, but in the first street she found a small side table going free that she actually liked and put it in the rear of the car. Thank goodness she'd hired a hatchback!

In the next street she found a proper dining table and six matching chairs, old-fashioned and the table had a scuffed top, but she could fix that. The owner wanted £50 for them, which she paid gladly. He pointed out a trailer parked further along the street with a sign on it. 'Deliveries made, reasonable charges.'

Clearly the locals had this well organised.

When she went along to the trailer, the owner came out and she bargained with him to take whatever she found to the leisure village later that day. She'd phone him up to collect any other things she found and pay extra for that service.

He seemed delighted to be offered a retainer of fifty pounds to act as her carrier and agreed that she could use his front lawn as a dumping ground till then, starting with the small table.

'You won't let me down?' she asked.

His wife had come out to join them and frowned at that. 'My Fred has never let anyone down in his life, and we live here, so he can hardly run away with anything, can he?'

'Sorry. I didn't mean to offend. I have a whole house to furnish and not much money, you see, so I'm a bit – anxious.'

'Marriage broken up?' the woman asked with a sympathetic look.

'Something like that.'

'Some men are bastards, but then some women are too. Me an' my Fred were lucky to meet, not lucky to stay together. We've worked at it.' She hooked her arm in her husband's and gave him a loving smile.

Lara couldn't help feeling a sudden stab of envy at their happiness, but she hoped she hadn't let it show.

The words stayed with her though. Had she and Guy worked hard enough at their marriage? No. She could see that now. He'd worked every hour of the day at developing his car yard and once the children were off their hands, she'd joined the company and taken projects all over the world. At first a month here and a month there, then longer stints. That was all in the past, so why on earth was she thinking about it now?

She carried on, finding bits and pieces, most of them free or at minimal cost. Twice she went back to get Fred to bring his trailer and collect bookcases and a clunky old TV table too big to fit in her car. Of course she didn't have a TV yet, but that was beside the point. Five pounds was a good price for this one.

By mid-morning she was tired and the best items seemed to have been snapped up. She decided she'd buy herself a brand new bed; well, she would once she had more of an idea where exactly she stood financially. Surely the police would find John and get at least part of her money back? Or was she fooling herself? They hadn't phoned her today. Did they work at weekends? Or did thieves have free rein then?

Fred nodded when she told him where she lived. 'I'll follow you home and don't worry if I fall behind. I know where that leisure village is. I play golf there sometimes. Do you play?'

'No. I'd rather go for walks and enjoy the scenery.'

By the time she got back, Fred had fallen behind. She saw a car parked in front of the next house whose door was propped open. She wondered if it was the owner, but she was too eager to take her smaller loot inside to hang around and introduce herself.

She put the kettle on, sure that Fred would welcome

a cup of tea or coffee when he arrived, then she started unloading her car.

She'd tried to find solid pieces which she could rub down and paint white. She wasn't stupid enough to leave them as they were and call it the shabby chic look, because it was a furnishing fashion she heartily disliked. Fancy deliberately putting scratches on your furniture as one of her colleagues had done! How stupid was that?

Fred arrived and started lugging things inside, sometimes needing her help. She went to help him with the dining table, which was very heavy, and without Fred's wife, the two of them had trouble getting it off the trailer safely.

'Let me help,' a voice said and a man came across from next door to join them.

With his help they got the table inside the house and he went on to help Fred with the other bigger things, so of course she offered him a cup of tea and a biscuit as well.

'Love something. I forgot to bring a snack with me.' He sat down with a sigh, looking rather pale.

'Should you have been doing that heavy lifting?' she asked, suddenly feeling worried about him.

'I just get tired easily. I'm not injured or anything like that. A cup of tea will work wonders. I haven't introduced myself – Ross Welby. My aunt used to live next door, but she died a few months ago. I've been too busy to clear out her house and of course I had to wait until I got probate, but I made a start on it yesterday.'

'I'm Lara Perryman. I've been working in Australia and come back to settle in the UK permanently.'

'You've bought some nice solid pieces today.'

She smiled. 'In among the tat and cast-offs. But they'll look a lot nicer after I've either repolished them or, if the surfaces are too badly damaged, painted them white. I, um, can't afford to buy new furniture.'

He nodded, accepting her vague explanation without comment, thank goodness.

Fred finished his tea and stood up. 'Got to go. Hope things go well for you, Lara.'

She paid him seventy pounds and he nodded as if he thought that fair. She saw him to the door and waved goodbye.

When she turned round, Ross was still sitting there clutching his empty mug, looking thoughtful, so she sat down again. She hadn't had time recently in her busy life for doing much socialising with neighbours but she'd vowed to take every chance she could to meet people in her new life, so she wasn't in a hurry to get rid of him.

'I'm sorry about your aunt, Ross.'

'Yes. Me too. She was a lively old bird and I really miss her. Look, I wonder if you could do a job for me? In return I can give you Iris's spare bed. It's a double and doesn't look as if it's ever been used. She bought it new when she moved in so that her friend could stay the night, only the friend died suddenly.'

'What's the job?' she asked cautiously.

'Clearing out her underwear and clothes. I can't bear to touch them, the underwear particularly. It's, um, rather old-fashioned and some of it's been used, though it's clean, of course.'

He'd actually flushed slightly as he said that and she relaxed a little. She'd met a lot of predatory men in her working life and this guy definitely wasn't one of those.

In fact, he seemed quite gentle, in voice and manner.

He was still too pale, though.

'Have you been ill?'

He hesitated.

She held up one hand. 'I'm sorry. I didn't mean to pry. It's none of my business.'

'If you're going to help me out – you *are* going to, aren't you . . . ?'

She nodded.

'Well, you're bound to notice how quickly I tire. I have chronic fatigue syndrome, otherwise known as ME. A lot of people don't believe in it, but—'

'It's all right. I do. I knew someone who had that. But she got better, slowly.'

'I'm hoping to do that. I've been going through a rather nasty divorce recently, but it's over now, at least I hope it is, so the stress levels should go down.'

'Divorcing is horrible, isn't it?'

'Very. You're divorced too?'

She nodded. 'Years ago. It wasn't acrimonious, not exactly, more chill and polite, but it was very unpleasant dividing up the goods and chattels. I was relieved when that was over.'

They were silent for a few moments, then she looked at his pale face. 'Perhaps you'd better go home and rest now. I can't start work on your job till tomorrow because I have a lot of new possessions to clean and arrange. I can't bear to live like this.' She gestured to the bundles of 'stuff' and pieces of mismatched furniture that made her lovely new home look like a junk shop.

He nodded and stood up. 'Fine by me.'

She watched him go, standing at the kitchen window, which overlooked the parking area. He looked utterly exhausted as he closed the front door of his aunt's house and got into his car, poor thing, and yet he'd helped her.

It sounded as if she could earn herself a bed and that would be a help. Even a small positive step was welcome.

She turned round and stared at the chaos, wrinkling her nose at the musty smell of the old, neglected furniture and who knew what else there was in the 'miscellaneous boxes' of crockery and kitchen paraphernalia. These pieces would need a thorough wash before she did anything else with them.

She was about to start on that when her phone rang.

'Donald Metcalf here, from the fraud squad.'

As if she'd forget who he was!

'Nothing to report, unfortunately, Ms Perryman. Any sign of that photo?'

'My daughter's going to go through her records tonight. She thinks she still has it.'

'Let me know as soon as it's available. Let me give you the address to email it to as well as my own direct email. If it's any comfort, we're setting things up with Interpol at the moment, given the scope of this Crichton fellow's thefts. I'd guess he's hiding out somewhere in Europe. People who commit fraud often do. Or he may have gone to South America. I'll keep you in touch if there are any developments.'

If, she thought, not *when*. As she put the phone down, tears came into her eyes but she blinked them away. She would *not* keep crying.

She went to change into her oldest pair of jeans and start cleaning her new possessions.

Thank goodness for the old radio and the talk-back show she found. She was so used to being with people it felt weird to spend so much time on her own. There didn't seem to be anyone around in the detached house on the other side of her row, as well as Ross's aunt's house next door being empty.

Lara spent the whole afternoon dealing with her new possessions. That was rewarding. She actually enjoyed washing the glasses she'd bought at knock-down prices: wine, champagne, tumblers, all sorts. It had seemed as if every alternate person had too many glasses and wanted to sell untouched packages of them. She hadn't had to pay much for them at all.

Who knew there was this other bargain world out there?

After that she gave in to temptation and unpacked the box of special ornaments and pieces of silver that she'd had stored at her daughter's for the past few years. Was she being stupid putting such lovely pieces out on view among such rubbishy furniture? She shrugged. Who cared? It would give her pleasure to see them every day.

But after she'd eaten, another evening hit her. A scratch meal and then what did you do to pass the time? She wasn't in the mood for reading, though she'd picked up a few dog-eared paperbacks as well as household items.

She would definitely have to hire or buy a television. She'd go online and have a look tomorrow, if Molly would let her use their Internet system again. Maybe even on a Sunday she could find something to hire – or would buying one turn out to be cheaper in the long run?

Who knew? This was a very big learning curve on frugal living.

All she did know was that she was too tired to go online and find out tonight.

Chapter Eight

When Ross got home, he went to lie on the bed, fretting at his desperate need for another rest. Still, the day had seen some progress made. He had to hang on to the idea that any job ticked off his list was a good thing at the moment, given how weak he felt. He would have preferred to work more quickly – who wouldn't? – but it wasn't going to happen.

The new woman living next door would probably be a pleasant neighbour for whoever bought his aunt's house. She didn't look the sort to throw wild parties and keep people living near her up all night. What was her name? Lara something or other. He couldn't remember her surname. He yawned. Nice name, Lara.

She seemed a bit uptight, but she was clearly short of money, so maybe that was why. Been there, done that in the early days of his first marriage. He and Diana had tried to make it fun to manage together, literally saving every penny they could in a big pot, but even so, it had got them down sometimes.

Being economical would be a lonely business on your own, and Lara was a bit old to be in that situation, surely?

She was sporting quite a good suntan so he guessed she'd been working overseas. Strange. People usually came back from that sort of stint with plenty of money – unless she'd just been travelling for pleasure.

The best thing about meeting her was that she was going to get rid of that damned underwear and all his aunt's other clothes for him.

He was woken by the doorbell ringing and before he'd come to fully, it rang again. He stumbled across to the window, still feeling dopey, and stuck his head out, looking down towards the front door. 'Fiona! Hi!'

'Hi, yourself. Are you in bed again?' she teased.

'Yeah! Can't get enough of it. I'm a sleep junkie. Hang on. I won't be a minute.'

He let his cousin in. It was always good to see her.

Head on one side, she studied him. 'I'll make you some coffee, Ross. I want you fully alert because something's cropped up that may be useful to you.'

'Mmm.' He led the way to the kitchen and got out a cake while she made the coffee.

She smiled at the sight of it. 'How have the mighty fallen! A bought cake!'

'Yup. I still miss Diana's cakes. And her.'

'I miss her too, you know. You married a great woman the first time. Diana felt as much *my* cousin as you are. She and I used to have a lot of fun shopping together.' Fiona plonked a beaker of steaming liquid down in front of him. 'Take a couple of swigs of that and then listen carefully.'

'You always were a bossy britches, even when we were kids.'

'I was the oldest cousin. I had the right to boss you others around because I was always left in charge and got in trouble if you misbehaved.' She took a sip then looked at him. 'Am I right in thinking you're going to be very short of money after you've paid off Nonie Jayne?'

'Yeah. It's what they call paying for your mistakes. With a vengeance.'

'Well, I know how you can earn some decent money without lifting a finger.'

He looked at her, frowning. 'Lead me to it. As long as there's no risk of losing what I've got left.'

'Don't look so wary. It's a way of using your biggest asset.'

'Huh?'

'This house, dumbo. Have another gulp or two of coffee.'

He did as ordered. People tended to do that when Fiona spoke in *that* tone of voice.

'You know my friend Tom Connors, the film producer? Well, he's scouting round for an eighteenth-century house to use as a location for a new historical TV series.' She made a sweeping gesture with one hand. 'And here you are with a house built mainly in that era, which you have neither the energy nor the money to look after properly at the moment.'

He realised he had his mouth open, literally, and snapped it shut again.

'They'll pay big time for you to get out of here and let them hire it for a few months. And they'll guarantee to look after the place, too. They'll put in a live-in caretaker and improve your security system at no charge to you because they'll be leaving expensive equipment around. Apart from the caretaker, the house will only be used for film shoots.'

'How much will they pay?'

The sum she named made his hand jerk and sent coffee splattering across the table. 'You're joking.'

'No, I'm not. They'll pay that much and still save themselves money. They don't want you to leave any valuables around but they'll pay extra if they can use your furniture. It'd cost them much more than that to build fancy sets and source reproduction furniture, you know.'

He found his voice at last. 'Tell me where I sign the contract and I'll run all the way there.'

'You can't do that till they've seen the house and approved of it. It's not a hundred per cent certain yet. I don't know the details of this series so I can't say exactly what they need, because that's being kept a big secret. But when I showed Tom a photo of your house and told him about the interior, he thought it looked promising.'

'I could go and live in Aunt Iris's house for a few months. This would be all profit.'

'Yes, that's what I thought. Good timing, eh?'

'It certainly is.' He waited for her to go on, mentally crossing his fingers and hoping that fate had moved across to stand by his side for a while.

'When can they come to view it, Ross?'

'Any time they want, unless you think I need to spiff it up a bit first.'

'No. They want a lived-in look.' She took out her phone. 'Shall I ring Tom and set up a visit?'

'Go for it.' He watched her, trying to work out whether

the meaningless grunts and monosyllabic comments she kept making were positive or not.

She held the phone away from her ear. 'How about Tom comes round now? He's only half an hour's drive away.'

'Fine by me.' Ross swallowed hard, closing his eyes for a moment, and next thing he knew she had her arm round his shoulders.

'Poor you. You've had a hard time with that bitch and the fallout afterwards, haven't you? And being ill on top of it.'

'Not been the best of years. But she's not a total bitch.'

'Oh?'

'No. She's rather stupid and greedy, but she has her good points. We were just the worst of mismatches you could ever make.'

'Well, that's all water under the bridge now. Let's see if Tom can cheer you up a bit. It always makes me feel good to be with him, he's so ebullient.' She moved away, smiling at him.

When Ross looked round the kitchen and jerked to his feet, she put her hand on his shoulder and pushed him down again, saying sternly, 'Do not even think of tidying up. Save your energy for dealing with Tom. I'll put the dirty mugs out of sight in the dishwasher and who cares about the rest? He won't.'

So Ross sat down again, finished his coffee and waited. Half an hour, he found, could seem a very long time.

Tom Connors was a thin, rather intense fellow of about Ross's own age, with hair gelled upright to defy gravity. Fiona had said he was just starting to make his name as a major filmmaker. When he got out of his car, he didn't come straight to the front door, but walked up and down outside, framing the house with his hands from various angles.

At last he came inside and Fiona introduced them.

Tom nodded, but wasn't really paying attention to them, instead was staring avidly round the room. 'Look, Ross, I'd prefer to go through the house on my own, if you don't mind, so that I can get a feel for it. Could you and Fiona maybe go out for an hour, then come back and we'll talk?'

'I'll take him for an early lunch at a café I know,' she said at once.

'I'm not really hungry,' Ross told her as they set off in her car.

'You can have a lemon and lime with a packet of crisps, then, and drive us back. I could murder a glass of dry white wine, early as it is. The kids at school have been über-lively all week.'

The hour passed slowly and they mostly watched the other customers, chatting only now and then. Ross was relieved when it was time to go home again.

They found Tom in the back garden, staring up at the house and prowling round the vegetable beds, empty this year except for a few perennials because Ross hadn't found the energy to plant anything new.

Tom greeted them with, 'This is perfect! Even this back garden, looking so neglected, is just what we need.'

It took Ross a minute to control a surge of hope and utter a choked, 'Good.'

'Did Fiona tell you how much I can pay?' Tom went on. 'It's not negotiable, I'm afraid. I'm on a tight budget and those period costumes cost a fortune.'

'How long exactly do you want the place for?'

'Nine months, with an option to extend if necessary for however much longer it takes to finish the filming. And of course, we'll pay extra at the same monthly rate if we go to that.'

'OK by me. An aunt just died and left me another house, so I'll have somewhere to live.'

Tom clasped one hand to his chest and rolled his eyes skywards. 'It was meant to be. *Meant!* That's such a great omen.'

Ross didn't go for the idea that things were 'meant to be', nor did he believe in omens, but now wasn't the time to say so.

'I'll tell my lawyer to see your lawyer and sort out the contract, if you'll give me his name,' Tom said.

'I think I need to find a new one. Mine's been dealing with my divorce and that's a different skill set.'

'I know one. She's really good.' Fiona reeled off the lawyer's contact details. 'Wait till I've had time to phone her about this, Tom.'

'You'll do that today?'

'I will indeed.'

'How soon can you vacate the house, Ross?' Tom looked round hungrily, as if he wanted to move in that very minute.

'As soon as the contract's signed. Couple of days if you can push it through fast.'

To Ross's horror, Tom threw his arms round him and plonked a kiss on his cheek, not a sexual thing just a great big sloppy kiss, but even that made him feel uncomfortable. He didn't usually go round kissing men. Well, he didn't do kissy-kissy with any strangers if he could help it. 'Great. I'll hurry my lawyer up and you do the same.'

Tom gave Fiona two similarly smacking kisses on her cheeks. 'I owe you one for this, Fiona my pet.'

And he was gone, whistling cheerfully as he went out to the car and stopping to take a couple more photos before he left.

Ross felt as if he'd been picked up and tossed about by a whirlwind. Fiona had that effect on people at times, and Tom was even more exuberant. But for once he felt energetic enough to let his excitement loose, cheering and dancing his cousin round the kitchen till she was breathless and laughing.

Fiona hugged him back, then pushed away. 'Stop that, you fool.'

'It couldn't have happened at a better time. How can I ever thank you?'

'By getting better. Now let me phone my lawyer friend and tell her about you.'

She ended the call with a beaming smile. 'She has a cancellation in an hour's time. I can't come with you but it's all very easy-peasy to set up. So you'll be able to rest and stop worrying this evening.'

'Thanks, kiddo.'

'My pleasure. Your parents were always kind to me. I'll come round and help you pack tomorrow. No, don't try to stop me. You know you'll struggle to do it in time all on your own. I'll bring a ton of bubble wrap and some boxes. We had a delivery at work and the stuff's just sitting there waiting to be reused.'

Ross sighed. 'I feel terrible having to rely on you so much. You're the best cousin there ever was.'

She smiled, looking a little sad. 'A spinster lady born and bred, there to help others. Yup, that's me. Every man I meet these days wants me for a platonic friend or an adopted sister.'

It was his turn to hug her. 'I've always been surprised you never married.'

She shrugged. 'I met a guy once but it didn't work out.'

He looked at her in astonishment. 'Morgan? Still?'

'Yes. I know it's stupid, but no one I've met since has ever come near him for me.'

'You never mention him.'

'Well, what is there to say? That I'm stupidly stuck in the past? That he's been gone for nearly twenty years and he's still as vivid in my memory as ever.'

'I'm sorry. You'd have made a good mother.'

'Some of us aren't destined to experience that pleasure, but at least I've enjoyed teaching other people's children for nearly twenty years and from time to time I enjoy helping younger folk to become teachers themselves when I supervise their pracs. I give them the best training I can because it's such an important job. So, you see, my life hasn't been wasted.'

'It's not too late.'

She took a deep breath. 'Let's not dwell on the past. You need to start thinking about which personal effects you want to take with you and which valuables you want to store at the bank. I'll come round to help you tomorrow – good thing it's a weekend. We should get quite a lot done if I come here early.'

She glanced at her watch. 'I'm meeting some friends this evening for a meal, so I have to go and finish a few things. If you stir your stumps, you'll have time to get some cardboard boxes from the supermarket before your appointment with the lawyer. Go round to the back entrance. They're always glad to be rid of them. This evening, if you can manage it, do a preliminary sweep of the house and decide what you want to put into storage and what you want to take to your aunt's house. Make sure you collect all your valuable antiques.'

'Yes, ma'am.' He gave her a mock salute, then watched her drive off. Fiona was like that when something needed doing. Somehow she took charge and you did as you were told. She'd had a brilliant teaching career already, winning awards for her innovative work and helping underprivileged children to achieve academic success. He'd thought many times how sad it was that she'd never married, hadn't realised she was still carrying a torch for the guy she'd lived with for a couple of years, a guy who had just vanished one day and never been seen again.

Ross felt quite galvanised by the thought of making all that money – and he also liked the idea of spending some peaceful months in his aunt's neat little house with a nearby lake to stroll round. Maybe he'd even take golf lessons. No, maybe not. He'd been pitiful at sport at school and couldn't see himself having any better hand–eye coordination now, even if he had the energy.

It seemed like another omen that at the supermarket he was given as many cardboard boxes as he could fit into his car.

The lawyer turned out to be rather like Fiona, a brisk

woman who took the particulars and said it didn't sound as if it'd be a difficult job, especially if Fiona approved of this Tom Connors.

That evening Ross even found the energy to go round the old house and make a start on gathering up the more valuable pieces of silver and china.

It'd be best to put most of these into secure storage, together with a few of the more valuable pieces of furniture. He'd keep a few favourite things with him, though, to enjoy looking at. The rest of his personal possessions, including his books, could sit in his aunt's spare bedroom.

Since he was giving Iris's spare bed to his new neighbour in return for helping him clear out his aunt's clothing, there should be adequate storage space. He wasn't taking all that much with him.

He didn't mind the thought of sleeping in his aunt's bed. He'd helped her choose a new one when she moved in. A woman as nice as her could have left nothing but good vibes behind, he was sure.

For the first time in ages, he felt hopeful and even able to laugh at his own weakness about Iris's underclothes.

But he still wasn't clearing them out. That was a major sticking point, for some reason!

In the morning the sales office didn't open till ten o'clock, because of it being a Sunday, and Lara, who'd been waiting impatiently, nipped across to see Molly as soon as she turned up.

'Could I please use your Internet access again? The other password didn't work this morning and I need to do some shopping online.'

'Of course you can. We change it every day, for security reasons. I should have thought of telling you that. What are you after this time?'

'I need to hire a TV.'

'Ah. We have a few small TV sets sitting in a storeroom at the hotel doing nothing. If you want one, you're welcome. They've only got twelve-inch screens, but they work just fine. Everyone wants bigger ones in the hotel rooms these days, but we've kept a few for emergencies. I'll call the reception desk and they'll get one out for you when they have a minute. Better wait till the afternoon to pick it up, though, because Sunday morning is always busy with people checking out.'

Lara blinked in shock. 'I can't ask you to do all this.'

'You didn't ask. I offered.'

'Were you a fairy godmother in a previous life?'

Molly chuckled. 'No. I was an unhappily married woman. I took a long time to get my act together after my first husband brainwashed me into thinking I was stupid.'

'You seem to have your life nicely sorted out now. And I don't know how anyone could ever have called you stupid!'

The other woman's voice softened. 'Yes, my life is good now. And I've realised that I'm not stupid. But I always feel that meeting Euan was the reward for taking my life in my own hands and doing something with it. You know what they say: if you want to be treated as a doormat, first you have to lie down and let others walk all over you. That's what I was doing with my husband and my grown-up children.'

She smiled in such a way that her whole face lit up. 'My son has also got his act together, learnt that he's not the only pebble on the beach and met a wonderful young woman.' The smile faded as she added, 'My daughter is – well, still in thrall to her father, who can switch on charm like a tap. I hope one day she picks up her own life and does something with it.'

'You can't live it for them, however much you love them. My son's rather selfish, such a go-getter, focused only on his career. I hardly ever see him.' It suddenly occurred to Lara that Joel took after her – and that there was nothing she could do to stop him making the same mistakes and narrowing his life as she had. Only time would do that.

'Well, you can hope that he'll learn to broaden his life, as I still hope for my Rachel. She won't even come to meet Euan.' Molly's expression was still rather sad.

Well, that was one thing she'd never done, Lara thought: acted as a doormat. But on the other hand she'd never helped people as Molly seemed to do instinctively. Perhaps she would be able to change, become a more caring person, a worthwhile grandmother for little Minnie.

She was finding out for herself what a difference even a small helpful act could make to a person at a time of crisis. Only . . . how did you do it, change your whole attitude to life?

'Oh, there's Ross,' Molly exclaimed suddenly.

They watched through the office window as her neighbour's car pulled up in front of his aunt's house and then they exchanged surprised glances when he began to unload cardboard boxes, full ones from the way he had to heave them up. Then he took in two battered suitcases, which looked equally heavy.

'Is he moving in, do you think?' Molly wondered aloud.

'It looks like it. I wonder what's happened to cause that.

He was talking about selling or renting the house yesterday.'

'We'll find out. Nothing stays secret in our little village. You wait till Cindy gets back from America. She always finds out about whoever moves in – though in the nicest possible way. You'll like her. She lives in that big house to the left of your terrace.'

'I was beginning to wonder if any other people were actually living here, it's been so quiet.'

'Some of them come and go because they have houses in warmer climates for the UK winter. Now that it's spring they'll probably start coming back. We've been lucky so far with our buyers. Nice, civilised people.'

Ross drove off as soon as he'd unloaded his car, then returned two hours later with more boxes. Lara didn't interrupt him, not even to offer a cup of coffee, though she couldn't help taking the odd peek.

She'd wondered if he'd be spending the night here, but he didn't. He unloaded the car a second time, then drove off again, looking tired but happier than before, as far as she could tell.

What had happened to cheer him up? Whatever it was, she hoped it continued. He had a very attractive smile.

In the late afternoon Lara drove up to the hotel to collect the television set. It looked silly on the big stand she'd bought yesterday, but never mind that. It was now at the right height for comfortable viewing. She plugged in the aerial, then the power, crossing her fingers as she switched the set on.

When a picture formed she let out an exclamation of joy. Leaning back in her chair, she began to find out how the remote worked and then had to retune the TV channels.

All she needed now was a glass of wine to sip as she watched it in the evenings. She might buy a bottle of cheap plonk and ration herself to one glass a day.

Any items of furniture more luxurious than what she'd found this weekend would have to wait, as so many things were doing, until she gained some idea of whether the police would be able to retrieve any of her money.

All she knew was she didn't want to go and work on projects for big companies any more, however much they paid. She wanted a home. The depth of that longing had taken her by surprise.

And there, she realised suddenly, was one change at least. She no longer had the slightest hankering to travel the world.

She also wanted to make friends. Could she count Molly as a friend? She hoped so. And she hoped her neighbours would be friendly too.

Chapter Nine

On Monday morning Lara looked out of the back window at the sunny vista and felt her spirits lift, even though she'd heard nothing else from the police. A wagtail came and hopped across her back patio, then looked up, as if inviting her out to play. It was one of her favourite birds, delicately pretty and seeming interested in anything and everything. She loved watching them.

Should she go for a walk round the lake now or after lunch? Before she could make up her mind, a car pulled up outside her house and she went to the kitchen window to see who it was. As her ex got out, she exclaimed, 'Oh no!' and looked at him in disbelief.

What on earth was Guy doing here? Had he come to gloat? And why was he driving such an ordinary little car? He usually swooshed around the countryside in large luxury vehicles, like the show-off he was!

She stepped back out of sight as he approached the house and when he rang the bell, she hesitated about whether to open the door or not. Then she got angry with herself for being a coward and flung it open as wide as it would go.

Neither spoke for a few seconds because they were staring at one another, finding out what the years had done to the person they'd once loved. His hair had thinned a little and was grey at the temples, but he looked his usual elegant self. He always had worn clothes well, even when they couldn't afford to buy ones as expensive as these clearly were. He wouldn't approve of her short, practical hairstyle, she was sure, or the extra pounds she'd gained since they split up. She wasn't fat, not even plump, but she was no longer slender.

He spoke first. 'Aren't you going to invite me in, Lara?'

She didn't want to and was sure he knew that, but she couldn't think how to refuse without seeming churlish, so stepped back and spoke mockingly – well, she hoped she sounded mocking. 'Pray come into my humble abode.'

He walked past her and moved slowly across the room, openly studying it. He stopped by the rear window, gesturing. 'Pleasant view.' Then he took another look round, raising one eyebrow at the jumble of oddments, as if to ask her what was going on.

'Um, would you like a coffee? I'd better warn you, I only have instant.' That should put him off staying. He'd been a coffee snob long before the coffee craze was invented.

'Yes, please.'

As she was putting the kettle on, banging things around, he said abruptly, 'Look, can we please bury the hatchet completely now, Lara? You and I have children and a granddaughter in common. Would it be so hard for us to deal with one another in a friendly manner, if only for their sake?'

She shot him a quick glance to check that he was being serious – and he was, she could always tell – so she took a minute to think about it as she got out the mugs and jar of coffee. Actually, she felt pleased that he'd been the first to suggest this, so in the end she turned round and inclined her head. 'Why not?'

She followed that up by, 'I presume Darcie told you what happened to me?' She wanted to get the discussion of *that* over and done with.

'Yes. Rotten luck. I'm sorry.'

He sounded as if he meant it and they were speaking without arguing or sounding stand-offish for the first time in years. Goodness, whatever next? Well, she had more to worry about than bumping into Guy occasionally at their daughter's.

He seemed to be waiting for her to speak, so she said, 'It's been a bit of a shock, I must admit. Do you still take one sugar?'

'No, thank you. I haven't done sugar for ages. It was settling round my waist.' He began walking to and fro, as fidgety as ever. 'You must have picked up this furniture from the Pass It On Day offerings. Good thinking.'

'Yes. One of the owners of this development told me about it. Very green of everyone and highly convenient for me that it happened this weekend. Do sit down and stop pacing, Guy. You're obviously here for some reason. What is it?'

'I've brought you a car. And no, you don't owe me anything for it. I got it very cheaply.'

She froze and was about to tell him to take it away again when he held up one hand.

'Don't refuse it, Lara. It's only a little runabout and you must need a vehicle. I presume that hire car outside is yours?'

'Yes.' She felt as if she was choking, and whether it was with annoyance or gratitude or some other emotion, she didn't know. Only she couldn't say no, simply couldn't refuse such a gift. She took the coffee across to him, then brought her own and sat down opposite. 'I don't know what to say.'

'Say you'll take the car and tell me more about what happened. Did that accountant steal much from you?'

'Nearly everything.' She closed her eyes and fought for control, achieving it – but only just.

'Oh hell, that bad! Lara, I'm so sorry.'

He really meant that. She felt something inside her soften still further. 'It wasn't only me he ripped off. There were several other clients involved, apparently. The police have got Interpol working on it with them but they don't hold out much hope of catching him.'

She watched Guy take a sip and try not to grimace, but didn't dare pick up her own mug of tea to do the same or it'd have betrayed how her hands were shaking.

'That's even more reason for me not taking no for an answer. Look, I really want you to accept the car. It's not an expensive one, for heaven's sake, and I can easily afford it.'

She surprised herself by saying, 'Well, all right, then. It'll be a big help. Thank you very much. If you're quite sure.'

'I am. It's four years old and not a luxury model, but it's got low mileage and as far as my chief mechanic can tell, the engine's in good working order. It even has a satnav installed already, an older type but it still works OK.'

He looked at her warily as he added, 'I've arranged for insurance and organised the licensing and stuff.'

'Generous indeed.' She swallowed hard, watching him take another sip of coffee and stare down into his mug.

When he looked up, he asked softly, 'Do you have any money left at all?'

'Yes. Luckily I had a redundancy payout when I left the company and I hadn't added that to my superannuation account, even though Crichton urged me to, because I knew I'd need money to set up in this house. It's enough to tide me over till I can find a job.'

'Good.' His look was sympathetic but thank goodness he didn't push for more information. She'd already told him more than she'd intended. But somehow, today, he was more like the old Guy, the one she'd fallen in love with and married all those years ago.

'You'll need to drive me back home, if you don't mind, Lara. I'll go over the car with you first, show you what's what and then you can see how it drives.'

'Thank you.'

He gave her one of his wry looks. 'I think I'd feel more comfortable if you shouted at me. I'm not used to this quieter you.'

One of the tears she'd been desperately trying to hold back escaped and left a cold trail down one cheek, but she made no attempt to wipe it away, hoping he hadn't noticed. 'I'm not used to it either. Only, what good would shouting and wailing do? What I can't get over is how kind people are being to me, complete strangers even. That's really surprised me.'

'People can be kind as well as nasty, even ex-husbands.'

After another gulp of coffee and a barely concealed grimace, he changed the topic firmly. 'What do you think of young Minnie?'

Safer ground. Lara could deal with talking about their granddaughter. 'She's gorgeous. Absolutely gorgeous. I'm so sorry I missed the first few months of her life.'

His expression softened. 'I saw her when she was a few hours old. My goodness, she could cry loudly, even then.'

Silence fell and Lara searched in vain for something neutral to say.

He had another drink of coffee before looking across at her with his usual shrewdness back in place. 'Let's look over the car and take it for a spin, then I'll shout you lunch.'

She shook her head. That was a step too far in her present fragile state. If they talked for much longer she might break down in front of him. 'It'd be a waste of your money. I don't have much appetite at the moment.'

'Then we'll take a rain check on it.' He unfolded his long legs and stood up, taking his coffee mug over to the kitchen area and tipping the remaining third down the sink. 'And you and I will live in family harmony from now on.'

'Yes.' She tipped most of her own drink down the sink, had been having trouble swallowing it.

Once outside, she listened to the instructions about the controls, then gasped as she had a sudden idea. 'Oh! I've just thought of something. Could you spare me another half hour or so, Guy?' At his nod, she explained, 'If I phone the car hire people, and you don't mind a small diversion, I can return the hire car to their depot in Swindon and get some of my money back. I've already checked that with them.'

'Good idea. Monday's a quiet day for sales and the team won't expect me to spend long at the yard, so I can spare as much time as you need.'

'Thank you. That'll be a big help.'

'I'd better drive your new car. I won't be insured on your hire car.'

After that, everything went so smoothly, she was amazed.

When she finally dropped Guy off, she realised he was living in a flat and stared at him in surprise. 'I thought you hated flats.'

'I hate gardening more. I could pay someone, I know, but there's a large, sheltered balcony outside my flat, as big as a room, and I thought it'd be OK when I want to sit outside. Since Julie dumped me, I don't entertain at home, but take people out to restaurants.'

She didn't say she was sorry about his breakup. She'd been glad when she heard about it from Darcie three years ago, and if that was mean of her, well, so was the way Guy had dumped her when she wouldn't give up her travelling job.

Water under the bridge now, she reminded herself. *I have to move on.* She realised he was holding something out and took it automatically.

'I'm at Flat 10, if you ever need me. Here's my card with my personal phone number and email address on it.'

'Oh. Right. All I have is a mobile phone at the moment. I haven't got round to having business cards printed, let alone getting an Internet connection.' Only then did it occur to Lara that she wouldn't need that sort of card now – unless she got a job that required them.

'Give me your number.' He entered it into his phone.

She took a deep breath and found it easier than she'd expected to say, 'Guy – thank you. I'm very grateful.'

'My pleasure. Really it is. And Lara . . . I'm glad we're no longer at odds. Life's too short.'

She was determined to wait till she was home to let the tears fall. They'd been threatening since he gave her the car.

Strangely, the urge to weep faded as she drove away from him. The car was easy to handle; she even liked the colour. Who'd have thought it of Guy?

Miracles still happened, it seemed. As well as disasters.

She'd start work the following day on helping clear out the house next door, if that was all right with Ross. That would get her a decent bed without spending money.

Today she still had time before the shops closed to buy some paint, sandpaper and whatever else she could think of to do up the furniture she'd bought. She could work on that gradually.

She had a moment's panic as she came out of the hardware store, when she couldn't be sure which car was hers. How stupid not to memorise the number! Thank goodness for remotes that made the car lights flash at you when you clicked them. This time she stood and learnt the number before she got in.

She had to get a grip on things, had to stop being so emotional.

When she got home, Lara decided to sand down the two bookcases first and then paint them. That would be a straightforward job to get her hand in with do-it-yourself stuff.

She had to soak off various labels and stickers first.

Who would put such things on bookcases? They must have belonged to children. It took her ages.

Keeping busy helped. A little.

But she cried later as she lay in bed, trying vainly to get to sleep. She couldn't stop sobbing for a long time. Her eyes were swollen by then and they'd still be red the next day. Well, who was there to care whether they were puffy or not?

It felt as if she'd stepped from one world into another since she'd arrived in England, and she didn't know how things would work out in her new personal situation or where she was heading long-term.

A word came into her head. *Fragile.*

Yes, that was the way she felt: fragile. And she didn't like it. She had always prided herself on being a strong, modern woman.

The next morning, which was a Tuesday, Lara woke early, feeling hungry. She realised she hadn't eaten a meal last night, just had a cup of drinking chocolate and a biscuit, so no wonder.

She dressed in her oldest jeans and a faded tee shirt, ready to start work next door. Well, she would be starting if Ross turned up and wanted her.

She was just finishing a boiled egg and contemplating another piece of toast when the phone rang.

'Mum? It's me.'

'Darcie. How lovely to speak to you. When did you turn into such an early bird?'

'When I had Minnie. She thinks the day begins at five o'clock and since her majesty is in charge here now, Carter and I join her. Look, I found that photo you wanted last night. I know you haven't set up your Internet yet, so all right to text it to you instead?'

'Yes. That'd be great.'

There was the faint sound of clicking.

'There. I've sent it. And Mum – did Dad get in touch?'

'Yes. He gave me a car.'

'Gave it to you, not sold?'

'Yes. Wasn't that kind?'

'Very. I hoped he would sell you one cheaply but this is far better.'

'Did you ask him to find me a car, Darcie?'

'Of course I did. He's very comfortable financially and he's in the car business. Seemed a no-brainer to me. I'm glad you didn't refuse it.'

'Part of me wanted to, but hey, if someone holds out a great big olive branch, it'd be wrong to knock it away. I think we've, well, you know – buried the hatchet.'

There was a loud groan of relief. 'Oh, good. That means I can ask you both round to tea at the same time.'

'Darcie . . .'

'Got to go, Mum. It's a real rush here in the mornings.'

Lara sat staring at the phone. Surely Darcie wasn't trying to get her and Guy together again? That relationship was water under the bridge. She could never trust her life and happiness to him again, whatever he said or did. And he needed a different sort of woman from her.

She'd have to make that plain to Darcie and to him, too, if he showed any signs of wanting them to get back together. No, surely he wouldn't do that. *He* had been the one to end their marriage, after all.

She hesitated, dreading looking at the photo of John Crichton, and was glad when the sound of a car outside indicated that Ross had turned up. She waited for him to get out and start to heave more boxes into the house. He must be bringing a lot of things with him.

As he was closing up the car, she went out to ask, 'When are you moving in?'

'Today. This is the last load. The people hiring my house needed it ASAP, you see, and they were paying well, so I got out quickly. Did you finish your urgent jobs yesterday?'

'Yes. And my ex has given me a car.' She indicated it and added, 'He has a dealership. Wasn't that kind of him?'

'Very kind.'

That was enough of talking about her. 'Do you want me to start on your aunt's things today or will you be too busy unpacking?'

'I was hoping you could make a start because I want to sleep in her former bedroom from now on, so it'd help if you could clear it right out before I unpack my clothes. Is that OK with you? We'll call the bed payment for clearing my aunt's room, but I wouldn't mind your help after that on some other clearing-out jobs. Molly suggested a suitable hourly rate.' He named a figure and stood waiting. 'All right with you?'

'Yes, that'd be fine.' She hadn't earned so little since she was in her twenties, but hey, beggars couldn't be choosers, and a day's work would cover her food and some of her other expenses for two or three days. Brilliant!

He was still looking at her as if uncertain of how she really felt, so she added, 'To tell you the truth, Ross, I'll be glad of something to occupy myself with, so I'm available for as long as you need me. I'm only hanging around waiting for the police to see if they can trace my so-called financial advisor. I'm not sure whether to go out looking for a permanent job or not yet. I won't need to if they get my money back, but if they don't, I'll have to find something. Look, I'll come round in ten minutes or so, if that's OK?'

'Fine by me. I'll start unpacking the mugs and kitchen oddments while I'm waiting, then I can offer you a cuppa as needed. My aunt had some fine old china tea sets, but the cups don't hold enough for me and I always used to be afraid of damaging them – well, I still am, they're so delicate.' He stepped back. 'Sorry. You don't want to know all that. See you in a few minutes.'

She went inside her own home again, steeling herself to open the photo of John Crichton that Darcie had emailed, scowling at the sight of him. It was a good likeness, though. How could such a wicked man look like an amiable grandfather? She hoped this photo would help the police to catch him – oh, how she hoped that!

Would they retrieve any of her money, though, or had he got it stashed away somewhere untouchable offshore? She sighed. *Don't go there, Lara!*

She sent the photo off to Donald so that he could share it with Interpol, then went next door to start her new job. The busier she kept, the better.

The living area of Ross's house was crammed full of furniture and looked even worse than her own. There was not only a lot of furniture but also what seemed like hundreds of ornaments. She'd never seen so many in one house. Empty cardboard boxes filled what was left of the floor space. She saw his grimace as he gestured to the room.

'It's a mess, I know, what with my stuff as well as my aunt's, but we'll work on her bedroom first. I can't move my boxes of clothes and personal stuff till I have somewhere to put them and the house is as cluttered upstairs as down.'

This house was the mirror image of hers in design, with a main bedroom that was light and airy, or would have been if it wasn't so heavily over-furnished. It contained a double bed with a very pretty bedspread and as many ornaments and trinkets as the downstairs room. They paused in the doorway to study it.

'My aunt was an avid collector all her life, right till the end. She could never resist a pretty ornament or piece of silver and luckily she had enough money to indulge herself. Her money's gone to another relative, but the house and contents are mine.'

His voice sounded soft with love. Lara liked the way he talked about the old lady. 'Do you want to keep all this furniture in the bedroom?' She asked that cautiously, still not knowing him well enough to guess.

'Heavens, no! I think the best thing to do first would be to take the bed I'm giving you next door to your place, which will clear some space for storage of this stuff in the second bedroom. Is that all right with you?'

'Good idea. And look, if you want somewhere to store any boxes of things, there's plenty of room in my third bedroom.'

'Thanks. That's kind of you.'

'Well, you're being kind to me.'

They smiled at one another for a moment or two, then he said, 'Come and try the bed out.' He led the way to the second bedroom where she dutifully sat on the bed and had a bit of a bounce, then lay down. As if she'd have refused it even if it was as hard as a rock! But it felt so comfy she beamed at him. 'It's great.'

It was easy enough to get a double bed next door and he helped her take her present single bed into the bigger spare bedroom.

When they got back to his house, they began removing ornaments from the tops of small tables and fancy little chests of drawers in his aunt's bedroom, and taking them into the next room. It didn't take her long to realise something. 'Do you realise that some of these small pieces are quite valuable, Ross?'

That stopped him in his tracks.

'Are you sure? I got a guy to look at clearing the house and he said there was nothing particularly valuable and even the price of silver had dropped. He didn't offer me nearly as much as I'd expected and my cousin Fiona said I'd get far more by clearing the place out myself and selling the better items on the Internet.'

'Some of the ones that are more collectible should probably go into specialist auctions, where you'd get more for them. This one, for instance.' She stroked an eighteenth-century chest of drawers with her fingertips. 'Look at the beautiful patina on that mahogany, and it's got the original handles, too. This isn't the sort of thing you send to the local salesroom.'

He looked at her in surprise. 'You sound as if you know about antiques.'

'It's been my hobby for years, but I still have a lot to learn. That's what makes it so interesting. I watch antiques shows on TV whenever I can and I learn a lot from them. They were showing all the main British shows in Australia on the free-to-air channels.'

Another pause while she picked up a couple of pieces of china and studied the marks underneath them. 'Some of the china is quite valuable and I love this 1930s figurine. I think it's bronze, not spelter, so it'll be valuable too.'

She couldn't resist stroking the lithe young woman with her uplifted arms and graceful pose. 'I know how to find information about it online. I have a few pieces of my own that I'd stored at my daughter's house and I found a few more in Australia, which I brought back with me in my hand luggage.' She'd travelled business class, which she regretted now that her money was gone, but at least she'd been able to bring back more luggage that way.

He frowned at the miscellany of items on the bed, then turned back to her. 'You know what? You're looking for a job and I'm looking to maximise what I get from this house. I'm thinking of my retirement too, especially if I – well, don't recover fully from ME. If I allow you a percentage of what you make, do you think you know enough to sell the various pieces, Lara? I certainly don't know nearly enough to do that to best advantage.'

She didn't hesitate. 'Yes. Especially if we do some of it online.'

'How about we split what we make fifty-fifty?'

'That seems unfair to you. I'd feel more comfortable with you getting seventy per cent to my thirty.'

It was her face he studied this time. 'You're an honest woman, aren't you?'

He sounded faintly surprised, which puzzled her. Did she look dishonest? 'Well, I try to be.'

He held out his hand. 'Make it sixty-forty, then. You'll be doing most of the work, believe me. And of course, I'll cover any expenses you have as well.'

She shook hands on the bargain, feeling bemused. 'I accept, then. And, um, I can do you a website to sell from. I wouldn't charge you for a simple one. I've worked with computers for years. It'll be quite easy for me.'

'Ah, but I'd insist on paying. You need the money and I need the service. No-brainer.'

She shook her head at him but he looked immovable, somehow, so she didn't push it. 'Oh, all right, then.'

He frowned. 'I've only got an old laptop at the moment. My old desktop died and I've been meaning to buy a new one to work from.'

'It's one of the top things on my list too. I'm thinking I may pick up some small jobs online. I can get you a discount on the computer, Ross, especially if we're both buying at the same time.'

'Done.'

She couldn't stop tears coming into her eyes. It was hard to take good luck after such a major piece of bad luck. And so much sheer generosity too, even from Guy.

'Oh, come here!' Ross said gruffly and pulled her into his arms. She tried to push him away.

He stilled for a moment. 'I'm not making a pass, Lara; I'm trying to offer you a comforting hug. You seem very alone in all this trouble.'

She'd been alone for years. She didn't seem to have the knack of forming close relationships easily. And a lot of ambitious men were chary of dating women managers who might become rivals. Giving in to temptation, she rested against Ross for a few moments, not saying anything just relaxing gradually. As she pulled away, she said, 'Thank you. It *is* comforting.'

It surprised her that she'd let a near stranger cuddle her, but Ross was so gentle and unthreatening, it had been like resting for a moment in a safe haven.

She blew her nose, then pushed her sleeves up. 'Come on. Let's get to work on clearing out this room.'

The trouble was, Ross was interested in every piece she knew anything about, so they didn't make rapid progress. There were a lot of pieces that could be sold individually. Not huge-value items, though one or two might be of what she thought of as medium value, in the thousands. But the money from so many trinkets and ornaments would certainly mount up for them both.

And they hadn't even gone into the rest of the house yet. Who knew what they'd find there?

She had a private bet with herself that even the attic would be full of *objets d'art*. Her own attic space was completely empty, designed for storage only, not occupation, so that her footsteps echoed on the uncarpeted floor up there.

Two hours later, she called a halt. 'It's past lunchtime and I'm hungry, even if you aren't, Ross. What's more, you look as if you need a rest.'

'I'm hungry too.' He sounded surprised. 'Let's go up to the hotel snack bar and I'll buy you lunch.'

'OK.'

How strange! She hadn't wanted Guy to buy her lunch yesterday but she didn't mind Ross doing it.

She enjoyed his company greatly over lunch. He was

well informed about the world and he treated her as a friend and equal, not a potential conquest. It turned out that he knew a lot about old buildings, but not nearly as much about antique furniture, except for the family pieces he owned.

As they were leaving the hotel after lunch, she got a call from Donald Metcalf and said, 'Excuse me for a moment, Ross. It's the police. This could be important.' She moved away.

Donald thanked her for the photo and told her it was good enough to plug into a facial recognition system they were trying out.

'Oh, good! I hope you catch him.'

'We'll do our best, believe me, but don't get your hopes up too high. Facial recognition is in its infancy. It's likely to be a while before we uncover anything, if at all. These investigations take time and patience, I'm afraid. In the meantime, you should get on with your life, Ms Perryman.'

'Right. I will. I've even found a temporary job. But thanks for keeping me in the loop.'

'I'll continue to let you know if anything happens. And please contact me if something occurs to you. Bear in mind that even a tiny detail could help our investigations.'

She sighed as she put her phone away and caught up with Ross, who had walked on a short distance to give her some privacy and was sitting on a low wall waiting for her. She explained what had happened, then studied him. 'You need to rest now, don't you?'

'Is it so obvious?'

'To me it is. I told you: a friend of mine used to have ME. I know some of the signs and effects.'

'You said she got better. How long did that take?'

'It didn't start to happen till she went to see a doctor with an alternative focus.'

'Really? My cousin said she knew someone like that, but my specialist warned me that anyone who says they can cure it is most likely to be a snake-oil salesman. He says they get a new theory about it every year or so, but nothing definitive. That's why they call it a syndrome, not a single illness.'

'Well, I'm no expert. All I know is she was really ill and got better gradually by nutritional methods, supplements of things like amino acids and minerals, not hit-you-hard-on-the-head drugs.'

'Hmm.'

When he didn't pursue the point, she let it drop. If it had been her, she'd have been online researching and evaluating every alternative method of treatment she could find – well, not those which sounded ridiculous or promised the impossible, she wasn't a fool, but some alternative approaches to health were well respected now.

'I'll knock on your door when I wake up,' he said as she left. 'Sorry about this.'

'It's not important. If you need a rest, take one. I've plenty to keep me busy.'

Chapter Ten

Lara went into her own house and stood for a moment feeling lost, unsure where to make a start, for all her brave words to Ross. It didn't seem like home yet, more like a campsite where she was surrounded by a few pieces of grotty furniture and various boxes.

Determined to shake off the feeling of melancholy, she went upstairs to put sheets on the new double bed. When she lay down to test it, she sighed in pleasure. There! This was a huge improvement over Molly's old single bed.

She didn't need to return that bed, though, because Euan had told her to keep everything they'd given her. So *voilà*, she now had a spare bed! That was progress of a sort – wasn't it? Well, a tiny step beyond basics, at least.

The trouble was, there was no one who might sleep in that other bed. She'd lost touch with her old friends in the UK one by one as she and they moved around the world. Not all at once, but gradually. Over the years, she'd either mislaid their addresses or else they'd moved and forgotten to let her know. She could have chased them round the Internet but had been 'too busy just then' and time had passed till she couldn't really remember what they'd had in common.

Some of her generation had lived their whole lives like flotsam and jetsam, washing here and there in random forays around the globe, depending on the whims of their employers or their own desire to travel. She'd been a bit like that too after her marriage broke up.

She'd made a few newer friends over the years, of course she had, but most of them were still embedded in The Company – which she always thought of as having capital letters. They lived in hub cities, not the English countryside, and anyway, now that she wasn't part of the same organisation the connection would drop away quite quickly. She'd seen it happen many times to other people.

Perhaps she could join some local group without incurring too much expense and make new friends that way? There was that tai chi class she'd seen advertised on the noticeboard at the hotel, or there would surely be other groups of various sorts nearby.

She could cope on her own without close friends, of course she could. She'd been doing that for years. But she wanted to change things, wasn't cut out to be a hermit.

What was she cut out to be now, though? She didn't know. She'd been intending to buy and sell antiques as a hobby, and had expected to make some money from it and perhaps friends too. But she couldn't afford to gamble money on purchases now and wouldn't have much time to scour junk shops for bargain items if she was working full-time again.

Until she had found a new direction in life, she had to hope that selling antiques with Ross would bring in enough money to live on for a while, because at least she'd enjoy doing that and—

Stop it! she told herself suddenly. *No self-pity. Find something to do. Stop obsessing about details.*

So she got out the new sandpaper, took one of the tatty old bookcases outside to the paved patio area and began to rub the woodwork down. After a while she brought out one of the old garden chairs and began to work on the lower parts of the bookcase while sitting down.

She wondered how old these two pieces were. They were solidly built of wood with beautifully dove-tailed joints, which was what had attracted her to them. Many years' wear had shown in the scratches and stickers all over them, as if heedless children had played with them. Luckily most of the damage was only superficial.

They would hold all her books, she reckoned, and perhaps some of her CDs and DVDs as well. It'd be good to get out her old favourites again. It was years since she'd seen some of them. She'd paid to have a shed erected in Darcie's garden and would retrieve the final few boxes from it the next time she visited her daughter.

She needed to organise her time better and get some sort of system into her days.

Why bother? that insidious little voice inside her head whined.

Because that's how I function best, she told it firmly. *Even now.* What was that old Latin phrase her father used to toss at everyone during times of crisis? Ah yes: *nil desperandum*. She would take that as her motto from now on. Don't despair about anything.

The trouble was, every time she thought of how much money she'd lost, despair edged its way in.

A few minutes later someone said, 'Why, hello there!'

Lara jumped in surprise and turned round.

A woman of about her own age was standing smiling at her from the grass strip that ran along the back edge of the line of patios. 'Sorry to startle you, honey. Do I have a new neighbour at last?'

'Yes. I bought the house a while ago but I've only just moved in.'

'Oh, good. It'll be nice to have someone new around. I'm Cindy Pavrovic. I just got back from the States. Are you into do-it-yourself?'

'Only because I have to be.' Lara took a deep breath and said it, because if she didn't tell Cindy what had happened to her, she was sure someone else would. 'I've recently had my superannuation fund stolen by my accountant, so to furnish my house I'm having to make do and mend, as they used to say in World War II.'

'Oh, that's too bad! I hope they catch the scoundrel.'

'That's my dearest wish at the moment, too.'

'Would you like a coffee? I've just bought one of those fancy machines and I'm dying to try out my barista skills on someone. I can bring the coffee across to you. I don't want to stop you working.'

'Um, I'm not really into coffee.'

'I'll bring you a cup of tea, then. It's a good excuse for a chat.'

As she was speaking, Ross came out of the back of his house and stood nearby, stretching and yawning, and they both turned to look at him.

'Have you two met?' Lara asked.

Her companions both nodded.

'I'm going to miss Iris,' Cindy said. 'She was such a delight to chat to and I loved looking at her collections. I'm just bringing a cup of tea for Lara. I'm having a coffee. Can I bring something for you as well, Ross?'

'Yes, please, if you don't mind. Coffee.'

'Tell me how you like it.'

She listened, waved to them and strolled back to the larger detached house just beyond the end of their row.

'Nice woman, Cindy. I don't know her very well but my aunt liked having her as a neighbour. I was coming to say we could start work again, but we can do it after we've chatted to Cindy.' He ambled across to study the bookcase she'd been working on. 'This looks as if it'll come good with a bit of work.'

'I hope so. I bought a pair of them, thinking that if I painted them both white, they wouldn't look too bad. But now I'm seeing what's under the mess, I might just polish the wood instead. It looks like light oak. Could have been made in the 1930s.'

When Cindy came back with a tray containing cups and a platter of 'cookies', they had a pleasant chat, then Lara and Ross went back into his house to continue clearing out his bedroom.

'Did you have a good rest?' she asked as they made their way upstairs.

'I went out like a light.'

'Well, you look better for it, I must say. I hope we didn't wake you.'

'No, I'd already woken up. When I heard the sound of your toil, I looked out of the window of the other bedroom to see what you were doing. You were looking rather sad until Cindy joined you.'

'I was feeling both angry and sad. In fact, I'm alternating between the two modes at the moment.'

'I would too, in your place. We should bring back the stocks and put rats like that guy who stole your money in them.'

That made her smile. 'Oooh, I'd love to throw a rotten tomato at him. Maybe I'll build that into my dreams.'

Once again they surveyed the main bedroom. They'd finished moving out the ornaments but there were still the clothes hanging in the wardrobe and the drawers of underwear to tackle. Lara opened the top drawer and studied the piles of knickers that had freaked Ross out. Well, it felt rather strange to her, too, to be investigating a complete stranger's underwear.

He picked up the roll of bin liners. 'You can shove those things into these bags, then I'll throw them away.'

She felt a bit embarrassed asking, but she had to be frugal. 'Well, if you don't mind, I could use some of the throwaway clothes for rags – not the knickers, I draw the line at that, but the other stuff. I'll need plenty of rags as I renovate the furniture and it'll save me buying cloths, not to mention being better for the planet.'

'Good idea. I do admire the way you're getting stuck into making a new life with whatever comes to hand, Lara.'

'Thank you. But please don't be too sympathetic or I'll start crying again.'

'Cry away. You've a lot to cry about.'

She shook her head. She'd wept all over him once, didn't intend to make a habit of it. This catastrophe wasn't going to define her every waking thought. No way!

Darcie looked at her father, who had come to see Minnie, as he often did. But the baby was having a nap now and her father was still sitting outside in a sheltered spot on their patio, staring into space. She went outside to join him. 'You all right, Dad?'

He started and turned round. 'What? Oh, sorry! I'm being a very poor guest. I was miles away.'

'Thinking about Mum? I keep worrying about her.'

'Actually, yes. I'm worrying too now that I've spoken to her. She was so unlike her usual brisk self.'

'Who wouldn't be, losing all that money? About a million and a half pounds, she said it was.'

He whistled softly. 'She didn't tell me exactly how much. She'd done well, hadn't she? Of course, there was the money her mother left her as well as her share of our house and her earnings, but still, you have to admire how hard she's always worked. I suppose she'll have to get another job now. Sad, that. She'd always planned to retire early.'

'Are you going to retire early, too?'

'Heavens, no! What would I do with myself? My mother would expect me to spend more time with her if I did, and that I couldn't stand. I'm fifty-five but she still treats me as if I'm ten and rather stupid with it. And that old folks' retirement home she lives in drives me mad. There's always someone organising the residents – and trying to organise their visitors as well.' He shuddered.

Darcie chuckled. 'Aren't you into sing-songs and parlour games?'

'Definitely not. I'm grateful that you have Mum round for a visit once a month. Did I thank you properly for that?'

'Several times. It's harder to fit in now that I'm working again, though. But Gran's good company most of the time, though she tells me off, too. I'm doing the wrong things with Minnie, apparently.'

She hesitated but had been thinking about something for a while. 'Did Gran ever cuddle you when you were a child? She says it gives them the wrong idea of life to be picked up so often and I especially shouldn't pick Minnie up when she cries.'

He had a think, then shook his head. 'No, I don't remember her cuddling me very often. She was far more interested in cuddling my father. I don't think she's ever been really happy since he died.'

'Life is cruel at times, isn't it, especially as people get older. And there are some nasty excuses for human beings in the world who don't mind hurting others.'

'Like your mother's financial adviser.'

'Yes.'

'She was trying not to cry for most of the time we were sorting out the car,' he said suddenly. '*Lara, crying!* That surprised me and it upset me too. The car is as much help as she'll accept from me or I'd offer her more.'

'I did wonder if she'd refuse to take even that,' Darcie admitted.

He tapped the side of his nose. 'I was smart and took care not to try to give her a fancy new car. Her need was too great to refuse it. I read her right on that.' He looked at his daughter and started to say something else, then shook his head and shut his mouth again.

She didn't press him to tell her what he'd been going to say. You could only push him so far. 'Do you still miss having a wife, Dad?'

'Did I tell you that?'

'Yes. One night when you'd had a drink or two.'

'Oh. Well, the answer is yes, but I don't miss Julie per se. If I ever remarry, I'll make sure it's a woman closer to my own age, one who's past the child-bearing years and above all, one who doesn't think the whole world revolves round her. Julie was pretty and fun, but the age difference affected us more than I'd expected and her generation have different views about their place in the world, not to mention how to rear children.'

Darcie didn't say *I told you so* but she thought it. She hadn't disliked Julie, but she hadn't really taken to her, either.

'I've seen a couple of guys I know remarry and start a second family, then regret it. I didn't fancy doing that. It's hard work rearing one child and rearing two is *three* times as hard, I always reckon, because they egg each other on to be naughty or quarrel over nothing. Well, you and your brother did. I don't have either the patience or the energy for that sort of thing these days.'

'Tell me about it! One is having a huge impact on us. Minnie and her needs seem to rule our lives with a rod of iron.'

'Not planning to have any more children?'

She shrugged. 'Perhaps one more, in a year or two. I'm enough my mother's daughter to want to keep my career going as well, though. Joel isn't planning to settle down at all so I don't suppose he'll give you any grandchildren.'

'Your brother may change his mind if he meets someone special.'

'I suppose so. I didn't think I wanted children till nature tricked me into it. Now, I wouldn't be without Minnie for anything.'

'She's adorable.' He stood up. 'I think I'll skip the meal you kindly offered me, Darcie, and go home, if you don't mind. I've a lot on my mind at the moment.'

'Oh? What are you planning now?'

He gave her one of his twinkling, fatherly smiles. 'I may not want to retire but I definitely don't want to spend the rest of my life selling cars. I've started looking at other options.'

She gaped at him. 'I thought you loved cars.'

'I do. But the world is full of interesting things. And interesting people. Your mother isn't the only one with a fancy to try a new path in life.'

After he'd left she couldn't help wondering if he was thinking of getting back together with her mother.

No, he'd never do that . . . would he?

Well, even if he wanted to, Mum wouldn't. Dad had hurt her badly. Though she had accepted a car from him now, at least, so maybe the feud really was over.

Oh, who knew what to think, especially about parents. All Darcie knew was that her mother was in a terrible situation and didn't deserve it, and her father had displayed his best side in helping her out. She was proud of him for that.

What happened next was in the lap of the gods.

Chapter Eleven

The car pulled to a halt and parked a short distance away from The Gatehouse. Nonie Jayne scowled at the building through the car window. It looked as serenely beautiful as ever in the spring sunshine. She'd always loved its elegant exterior, even if it was horribly old-fashioned inside. But *he* hadn't allowed her to change any of the interior décor, let alone replace the old fittings.

Gil's voice from the driver's seat made her jump. 'It's a nice house, isn't it?'

She looked at him. 'If you like old ruins. It's not as pretty inside. The nicest thing there, as far as I'm concerned, was that it contained a lot of valuable old pieces, including some old silver that he gave me. And then he lied and pretended he hadn't done that.'

Gil chuckled. 'You like to stick to that story, but we both know it isn't true.'

'Look, you can't—'

'Doesn't matter to me. I like money better than anything

else and so do you. Just out of interest, I have ways of selling objects without attracting notice that you may not know about.'

'Oh? Do you really?'

'Yes. I think you and I could help one another here and then maybe we could go on helping one another. You didn't do your homework properly with Ross Welby, did you? He wasn't as rich as you'd expected.'

'I thought I had and—' She broke off, watching in puzzlement as a people-mover vehicle drew up in the drive and eight scruffily dressed people got out.

'Who are they?' Gil asked.

'I haven't the faintest idea.'

'They don't look as if they're here to take tea with anyone.'

'No. And what's that equipment they're carrying?'

'Who cares? We're wasting our time hanging around if he's got the painters in.'

'That's not painting equipment. Let's wait a bit longer and see what happens.'

A few minutes later a van drew up with *BellSaga Film Company* on its side in bright, sparkling letters. Nonie Jayne leant forward, surprised. 'A film company! What's that doing here?'

'I doubt it's a big company, not with a van as small as that. Was your ex into making films?'

'No. All he cared about was preserving old buildings. You couldn't get a word out of him when he was working on a project.'

Another man opened the front door of the house to the group of people who'd arrived and they greeted one another with a lot of kissy-kissy.

'Who's that?' Gil asked. 'He looks at home here. Have you ever met him before?'

'No.'

'You said your ex was short of money. Perhaps he's moved out and put tenants into this place.'

'Ross would never let strangers loose among his precious antiques. Only – perhaps he knows these people. I was so unlucky in my timing. He inherited another house from his aunt *after* we split up.'

Gil didn't answer, because he'd taken his smartphone out and was tapping on it.

'What are you doing?'

'Looking up that film company. Ah! They make movies and documentaries for TV. I bet they've hired this place for some filming. It'd be a lot cheaper to do that than to build a whole set.'

'If Ross is away, they wouldn't notice if one or two small pieces went missing. This could be a good time to see if you really can help me get hold of what's due to me.'

'We'll wait a while, keep an eye on them, but we'll do it from that little side street further along and you can tell me all about the sorts of things he has in his house.' He started the car, drove round the block and came back via the other end of the street.

Once they'd stopped, they sat watching.

'We'll get your things for you,' Gil said after a while. 'But we'll need to find enough to make it worth *my* while as well. After that, we'll talk about other jobs you and I could do together. A woman as beautiful as you can, if she's smart, make good money.'

'I've not done badly.' She smiled at her reflection in the

tinted window. Yes, she was still beautiful, but looks didn't last for ever, so she had to find her next husband while she was in her prime.

Or find out what Gil could do for her. No need to make a decision now. But she wasn't going to dive into crime. Taking her fair due was one thing, risking jail was a step too far.

She'd planned to give herself a few months off marriage after she got the money from Ross, because it could get very tiring pandering to a man and making him think she loved him 24/7.

She glanced sideways at Gil. He didn't look rich. She had a nose for that.

He might think he was going to use her but two could play at that game.

A few days' hard work got all the ornaments and collectibles that had been stored in Ross's aunt's cupboards roughly sorted out. Lara stood there with her hands on her hips after they'd carried the last boxes down, staring round the living area, trying to work out how to organise this.

'Cheer up, Lara. We're making excellent progress.'

'Do you really think so? I was thinking we'd taken far too long to get to this stage. All we've done is put similar objects into groups, more or less. We can't tell for sure which are more valuable till I do some research online.'

'I reckon we've found at least a thousand ornaments. We've also cleared out my bedroom completely, which I really appreciate, and all the cupboards and drawers upstairs, except those in the attic.'

'But this living area and the spare bedroom are in an even worse mess now than before with all the piles and boxes dumped in them. How you stand it in the evenings, I don't know.'

'Needs must. It doesn't worry me too much because I've usually got my nose in a book or I'm dozing in front of the TV. Tonight, however, I think you and I should celebrate progress by going up to the hotel to eat in a bit more comfort.'

She shook her head. 'Thanks, but eating out is too expensive for me at the moment.'

'Lara, you've done far more than I expected and done it twice as quickly. Plus you're easy to work with, no tantrums or fuss whatever happens. I think that's partly why I'm feeling better now than I have for ages. Last year was . . . bad. I want to celebrate and it's no fun doing that on your own. Tonight will be my shout and you can regard it as a bonus for working more quickly than expected. You must have earned bonuses before, surely.'

As she opened her mouth to protest, he folded his arms and declared in a mock fierce voice, 'You're coming for dinner with me if I have to drag you across to the hotel by your hair.'

She knew he'd never treat a woman like that and anyway he was trying not to grin as he spoke and failing. She was tempted to agree.

He added pleadingly, 'Joking apart, I'm going stir crazy here. I want to chill out, eat something I didn't cook or heat up and chat to a few people in the bar. Bear with me. I'm not taking you to the Ritz, just to the hotel.'

'Oh, all right. You're not the only one going stir crazy, actually.'

'That's great. It won't hurt you to loosen up a bit and

it won't make you any less efficient to take an evening off, I'm sure.'

She leant back on the sofa. 'People often say that sort of thing to me. I'm not very good at sitting around doing nothing, I'm afraid.'

'We won't be doing nothing. We'll be having a civilised conversation and chatting to Molly and Euan. I met her when I went for a stroll this afternoon. The two of them eat meals at the hotel regularly, so we've arranged to meet for dinner.'

'Oh.'

Now she was studying him as if trying to work out what he was after. The woman had never learnt to trust people easily, had she? 'Hey, how about I invite Cindy too? What do you think?' He was pleased to see Lara relax a little at that.

'I think she'll jump at the chance, Ross. She's a very gregarious woman.'

'We're meeting them at seven. Is that all right with you?'

'Yes. Perhaps one of them will know where I should go to look at antiques.'

'It's a social get-together, not a business opportunity.'

'Can't it be both?'

'Only marginally. You know, I'm going to give myself the challenge of teaching you to relax.'

'Many have tried.'

'I'll be the one who succeeds.'

There was a silence with such pregnant undertones that he wasn't surprised when she hastily changed the subject.

'I shall need to catch up on local prices before we go any further so it'd be useful to talk to them about where to look. It's all right watching antiques shows on TV but some of them are years old and we need to find out what prices are like *now*, and more specifically round here, both in shops and at auctions. They may know if there are any antiques centres nearby and a place that holds auctions.'

'There's an antiques centre in a nearby village. I forget its name but I do remember how to get there. It was once part of a dairy farm and they converted some of their barns into a sort of warehouse. Like a lot of farmers these days, they wanted to bring in other revenue streams. I think the daughter of the house runs the centre.'

'If you can find out its name online, I'll go and look round it.'

He couldn't resist teasing her. 'I'll take you myself if you're a good girl.'

'I don't need to drag you all over Wiltshire. Just get me the address and I can go on my own.'

'I may be in convalescent mode but I still need something to occupy my time.' Ross watched her run her fingers through her hair in a nervous gesture. 'Didn't you have friends to relax with down under? Most people build social and relaxation time into their lives.'

'I've been in charge of projects for several years and I was the one telling the people I worked with what to do, which made it a bit difficult to socialise with them. Fortunately I've never been a party girl, so that didn't upset me too much.'

'I'm glad you're not that way inclined. My ex was very much into that sort of life and loved to attend expensive social functions or eat at restaurants where one lettuce leaf artistically arranged seemed to cost a small fortune.'

He shook his head, annoyed with himself. 'There I go again. I wish I could stop thinking about her. I'm still not totally free, you see, not till the financial settlement is finalised and we get the decree absolute. I'm worried she's going to appeal against the arbitrator's decision.'

'At least Guy and I didn't quarrel about finances when we split up, I'll give him that. Not after the bargaining was over anyway. And he's been generous about the car. Don't tell me if you don't want to, but what was your ex like?'

He sat considering, then got out his smartphone and flipped through some photos. 'Beautiful. Dark hair and a really classy dresser. This is her. I only keep it because it's a good shot of my cousin Fiona, not because I regret my divorce to Nonie Jayne.'

'Wow, she's gorgeous.'

'Yeah. On the surface, anyway. I was blown away at first by her looks and charm. But once you've seen her throwing a hissy fit to get her own way, the beauty seems to fade. She could look really vicious if crossed.'

He put the phone away. 'If that's settled, I'll go and see Cindy about joining us for dinner tonight, then have a short rest. How about we three meet at five to seven and stroll across to the hotel together?'

'Fine by me.'

Lara went back into her house, feeling restless. She wasn't accustomed to having so much free time and nothing whatsoever needing her attention. It was no use starting work again on the bookcases. She was going out soon so didn't want to get her clothes and hands into a mess.

She went up to her bedroom to choose what to wear

and came down again to watch the news channel. She'd make sure she ordered the cheapest dishes on the menu tonight. She hated being the object of charity, still didn't feel comfortable about having accepted a car from Guy.

She studied herself in the huge wall mirror she'd bought for £10 on Pass It On Day. The frame needed a little attention but she'd got it very cheaply and could fix it up herself. She was looking good, if she said so herself. She'd lost some weight in the past week and it suited her.

Being extremely upset did that to you.

When Lara went outside to meet the others, she found Cindy already waiting but there was no sign of Ross. 'Nice to see you.' She was a bit dazzled by the amount of bling the American was wearing but some of the jewellery was really nice. She might look out for some pretty beads among the antiques. Her outfit was too plain.

Cindy beamed at her. 'Nice to have neighbours who invite you out. Ah, here's Ross. Did you fall asleep?'

'I had a nano-nap, but I'd set the timer, so it woke me up.'

'I can't do that,' Lara said. 'Take naps, I mean. I never could. My mind simply won't switch off in the daytime.'

'I find it refreshing to lie down and relax at least once during the day,' Cindy said. 'You should try it, Lara. You don't need to sleep, just let the tension go.'

She made a non-committal noise. She'd tried that. It didn't work for her.

As they turned and began strolling across to the hotel, she let Cindy and Ross bear the brunt of the conversation, envying the easy way they chatted, even though they hardly knew one another. If the walk had been longer, she'd have forced herself to do more than just murmur agreement, but the hotel was only a few minutes away and this wasn't a business meeting.

It was a lovely evening but chilly enough that she was glad to be wearing a light jacket. She was still getting used to the cooler climate here after the heat of an Australian summer and autumn.

The hotel's interior was pleasant and welcoming, with a big flower arrangement in the reception area and paintings on the walls. There was a sitting area beyond it which led into a bar and an airy dining room to the side of that.

Euan and Molly were waiting for them in the dining room with glasses of white wine in front of them and the bottle chilling in a cooler next to their table.

When they were offered a drink, Ross smiled ruefully. 'I'm afraid wine doesn't agree with me at the moment.'

'What can we get you instead, then?'

'Ginger beer would be nice.'

Euan raised one hand and the waitress hurried across immediately to take his order.

'How long are you back for this time, Cindy?' Molly asked.

'A few months. I'm getting tired of flying to and fro.' She turned to explain to Lara. 'My youngest son and his wife live over here and are expecting another child, so I want to be around for that.' She chuckled. 'They said the second one was their last but nature has tricked them into a third. My daughter-in-law is not amused by it and it'll help if I'm around to look after the other two while she produces the little dear. I like children. Do you have any, Lara?'

'Yes, two, though they're well past being children now. Darcie lives nearby and has a delightful baby daughter, but Joel isn't married and travels a lot for his work.'

Lara was relieved when the focus shifted away from her. Her companions were very easy to chat to, if you had something to chat about, but she needed a respite from the main thing going on in her life. She'd no doubt be lying awake again for part of the night worrying, as she had done every other night since she'd arrived in England.

As they finished their desserts, she suddenly felt very tired and could see that Ross was fading.

'Would anyone like a liqueur?' Euan asked.

Lara shook her head. 'Thanks, but I'm only just out of jetlag and I'm running out of steam for today.'

Ross glanced sideways at her and then across at Molly. 'I think we'll leave you three to it.'

'We can walk Cindy back to the village,' Euan said at once.

Lara let out a long sigh as they strolled back to what everyone onsite called 'the village'.

'I enjoyed their company,' Ross said.

'So did I. But I really am tired now.'

It was still not fully dark because twilight seemed to linger in the UK, unlike Australia with its abrupt daily descent into darkness. When Lara stumbled, Ross quickly grabbed her, then offered his arm. 'Hold on to me. I've got good night vision.'

'I haven't, I'm afraid.' She hooked her arm into his and it felt comfortable, so she left it there.

'I've been watching you, Lara. This is getting you down, isn't it?'

'Yes.'

'I'm not surprised. Isn't there any word from the police yet?'

'No. I'm beginning to wonder if they'll ever trace him. He's been very clever.'

'The police can be clever too and very persistent, especially with the more serious crimes.'

She could only shake her head. She didn't dare let herself hope.

'*Nil desperandum.*'

'My dad always used to say that.'

'Well then, it's obviously the correct advice. And here we are. Home.'

'Thank you for a lovely evening.'

He stepped away from her. 'Thank you for your company. Nine o'clock tomorrow morning suit you?'

'Yes. Or before that, if you're ready. I'm an early riser.'

'I used to be. Now, I never know when I'll wake up – or when I'll get to sleep. Go inside now and I'll wait to see you lock your door as a gentleman should.'

'Thank you, kind sir.'

Lara sketched a mock curtsey and opened the door. But for some weird reason as she turned to close it, they stood staring at one another. She admitted to herself that she didn't want to go inside and be on her own again.

When he raised one hand and turned away, she nodded, forcing herself to close her door again.

As she put the lights on, she thought what an easy person he was to be with. So were the others. She'd fallen lucky with her neighbours.

She looked round. Even with such tatty furniture, for the first time it felt – well, like a home.

She didn't linger downstairs but took her book up to bed

with her – and wished she still had the warmth of Ross's hand to hold instead.

Now, don't be a fool, she warned herself. But to no avail. She really liked him.

She woke in the middle of the night, angry with herself because she'd been dreaming about Ross: his kindness, his charm and his intelligence. She didn't usually dream about men in that way. Oh dear! She was no better than a stupid schoolgirl with a crush on the lad next door.

How strange! Guy was the only other man she'd dreamt about in that way.

Her whole world was topsy-turvy at the moment, so why not her dreams too? Well, Ross wouldn't know about featuring in them, would he, so what did it matter? Even a practical, middle-aged woman was allowed to dream.

The moonlight was so bright she didn't need to switch the lights on as she went to use the bathroom.

On her way back she looked out of the window at the moonlit scene. It was so beautiful she lingered.

Then a shadow moved and a figure in dark clothing wearing a hoodie walked along the far edge of the grass. Who would be out there at this time? The person seemed to be coming from the hotel towards the village.

The hotel had a good security system, but there was nothing in the unoccupied individual houses such as hers. A shiver ran down her spine. She'd better get some stronger bolts fitted to the doors. It didn't hurt to be careful. And she'd mention the prowler to Ross.

She went into the next bedroom and switched on the light to show that people were wakeful here, then hurried back to the other room to watch. The figure had turned round and was running away towards the lake now.

That was not a good sign.

She watched for a few minutes longer but there was no sight of the person coming back or of anyone else hanging around for that matter. Perhaps it had been one of the hotel's security staff? No, they'd not have run away when she switched the light on.

But why would anyone be walking round the houses? Checking them out?

Did someone know Ross's aunt had had a lot of valuable collectibles and antiques? She'd definitely tell him about this prowler in the morning, just in case.

Getting back into bed, she tried to get to sleep, but it was a while before she managed it because she couldn't get out of her mind the way the figure had turned and run away when she put the bedroom light on.

She was definitely going to get some heavy duty bolts fitted. She couldn't afford to have a monitored security system installed, but maybe she could buy an alarm and attach it to her doors herself? She'd had enough practice with electronic gadgetry over the years.

Thank goodness there were people on either side who would come running if she shouted for help.

She was still trying to work out what was going on when she fell asleep.

Chapter Twelve

Sandra had come into John Crichton's life when he was going through a very bleak time after the death of his wife. His secretary of many years retired suddenly and he had to find a new person. Sandra was head and shoulders above the other applicants and he had no hesitation in hiring her. She didn't have job references, but she was a widow, needed to earn money and was well qualified.

At first he hid what he'd been doing from her. Well, it was just a game, wasn't it? He'd started working out how to diddle his clients and get away with it, just to keep his mind busy. He'd grown so bored after his wife died.

But Sandra was good at her job and inevitably she found out what he'd been doing. To his relief she joined in the game, and they had fun plotting and planning together. That led to a few dates and she didn't seem to mind that he was twenty years older than her.

Then one day she said suddenly, 'You know, we could actually do this, John. Get rich and make fools of all these earnest savers who bore you to tears with their fiddling worries.'

He didn't believe her to be serious, so laughed. 'I suppose we could.'

She didn't pursue the matter but the seed had been sown, and when she went away for a few days to visit a long-time friend who was ill, he found himself working on the details again, this time more carefully, checking out possibilities, wondering if he could really get away with it.

The excitement made his heart skip a beat, then go faster. It thrilled him as nothing had done for years. But he still held back. He wasn't a criminal, was he?

One day some months later, following an afternoon appointment with a particularly obnoxious client, he ushered the stupid bitch out, then turned back to Sandra and said in a harsh voice he hardly recognised as his own, 'Do you really think we could do it, run off with their money – starting with hers?'

She stared at him open-mouthed, then a smile lit up her face. 'Yes, I do. And why not? I think you're as bored with this careful life as I am.'

'Oh yes. Very bored.'

She grabbed his hand. 'I'm not bored with you, John darling, never think that, but some of these customers think having half a million pounds in the bank entitles them to demand your attention for the slightest thing and they treat me like a rather stupid shop assistant. I don't know how I keep my mouth shut sometimes.'

That made him even angrier, because he'd seen some people talking down to her.

The game turned into reality as easily as that!

They got married and then took their time, working through every detail, checking every potential action more than once. He didn't intend to get caught. Oh no!

And he wasn't putting Sandra's freedom in danger, either.

Step by step they planned and re-planned what to do. He took care of the financial side of things, she dealt with the practicalities of getting away afterwards.

They laughed at the obnoxious customers now, shrugging away the thought of how this would affect the nice ones.

'You can't make an omelette without breaking a few eggs,' Sandra would say, then whirl him round in a triumphant dance.

She made him feel ten feet tall, and he was intoxicated, enjoying himself more than he could ever remember in his whole life.

The morning it all began for real, John transferred his clients' money into his new account and it felt like an anti-climax, it all went so smoothly.

He went to Paris that same afternoon, travelling by train and leaving Sandra to 'shut up shop', as she called it.

He nearly went mad during the two long days he spent on his own in the small serviced flat she'd rented under their new names, waiting for her to join him. Suddenly his fantasy had turned into reality and just as suddenly he started to be afraid, absolutely terrified of something going wrong.

He didn't dare go out in case he ran into someone he knew, so ordered meals to be sent in from the café on the ground floor. He didn't finish one of them. Most of the long daylight hours were spent staring out at grey skies, feeling hemmed in by the taller buildings surrounding the four-storey block of flats.

He lay awake half the night.

He didn't enjoy watching French TV, because they spoke too fast for him to understand what they were saying. He'd never been good at languages. With some difficulty he managed to download a couple of English-language movies, but couldn't settle to those, either.

He watched the occasional comings and goings of other tenants in the courtyard below and on the third day positioned himself by the window to watch for Sandra long before she could possibly be due.

When he saw a blonde-haired woman getting out of a taxi, he sighed and looked away, then looked back in shock. Was it? Yes, it was Sandra!

He buried his face in his hands and muttered, 'Thank goodness! Oh, thank goodness.'

She looked very different with the new short hair style and her brown hair transformed into a gleaming silver blonde. Even her clothes were different in style. She looked younger, far younger than she had before, and that upset him because his mirror had told him that morning that he was looking haggard and old.

He was waiting for her with the flat door open and when she got out of the lift, he hurried to carry her luggage, not daring to hug her even till the door of the flat was safely closed.

'You came! You came!'

She leant back in his embrace and smiled as she traced her fingers down his cheek. 'Silly boy! You've been worrying, haven't you?'

He nodded and gave her another hug.

'You should have trusted me. Your new persona and passport didn't set off any alarms and neither did mine.'

She'd waved one hand airily when he asked how she'd managed to obtain these new identity papers. The ease with which she seemed to have done it worried him more than a little. He wouldn't have known how to begin. How come she'd known? Not just passports but driving licences, lots of bits and pieces of documentation had appeared by magic, though at some cost.

She'd chosen their new names and he was now Anthony Grey, while she was Mary Grey, née Jamieson.

As Grey, he had an appointment the following day with a leading plastic surgeon Sandra had found for him. They both listened intently to what the fellow said.

'Everything you ask is possible, *monsieur*, but before we can do the work, there are some tests we need you to take. You are not a young man and it's best to be careful.'

'Oh? What sort of tests?'

'A survey of your general health. We need to be sure you can cope with a long time under anaesthetic. My secretary can book you in for next week.'

'Can't you do the tests sooner?'

'I'm afraid not.'

It seemed a very long week, even with Sandra to cheer him up.

On the day of his appointment she dropped him off at the clinic and went out shopping for new clothes for him while he took the tests.

Then he had to wait around for the results. He was surprised that Sandra hadn't yet returned. What was taking her so long?

When the door to the luxurious little private waiting room opened and she came in to join him, he felt better at once.

She was carrying some expensive-looking, monogrammed carrier bags, which she placed on the floor before coming across to kiss him. 'Nearly there now, Anthony darling.'

It took him a few seconds to realise she was using his new name. 'Yes, um, Mary. I do wish they'd hurry up with the results, though. I finished the tests nearly an hour ago.'

She came to sit beside him, taking his hand. 'Hang in there, love. It'll all be worthwhile in the end.'

'Mmm.' Her arrival had cheered him up, as her presence always did.

The surgeon came in to see them a short time later, accompanied by a nurse, and they took seats opposite, looking so grave that John's heart skipped a beat.

'Something unexpected 'as come up, I'm afraid, *monsieur*.'

The surgeon's English was good, with only a slight French accent, but it still took a few moments for what he'd said to sink in. John's heart began to thump in his chest. What could be wrong? Surely the police couldn't be on to them already?

It was Sandra who asked, 'What do you mean?'

'There is a problem with your heart, *monsieur*. I'm afraid a series of operations, such as you 'ave requested of me, would not be possible for you. The risks would be too great.'

The room spun round and everything went black.

When he came to, John was in another room, lying on a narrow bed. He was attached to a heart monitor and even he could see from the visuals that his heart was beating irregularly – well, he could feel it doing that. It'd been behaving that way for years.

The surgeon stood beside him, watching the screen, frowning. 'This incident only confirms that your heart is not up to such operations, I'm afraid. You can see how erratically it's beating.'

'Surely there is something that can be done about that?' John gestured to the pulsing, jagged peaks and troughs on the screen.

'Not as much as would be needed, I'm afraid. Your heart is showing wear and tear on a basic fault that you were probably born with. You must have noticed the irregular rhythm, surely?'

'I've had that all my life. Never thought much about it.' He'd always hated doctors messing around with him. Only the most extreme need had brought him to seek this man's services, the need to change his appearance completely.

'You should 'ave paid attention to the signs earlier. Now, it is probably too late to repair the fault, but you should consult a cardiologist, who will help you manage the condition. If you live quietly and carefully, following his advice, you will enjoy many years yet, I'm sure.'

John turned to Sandra, who was looking as shocked as he was feeling, then asked the surgeon, 'What if I'm prepared to take the risk of an operation?'

'You may be but I am not, *monsieur*. None of the major procedures you were contemplating could even be considered. No reputable surgeon would undertake them after seeing that.' He waved one hand towards the screen.

'But I—'

'Please allow me to finish. If you go to a less skilled surgeon, the sort who will do anything for money, the operations will probably kill you.'

He looked so smugly certain as he said this that John had a sudden urge to punch him in the face. Instead he turned sideways to look at Sandra.

She shook her head as if to warn him not to say anything else, then turned to the surgeon. 'You're sure a cardiologist couldn't help us prepare for, perhaps, a lesser operation or two?'

'A cardiologist will be able to help your husband get the most out of his life, *madame*, but no one can perform miracles. Some things are' – he gave a very Gallic shrug – 'beyond our power to correct. One day, perhaps, but not for many years.'

'Thank you for your honesty, *monsieur*. We shall have to manage without the operations, then. It was only vanity, after all, because Anthony is older than me and doesn't like to look it. I shall still love my husband, whatever he does.'

She hadn't once let his real name slip, John thought. She was better at this than he was. Since he couldn't think what to say or do next, he let her take charge and get them out of there.

The bill shocked him because it was huge, but Sandra paid it without blinking, using the new credit card he'd provided her with.

'You'll have to transfer some more money to this account,' she said cheerfully. 'I'm afraid I spent rather lavishly on new clothes.'

When they left, they took with them a referral letter to a woman who was one of the top cardiologists in Paris.

'I'm not seeing anyone else,' John said as they sat in the taxi.

'Shh now, we'll discuss it later.'

He stared down at the envelope, tempted to throw the damned referral out of the window, but she took it from him and put it in her handbag.

He leant back and closed his eyes, wishing they were anywhere but Paris.

He felt very English today; he didn't know why.

And was regretting what he'd done.

Back in the flat, he flung himself down on the uncomfortably hard sofa and, after a moment's hesitation, she sat beside him and put her hand in his.

He patted her beautifully manicured fingers. 'I'm sorry to let you down, Sandra. It's all been for nothing.'

'You haven't let me down, John dear. We did make sure we had an alternative, just in case. It'll have to be South America after all.'

'South America!'

'Yes. We'd better both start learning Portuguese, hadn't we?'

'I don't want to go there and I've never been good at languages, anyway. You've heard how badly I speak French and I studied it for years at school.'

She patted his hand. 'You'll soon learn a language

which is being spoken all round you, day in, day out.'

'I don't *want* to learn Portuguese and I hate the thought of going to live in South America. That's why I was going to have the plastic surgery.'

'I know, darling, but it'll be all right and you'll feel better once we get settled there. You'll see.'

She stood up and he shot her a quick, anxious look.

'I'll make us a nice cup of tea, shall I?'

He watched her move gracefully around the kitchen area. She was not only younger but much fitter than he'd ever be. Why would she want to stay with him now?

As she handed him his cup, she said abruptly, 'I'll have to go and see my contact here. We should start putting some new plans into place. No use waiting. We should leave as soon as possible. Will you be all right?'

He said yes, of course he did. He'd say yes to anything she wanted. Maybe he was an old fool, but he needed her desperately. She made life exciting, made him laugh. Perhaps even now it wouldn't be too bad.

If things worked out.

If nothing else went wrong.

Not for the first time, he wondered how she'd found all these contacts. It had certainly cost him a lot to pay for what they provided.

Oh, what did it matter as long as they got away?

Only it did matter, he found, as he sat there with his thoughts whirling round like dervishes in his brain. He only had her word about her past life. What if she was . . . a criminal?

Oh, he was being silly. This was Sandra, *his Sandra*.

Then he reminded himself that they were both criminals now.

With a sigh, he switched on the television, snuggling down on the sofa to watch a football match. At least you didn't need to speak French to know what was happening in sports programmes.

But he couldn't even concentrate on that and he usually enjoyed football, because he kept looking at his watch, wondering what she was doing, why she was taking so long.

Would he be safe without the plastic surgery? There was this facial recognition stuff the police could now use. He'd read about it, seen it on TV. You had to be extremely careful of what you did and where you went.

Facial recognition was still in its infancy, but it would improve quickly, he was sure. Technology seemed to be on the gallop these days, changing the world faster than a plain man like him could keep up with it.

Sandra had assured him that plastic surgery would change him so that neither machines nor humans could ever identify him again as John Meyer Crichton, late of London.

It had all been in vain, though, damn it! He was richer now than he'd ever expected to be, far richer, yet he couldn't do much with all that money, let alone make Sandra's life a happy, interesting one. He had to *live quietly* because of his heart. And live in a foreign country, whose language he didn't speak.

Fate was catching up with him, he realised suddenly. He was going to pay for his crimes one way or another. Only he had to somehow make sure *she* could get out of this mess safely.

But South America! Oh dear, that was where criminals went in bad movies. The Great Train Robbers had gone there too in real life, if he remembered correctly.

Why the hell had he done it? He'd been making a good living.

Oh, he knew why: he'd done it to show off to his younger second wife, that was why, prove that he was still a bit of a lad.

Would she even stay with him now?

His heart hiccupped in his chest and he pressed one hand against it till it settled down again.

Then another worry crept into his mind. What if she was just pretending to love him? What if she took the money and vanished?

No, Sandra wouldn't do that – would she?

Well, she couldn't at the moment because he had to be involved in their major financial arrangements for money to be transferred. They'd planned to share control of the money once they were safely away because he didn't want any suspicious changes to show in his bank records before that.

Maybe he wouldn't share control with her yet. He didn't want her to be able to leave him high and dry if he became too big a burden. And he also didn't want anyone to blame her if the two of them were found out. He would tell her that he was doing this to keep her safe if they were caught.

He'd make a will leaving everything he owned to her, of course he would, but he'd keep the money under his own control. He knew more than she did about banks and figures and money transfers, so it'd be relatively easy for him to make sure she couldn't steal the money from him.

That decision felt right, made with his brain not his heart.

He began to think it through. At least he could still plan better than most people, weak heart or not. He'd already proved that.

When he felt hungry and looked at his watch, he found that three hours had passed. Where the hell was Sandra? She should have been back by now.

Chapter Thirteen

The next morning, while she was finishing getting ready to go out and look round the antiques centre with Ross, Lara heard a car draw up outside. Naturally she went to peer out of the bedroom window. You did that automatically when you lived so close to your neighbours, she'd found.

She immediately jerked back out of sight. Oh no! It was Guy. What did *he* want now?

Well, it wouldn't be right to pretend not to be here because she owed him for the car, so she ran down to answer the door, waiting for him to say why he was there.

'You're looking more rested today, Lara.' He studied her openly. 'You're certainly wearing well. Aren't you going to invite me in for a cup of coffee?'

'I'm just getting ready for work. And why are you calling at this hour of the morning, anyway? Unless you've changed your modus operandi totally, you're usually in the office at this time of day, seeing that everything starts smoothly.'

'I've changed, as I'm sure you have, too.'

He was still waiting, head on one side, a challenging half-smile on his face, so she said, 'Oh, come in, then.' She waved one hand towards the furniture. 'You have the choice of a garden chair at the kitchen table or an uncomfortable armchair with a view of the patio.'

He took the garden chair, sitting near the kitchen area watching her, rather too close for comfort. You could never ignore his presence.

She put the kettle on and stayed at the other side of the table, waiting for him to explain why he was here.

'I thought you and I might take young Minnie out to the park this coming Sunday, like other fond grandparents do. Apart from the fact that you'll want to get to know her better and she's a great little kid, I think Darcie and Carter might welcome some time on their own.'

Lara had been going to refuse to go out with him, but had to ask, 'Why? Aren't they getting on?'

'They're getting on just fine, but like all young couples, they need time together. I've been thinking of taking young Minnie out, but I will confess to chickening out about doing it on my own. I'm no good at changing nappies.'

'You never were.'

He shrugged and grimaced. 'That wasn't feigned. Dirty nappies really did make me want to throw up, still do. Anyway, how about it?'

She didn't know what to say. It'd be lovely to see Minnie and she should have thought of taking her granddaughter out herself. 'All right.'

'Don't overwhelm me with your enthusiasm.'

'I won't.' She plonked a cup of instant coffee in front of him and sat down. 'What time and what is there to do at this park?'

'I'll pick you up just before ten in the morning, then we'll grab Minnie and take her to the park near my flat. It's an upmarket one, with a special playground for littlies: strap-in swings, a very low slide and rubbery stuff on the ground in case they fall. Talk about occ. health and safety taking all the fun out of playing pirates! You might like to wear jeans or shorts.'

She felt uneasy, because she was sure there was something behind this, but she couldn't think of a reason for refusing and she did want to see Minnie, so she said, 'All right.'

He took a sip, managing not to grimace.

She didn't attempt to hide her amusement. 'I still don't drink coffee myself, Guy, and I get so few visitors, it's not worth buying the fancy stuff.'

'Hmm. I'll have to get used to this sort, then.'

'Why would you want to?'

He didn't pretend not to understand. 'Because of what I said last time. Grandparents who get on with one another make for happy family get-togethers.'

'You never used to care about our children when they were little. You were utterly work oriented.'

'And by the time I realised there was more to life, they were nearing the end of high school and you were just as work oriented as I had been.' He held up one hand to stop her carrying on. 'Can we let those particular sleeping dogs lie? I paid for my various mistakes big time. Let's start off a new phase of our lives as friends, eh? I've always enjoyed your company and we've never been short of something interesting to chat about, have we?'

She shrugged, then confessed, 'I don't feel able to chat

about anything that'd interest you at the moment, Guy. My mind's in turmoil.'

'No news from the police?'

'Nope. Not a single thing.'

'I'm sorry to hear that.' Then he caught sight of his watch and stood up. 'I have a meeting scheduled in half an hour, so I'd better get on with my day and leave you to yours.'

She hid behind the curtain and watched him go. Big swooshy car this time. It suddenly occurred to her that he was still a good-looking man.

Why hadn't she dreamt about him? Why was it Ross who had joined her in a rather exotic dream?

Because the thing she'd had for Guy was over and done with. The sight of him no longer made her heart beat faster. Surely he didn't want to revive their relationship?

No, of course he didn't. This was what he'd said: wanting to keep the family together, for Darcie and Minnie's sake. And Carter's too, she supposed, only she didn't know her son-in-law very well. He'd happened along during her travelling years. She'd met him when she came back between projects and had come home to see Darcie married, naturally. But she'd never spent much time with him and no time at all, now she came to think of it, on a one-to-one basis.

It had been a nice wedding but not fancy, at the couple's request. They were such a sensible pair, not into wasting money on weddings when they needed to save up for a house deposit.

Guy had given them a big chunk of money as a wedding present.

She had never been in his league financially so had given them what she considered reasonable and Darcie, bless her, had asked if she was sure she could afford that much.

Guy had still been with Julie then, so Lara had felt rather alone at the local pub after the registry office wedding.

Oh, why was she going through all that stuff again? Coming home had certainly stirred up the embers of her life.

She might ring Guy and say she preferred to take Minnie out on her own. Or she might not. She felt disoriented at the moment, was having trouble finding the old Lara. Probably it would be better for the baby to be with someone she recognised as well as a strange grandma.

It was a relief when Ross rapped on her kitchen window and held up five fingers. Lara rushed round checking that all the windows were closed and the patio doors locked before grabbing her jacket.

She was looking forward to checking out the antiques centre and making a start on understanding current prices of old china and small silver items. It'd be good to have something else to occupy her thoughts.

Just as she was leaving the house her phone rang. She nearly didn't answer it, but it might be the police. She saw Ross waiting outside and held up the phone as she put it to her ear.

'Lara? Donald Metcalf here.'

'Oh, hi.' Thank goodness she'd answered it. She waited, hardly able to breathe, so desperate was she for news, any news.

'Just thought you'd like to know. We're pretty certain we've traced your accountant to a cross-Channel ferry. Bit of luck that a colleague was checking something else out and happened to recognise Crichton on the CCTV footage. We've checked out vehicle registrations for that crossing and he wasn't listed as owning any of them. And he certainly didn't travel under his own name. We have a list of passport holders, but it'll take a while to check them all out.'

'Pity.'

'Unfortunately, we don't know where he went in Europe after that, though it's most likely he went to Paris first. It's such a hub for rail travel. We didn't see any sign of his wife, though, and she wasn't at the London office that day, either.'

'Thanks for telling me, anyway. I appreciate that.'

'I'll always keep you informed, Lara. We do understand what this sort of theft means to the victims. It strikes people very hard to have a lifetime's hard work wiped out. We're doing our best for you, I promise.'

To her annoyance, she was so close to tears she gulped loudly enough for him to have heard, but he didn't comment, thank goodness.

'I'll get back to you if we find anything else out. It's a good sign that we've got something to start from, gives us a better chance of finding him.'

'Just one thing, Donald. You said Sandra wasn't on the ferry. Look, she had shoulder-length brown hair and if I were her, I'd probably have changed the style completely. Try blonde or red hair and a short style.'

'We've only got some CCTV from the office block with her on it, brown hair and all, and there were no photos of either of them at their home, so she's going to be harder to trace. It's a bit of a pain how women can change their hairstyles and colours so easily and nobody blinks an eye. Look, you'll know what she looks like better than we do if she was his receptionist. What sort of clothes does she wear?'

'She always wore classic, understated outfits when she was in the office. Mousy-looking, I thought. Maybe you should look out for her to be wearing a lot of bling and fashionable clothes.'

'Worth a try. Let me know if you have any more thoughts about it, anything at all.'

As the call ended she wondered if he thought her a fool for trying to teach him his job. Of course they'd figure that Sandra would have changed her appearance. Only they had no real photos of her to work from.

Actually, he'd sounded as if he meant it when he said she'd been useful.

She sighed. She was clinging to every shred of hope but she had to face the fact that she would probably not get her money back, even if they caught John.

Damn him and all thieves like him! They stole more than just money.

Donald put the phone down and shared what Ms Perryman had told him with a female colleague.

'Worth bearing in mind, since she's seen the woman in the flesh. We should run any photos of possibilities that we collect from CCTV past Ms Perryman.' She looked at him. 'What's wrong, Don?'

He thumped one clenched fist down on his desk. 'The poor woman was holding back sobs. I heard her gulp a couple of times. I hate this sort of crime.'

'I hate terrorism and murder a lot more, but I know what you mean. This is a particularly unkind type of theft because it mainly hits older, more vulnerable people, decent folk who've worked hard and been frugal.'

Chapter Fourteen

Lara got into the car and let out her breath in a long, slow sigh as Ross drove her out of Marlbury and into the beautiful Wiltshire countryside. Today she glanced only briefly at the old houses with their tall gables that they passed occasionally. She was more concerned to bring Ross up to date on what Donald had told her about John Crichton.

'Well, it's something at least that they've found out he's left England,' he said when she'd finished her tale.

'Yes.' Then she remembered the figure she'd seen last night and told him about that as well.

'Strange. I don't suppose it can be—' He broke off abruptly.

'Can be what?' she prompted.

'My ex. I had to stop her stealing some of my family's most valuable silver pieces.'

Lara looked at him in shock. 'But I thought the arbitration had settled your payment to her.'

'They might have, but has she accepted it?' He frowned, then shook his head. 'No. Even she wouldn't be so stupid, surely.'

'Well, I have no idea who it was but I'm going to get some strong bolts fitted to my doors and the downstairs windows too.'

'I'll fit them for you.'

'You should get some too, Ross.'

'I will. But we'll not do it today. I've been looking forward to an outing.'

'You're right. I doubt anyone will be prowling round during the daytime. There are too many golfers around. I've been looking forward to visiting an antiques centre too.'

'You seem to love antiques, Lara.'

'Yes, I do. I was going to buy and sell smaller items on the Internet after I retired. Only in a casual way, for my own pleasure, but I'd hoped to make a bit of extra money from it because I've proved quite good at spotting a bargain. But anything we find today will be yours, of course, since you're employing me. I'll still enjoy the hunt, though.'

His surprise was evident. 'Are you expecting to find things to *buy*? I thought we were just going to scope out prices.'

'I always keep my eyes open, so we might or might not spot something worth buying. Since you're employing me, the profit will be yours.'

'I don't agree with that. I'll pay for anything you find today and we'll split the profits fifty-fifty.'

As she opened her mouth to protest he cut in. 'Don't argue. It's only fair because I don't have your knowledge of antiques so I could never do anything like that on my own.'

'Oh. Well. All right.'

A couple of minutes later, he said, 'You're an amazing woman, you know. What other secret skills are you hiding?'

She felt flustered and was glad when they drew up at the antiques centre just then and she could ignore his question. There were no secret skills that she could think of. She was rather a boring person, really – a workaholic. Like her son.

She looked round. 'This still looks more like a farm building than a shop, doesn't it? If it weren't for the sign I'd have driven right past.'

'That's rather the point of having such a big sign. And this one is not only eye-catching but much cheaper than changing the buildings.'

Ross parked neatly near two other cars. He seemed brighter today, Lara thought as they walked towards the door. Perhaps he was starting to relax now that he'd had a positive outcome to the hearing and rented out his family home profitably. Less stress was always helpful.

She stopped just inside the doorway of the centre and he stopped too.

'Something wrong, Lara?'

'No. I'm studying how the centre's laid out, that's all. Let's start in that part to the right, where there are display cases. We can't look at every single item in a space this big, nor do we need to. We're not here to check out big furniture. Your aunt collected small objects mainly and those glass cases have lots of things in them which must be more valuable than what's on tables or shelves or they'd not be locked away. Your aunt's items are of really good quality, even if not hugely valuable.'

'Good thinking. Just lead the way and I'll follow meekly behind you. This is where your expertise puts you in charge, your ladyship.' He tugged an imaginary forelock at her and they both chuckled.

She pulled out a notebook with attached pen. 'I won't remember all the details, so I came prepared. This suits me better than an electronic device because I can tear out the notes later and put them with the same type of memos at home.'

'Why am I not surprised?'

She looked at him uncertainly.

'It was a left-handed compliment, teasing you about your efficiency.'

'Oh. That's all right, then.' She wasn't used to being teased, but it felt good.

They moved slowly along the first few display cases, with her noting down prices of relevant items. At the end she stopped and looked at the scribbled figures. 'I think your aunt's collection might be more valuable than I'd realised if these prices are typical, though of course these are retail prices. You wouldn't get this much for them at auctions, where prices can fluctuate unbelievably.'

'It'd make me very happy to get more for them. An old house like my family home is always money hungry. You wouldn't believe how much I spent catching up on maintenance when I inherited it.'

After an hour or so, he called a halt. 'They've got a refreshment area over there and a couple of tables. Let's stop for a break and a snack.'

'Oh, sorry. I keep forgetting that you need to go carefully.'

'I slept well last night and I'm feeling pretty good today, but I don't want to push myself too hard. Anyway, I'm thirsty.'

They stood in front of a self-serve system, which seemed

to rely on customers' honesty because there was an open box for payments.

As she was about to sit down, something caught Lara's eye on a table of oddments nearby. She dumped her cup down next to his and hurried off, calling over her shoulder, 'I'll be back in a minute.'

Only, she didn't come back. He watched her pick up a few things, study them and put them down again. Then she moved on to study some pieces of furniture before picking up two wine glasses on her way back and bringing them to their table.

When she sat down next to Ross, she said in a low voice, 'I think your aunt's tallboy is worth rather more than we guessed. There's one like it for sale at just under £500.'

'*What?* We won't get anything like that at an auction.'

'No, but by selling online, we can ask a lower price and still keep more of it for ourselves, because we won't be paying commission. Though we may have to wait to sell some items, of course.'

'Good thinking.' He gestured to her hand, which was curved protectively around the two glasses. 'What have you got there?'

'Oh, just two old glasses. We may make a pound or two on them.' She gave a quick shake of the head and changed the subject quickly.

He took this to mean she didn't want to discuss the glasses now. Were they valuable? They weren't very big and looked rather scratched.

Ross had been watching her with great interest, seeing a new side to the unhappy woman who'd needed a comforting hug so desperately. Today her eyes were bright and her whole bearing was that of a person enjoying herself. Her enthusiasm for old things was very attractive. Well, enthusiasm for anything was usually attractive, he'd found.

She certainly seemed to know her stuff about antiques, too. She reeled off figures, knew what era many items were from before she even picked them up, and showed him makers' marks he hadn't even noticed on some items.

'Why on earth did you go into management and sales when you're so good at this stuff and you obviously love it?' he asked before he could stop himself.

'To make enough money to retire early and be independent financially. I saw how my husband relished the financial rewards of his hard work as he grew more successful and I wanted that security. Besides, I didn't know nearly as much about antiques in those days. It was just a hobby I tried to squeeze into a busy life, so I didn't even consider trying to find work in that area.'

'Didn't you discuss your career with your husband?'

'Guy was working so hard I rarely saw him and he said there was no need for me to work that hard. But I was determined, so I tried to figure out how I could do better for myself. He wasn't mean with money, but I wanted to be independent.'

'You know, I think I'd have felt the same.'

'Over the years I picked Guy's brain about business and management without him realising and I attended a few management courses. I gradually changed how I was working and made it clear I was available to travel. I took a big step forward when I was given my first overseas project to *manage* and made a success of it.'

'How long did that take you away from him for?'

'Three months. He was furious about me going off for so long but I enjoyed being in charge of the project and the kids were more or less off our hands by then. He could well afford to hire a housekeeper.'

'Was that why you split up – you working away, I mean?'

'It was the final straw, but we'd been growing apart for a while. Guy didn't like living alone and said I should rethink what I wanted. *He* wanted a wife to look after things on the domestic front so that he could go after the money unhampered by such things as managing a house or answering distress calls from kids at uni. And he wanted the physical side of marriage, too.'

'Was it worth the breakup of your marriage?'

She shrugged. 'I was ambivalent at the time. Now, I think it probably was. I'm a much stronger person because of it. But who can ever know for certain where another life choice would have taken them? I just wish I'd been more careful about choosing a financial adviser.'

She shook her head and stared down at her clenched hands for a few moments, then asked, 'What made you marry a woman like Nonie Jayne?'

He took that change of subject as a signal that she'd shared enough personal information, so gave her his usual summary answer before suggesting they get back to their investigations. This time they grabbed a shopping trolley to accommodate their purchases, which included one or two inexpensive items for Lara's house. She'd found a very pretty tray and a bargain box of household oddments.

'You sure you don't mind me doing this while I'm supposed to be working for you?' she asked. 'Only you don't often get things as cheaply, and I don't have any odd dishes and bigger bowls.'

'I don't mind at all. Stop worrying. I'm enjoying our outing.'

By one o'clock, Lara had filled several pages of her notebook and put a few antiques in the trolley. Ross trailed behind her, starting to feel tired now. She was incredibly focused when she was doing something. He'd rarely seen such utter concentration.

When she showed every sign of carrying on without a lunch break, he grabbed her arm. 'That's me done for the day, I'm afraid.'

'Oh yes! Sorry, Ross. I forgot.'

'I've only just started to sag. I've not done too badly.'

As they got into the car, he realised she was fizzing with excitement and holding the bag containing the two glasses with great care.

She turned to him gleefully. 'I didn't say anything in there in case someone overheard and wanted to charge us more, but I think these might be quite valuable. They're not exactly traditional in size and shape but they look quite old.'

'How can you tell?'

She waved one hand as if trying to drag the words out of the air around her. 'I don't know. I just – have a feeling sometimes. And at a pound each, what have we to lose?' She peeped into the bag to study them again. 'I'm pretty sure they're mid to late eighteenth century and since they haven't any damage at all, they may be worth over a hundred pounds each, possibly more.'

He could only gape at her. 'You're joking!'

'I never joke about money. We'll have to have them appraised by an expert, of course.' She continued to clutch the bag. 'Drive carefully. We don't want to damage them.'

When they got home, she slid out quickly. 'I'll take the glasses inside, then come back for my bits and pieces. You go and sit down.'

He ignored that and helped her carry her oddments in, but was quickly ushered out again.

'I need to get on with some of my own stuff now, if you don't mind. I'll take photographs of the glasses and send them to a guy I know first, though. It may be a day or two before he gets back to me. You look like you need a good rest.'

'You seem excited.'

'I am. If I'm right about these, it'll pay for my food for a week or two.'

'Is that how you think of them?'

'At the moment it's how I think of everything.'

'Well, let's hope we get good prices for them *and* for my aunt's things.'

But she'd already gone into her house.

Ross smiled as he unlocked his front door and carried his things inside. She was such a focused person. What would she be like in a relationship?

He stared in the direction of her house, puzzled. What had made him think of that?

No wonder she'd been a success as a project manager – and hadn't made a success of marriage to an equally focused person. To his mind, you needed two people to put their efforts into a relationship, not one and a half. The old phrase 'give and take' was spot on about what was needed on both sides. That was how he and his first wife had been.

He was enjoying Lara's company and there didn't seem to be any nasty edges to her. It'd be hard to live at such an intense pace all the time, though. It'd be interesting to try to coax her into relaxing and see whether that made her happier – if you could be happy after all your savings had been stolen, that was.

He did hope the police would catch this Crichton guy.

He sent a wish for that flying into the ether, then smiled at himself for doing it. Diana had always done that, said it never hurt to send good vibes out. Ah, he missed her wisdom and kindness so much still. He didn't miss Nonie Jayne at all.

He sat down with a cup of coffee, going over the morning. Why had Lara's ex dropped by today? Was he trying to get them together again? Ross frowned. He didn't like the idea of her going off with that fellow. Two workaholics getting together again was a recipe for disaster, surely?

It was none of his business, of course. She was his neighbour and employee, not his girlfriend. But he thought they might become good friends, perhaps more. He was attracted to her, but it would take more than physical attraction to keep his interest, so he wasn't rushing into things.

Nonie Jayne had been gorgeous-looking and good in bed, so beautiful he'd been bowled over by her looks. But she'd turned out to be a poor conversationalist, without an original idea in her head. She'd preferred to watch old movies on TV in the evenings rather than chat and had rarely watched the news or cared about the international situation.

He'd been stupid to get involved with her. And bored after the first flush of enthusiasm.

His first wife had been as much a friend as a lover and that had been a far more satisfactory basis for a relationship.

The question was, did he want to get involved with someone else? Ross smiled ruefully. Well, he'd vowed not to when he broke up with Nonie Jayne, but did you get any choice about being attracted? Not really.

He could feel his smile fading. You got a choice about what you did with an attraction, though. He'd try to make very sure of someone before he stepped into any close relationship in future.

But he did like Lara, faults and all.

A yawn cut off his increasingly tangled thoughts and he went for a lie-down.

On the Sunday, Lara had intended to drive herself to Darcie's, so that she wouldn't be dependent on Guy for when she came back. However he didn't return her calls, even though she left a voicemail message *and* texted him to say she'd rather meet him there.

Unfortunately she got lost in the task of creating a website for selling Ross's antiques and collectibles online, and to her annoyance, Guy arrived to pick her up before she'd even begun to get ready.

Scowling, she flung open the front door. 'I left a message that I'd drive myself over to Darcie's.'

'Seems silly to do that when you're on my way there.'

'Don't be daft! I'm not on your way – unless you've moved house since I dropped you off at your flat a few days ago.'

His voice was mild. 'You don't know where I've come from today. Did I say I drove here from home?'

'Oh, you always have an answer when you want your own way, don't you?'

He grinned. 'I try to have.' Then his grin faded to be replaced by a sympathetic look. 'Had some bad news from the police?'

She managed a shrug. 'One sighting, then he vanished again.'

'That's tough.'

Before she could stop him, he put an arm round her shoulders and gave her a quick hug. She only just stopped herself responding. Stepping quickly away, she busied herself making sure she had everything she needed in her shoulder bag.

'Right. Let's go.' She led the way out briskly, but spoilt her gesture by forgetting to lock the front door till he reminded her.

'Chill out, Lara! We're not bound to an exact time of arrival at Darcie's.'

Why did men keep telling her to chill out or relax? She preferred to keep busy. Especially now. It kept her mind off her problems.

Ross was just leaving and waved one hand to them. 'Have a great time with your granddaughter, Lara.'

She contented herself with a quick wave in response.

Guy fussed around, closing her car door for her, then getting into the driving seat. 'Do you tell that man everything you're doing?'

'We chat. All the neighbours do here. Everyone's going round to Cindy's tonight for drinks – she's another neighbour.'

'Lucky you. I don't know any of the neighbours in my block of flats.'

'In my experience, one rarely does in what they call executive flats. This place is the best I've ever discovered for a single person to live in.'

'But they're such small houses.'

She looked at him in surprise. 'Not all of them. Cindy's house is quite big, actually. It's that one.' She pointed. 'Only I couldn't have afforded one of those unless I wanted to work for the company for another year or two. Which I didn't.'

'What will you do now that things have gone pear-shaped, get a job?'

She shrugged. 'I suppose so. I'll take my time about that because at least I don't have a mortgage, so I'm hoping I can find something I quite enjoy.'

'I hope they catch that sod who stole from you.'

She could hear the sincerity in Guy's voice and was touched. 'Mmm. So do I. I'll manage, whatever. I always do. I've got good marketable skills. Unfortunately I won't earn as much this time round. Anyway I don't want to climb any more corporate ladders. I'll do project work, I suppose, till I'm mature enough to collect the old age pension.'

She hadn't even begun to investigate that, didn't even know how the rules worked in more than vague general terms.

'Perhaps you can set up in business for yourself.'

'What with? You need capital, money to live on for at least a year and money in reserve. The lack of financial backup is one of the main reasons small businesses fail within the first year. I don't intend to risk losing what little I've got left. Having that house is one of the things keeping me sane.'

She blew out a breath, trying to blow out her tensions with it. 'Anyway, I'm determined to enjoy this morning so let's not talk about that any more.'

'We'll both enjoy ourselves, I'm sure. Hard not to with such a cheerful baby.'

But when they got to Darcie's, their daughter opened the door and flapped her hand at them as if to push them away. 'Stay back. Plague warning.'

'What's the matter?'

'Minnie's been sick three times this morning, poor little thing, and Carter has just thrown up as well. Best if you don't even poke your noses inside. You don't want to catch whatever it is.'

'Definitely not.' Guy stepped smartly backwards. 'It's going round. One of my salesmen was off with it on Thursday. He caught it from his young son. If it's the same thing, it's short-lived but violent.'

'Well, the shorter the better. Oops!' Darcie clapped one hand to her mouth and closed the door again hastily.

Chapter Fifteen

For a moment or two neither of them moved, then Guy gestured towards the car and Lara walked slowly back to it.

She slid in, feeling let down. 'What a waste of a morning! I'd been so looking forward to getting to know Minnie better. And you're wasting time, too. You wouldn't have to drive me back now if you'd done as I asked and left me to make my own way here.'

'I don't mind. I've nothing better to do.'

'You can always go in to work. You used to do that most weekends, even when we were together.'

'I only go in on Sundays now if I'm needed because I have an excellent manager and I'm financially secure.'

'Lucky you.'

He winced. 'Sorry. I didn't mean to rub salt in your wound.'

'No, it's I who should apologise for being so touchy. What happened to me wasn't your fault.'

They drove in silence for a few minutes and she lost

herself in her thoughts. When she looked up she couldn't work out where they were.

'This isn't the way back, Guy.'

'No. I thought I'd take you out to lunch. You refused an invitation when you first arrived but there's nothing to stop you joining me today.'

'Only the fact that I don't *want* to have lunch with you.'

'Am I that bad? Or are you still that bitter?'

She had to think about that, then shrugged. 'Neither. I'm just not in the mood for socialising.'

His voice grew sharper. 'You'll be in the mood for going out tonight, though, I bet.'

'That's because of Cindy. She's very hospitable and it's hard to say no to her – though it won't hurt me to get to know the neighbours. In fact, that's part of my plans for the future.'

'Well, I haven't got any plans for the rest of the day so please have lunch with me, Lara.'

She gaped at him, surprised to see him flush slightly. It wasn't often he'd ever pleaded for anything, but today there was something needy in his tone of voice that made her hesitate to turn him down. 'Why?'

'Because I'd welcome the company. You're usually interesting to chat to and I've had a week of stupid clients and an even more stupid salesman, whom I had to sack. I don't allow lying to clients, as you know.'

'No. I'll grant you that. You've always traded honestly. The jokes about used car salesmen would never have applied to you.'

'Wow. A compliment from you, Lara. I wish I could frame it! Go on, join me for lunch.'

'Oh, all right. But nowhere fancy.'

'A pub lunch suit you?'

'Yes, but won't the pubs be crowded on a Sunday?'

'I can check with a couple of places I visit regularly.' He pulled over at the next layby and took out his phone.

Why had she given in? she wondered. It was one thing to meet Guy in family situations but them going for a meal together felt – weird. He was obviously determined to mend more than general family relations.

Or he really was lonely.

Or both.

Well, going along with him was small stuff compared with her other problems. And he had always been interesting to chat to as well, she'd give him that.

He proved that hadn't changed during the simple lunch they ate in a sheltered corner of the pub's gardens and their conversation never faltered: politics, self-drive cars, the idiotic hairstyles one of his young salesmen wore, gelled to stand straight up as if to defy gravity and, Guy suspected, to make this particular guy appear taller.

They didn't order wine because neither of them liked to drink alcohol in the daytime, so he ordered a bottle of sparkling elderflower instead. Lara sipped hers with relish. She'd missed that quintessentially British drink when she was overseas.

She was surprised when Guy glanced at his watch and said, 'I'd better get you home now, I suppose. Didn't you say your drinks party starts at five o'clock?'

She looked at her own watch. 'Wow! I didn't realise it was so late. Thanks, Guy. I've really enjoyed myself.'

'My pleasure. Um, can you bear to do it again?'

There was a nervous edge to his voice again, so she said, 'Yes.'

'Good.'

She watched him frown as he went back to his car after seeing her to her house. OK, she was peeping out of the kitchen window again. But she didn't think he'd noticed.

Why was he frowning?

And why was he seeking her out like this?

Fancy such a successful businessman admitting he was lonely.

Well, join the club. She'd been lonely for a good while. Not that she had let it get her down. Of course she hadn't. Well, not often.

Loneliness was apparently one of the problems of the times for older people. She shrugged and put her feet up with a book on Georgian silverware for half an hour before getting ready for Cindy's drinks party. It'd have been called a 'sundowner' in Australia. Cindy had called it 'late afternoon drinks and nibblies'.

While she was changing her clothes, Lara grimaced at herself in the mirror and ran her fingers through her hair. Either she should get it trimmed or grow it longer. The latter would be cheaper in the long run, if she could stand a few months of untidiness.

She didn't feel like socialising now. For two pins, she'd grab a bowl of cereal and have a quiet evening at home, only the others would see that her lights were on and she suspected that Ross would come and fetch her if she tried to do that. He might be quiet but he wasn't timid about making friendly gestures.

To have two social events in one day was incredibly rare for her. She hoped the other people at Cindy's would be good at small talk. She certainly wasn't when it came to strangers, whatever Guy said about enjoying her company. But then, he wasn't a stranger.

Ross didn't seem like a stranger now, either. It had surprised her how easy she found it to chat to him.

She clicked her tongue in annoyance at herself. Why was she worrying about tonight anyway? She'd bet Cindy would keep the conversational ball bouncing if things slowed down.

Who else would be there? Not many, surely? There were only a few houses built in the small development, though others were under construction, some nearly finished.

Taking a deep breath, she opened the front door, muttering, 'Just do it!'

When he left Lara's house, Guy stopped at the sales office, parking on the other side of it and hoping she hadn't seen him stop there.

She'd piqued his interest in this leisure village and he wanted to check what the bigger houses were like. He didn't really want the hassle of moving house again but that block of flats was so quiet even his thoughts seemed to bounce off the walls and it didn't make him feel good to go home to it.

What's more, he'd been wrong about the balcony being like a garden without the work of maintaining it. Sitting out there you heard a lot of traffic noise from the town during the daytime and there seemed to be traffic buzzing along the motorway half a mile away on the other side at all hours, day and night. And the balcony certainly didn't smell like a garden.

It had surprised him how incredibly dusty it was, too, due to a nearby building development, he suspected. So he had to dust the chair and table whenever he wanted to sit out there.

Only he didn't want to sit out there, he'd found. It was no fun talking to yourself and he'd never seen anyone sitting on the other balconies. At least if he stayed indoors he could have the television on in the background.

Should he consider moving? Who knew? He had no idea what he wanted from life these days. They talked about mid-life crises. Well, he was having one, wasn't he? He'd admitted it to himself a while ago and betrayed it to Lara today.

The woman behind the desk in the sales office looked up with a smile as he went in. Lovely smile it was, too.

'Can I help you?'

'I was wondering if you have any brochures about the houses in this development – the bigger houses, not the terraced ones.'

'Yes, of course we do. You're a friend of Lara's, aren't you?' She gave him an apologetic look. 'I can't help seeing everyone who comes and goes over there.'

'Yes, I know Lara.' He didn't enlarge on that. 'Her house is very nice and well-finished but it would be too small for me.'

She got out a brochure and opened it to show him the five styles of detached houses that were currently available. 'There's a lot more information on our website, of course, and we're happy to vary the interior layout of the houses.

We have one almost finished and we're part way along building another.'

She tapped the brochure. 'This one, the Byron. My husband is in there at the moment with the foreman doing a careful check of all that has been done or I'd offer to show it to you. If you're interested after you've read the brochure, do give me a call, then either he or I can show you round it.'

'Thank you.' He spent a moment studying the posters on the wall, which showed what the finished development would look like. He hoped Lara hadn't seen him stop here. His interest in the houses had nothing to do with being near his ex-wife. He was just facing up to his own loneliness, trying to do something positive about it, following up a possible lead.

He wasn't the sort of man to live on his own, he now admitted. And he'd made a mistake marrying a younger woman like Julie. Oh, they'd got on all right but there had been yawning differences between their understanding of the world and how they wanted to spend their time. What had finally torn them apart was her sudden longing for having children before it was too late. At least two, she'd said.

No way! He'd had a vasectomy the very next week without telling her, to make sure there could be no accidents. She'd gone mad when she found out. That had been the beginning of the end.

He sighed and realised he was standing staring into space, so nodded to Molly and left. No sign of Lara, thank goodness.

When he got home he spread out the brochure and

studied the plans, then got online and studied every detail of the development and how it was going to look.

Compared to most people, he had it easy, didn't he? If he wanted to live somewhere other than this damned flat, he had plenty of money, didn't even need to sell this place. He could buy any house in the leisure village and pay cash.

Only would that really solve his loneliness problem? Had Lara been right about the sociability of the first people to settle there? Would they include him? Would she be upset if he moved there?

Money didn't buy you friends. It took time and effort to find and connect with people you liked. But propinquity might make taking the first step easier. He liked that word. In fact, he had a new hobby, one no one else in the world knew about: he was trying to write poetry! How his father would have laughed at him for that! His father had believed in 'the bottom line' and regarded the arts as a rubbishy waste of time.

But Guy was finding it a pleasure to play with words, fascinating to read and reread the poetry of others through the ages, even more fascinating to try to write his own poems. He'd hated studying Shakespeare at school and (thanks to his father) scorned all poetry as 'girly stuff'. Most of the lads at his boys-only school had been rather sexist. Nowadays he didn't consider himself sexist – well, he was trying hard not to be.

Lara would laugh at his poetic efforts, he was sure. But not nastily. Even though she could have won an award for being Mrs Efficient, he didn't think there was a nasty or dishonest bone in her body. She had changed, seemed softer, less guarded.

He didn't want to get together with her again romantically. Or did he? No, of course he didn't! Well, he thought he didn't. He wasn't a hundred per cent sure of anything these days. But perhaps they could become friends again?

He looked across the room, seeing himself in the mirror and studying his face, trying to see himself as a stranger would. He frowned and the man in the mirror frowned back, then gave him a rueful smile.

Like Laura, he was changing. Work was no longer the be-all and end-all of his life. But what was? Damned if he knew.

He had to find another focus, though, because he was going quietly mad in the long, lonely evenings.

Lara locked her front door and started walking towards Cindy's house, jumping in shock as someone spoke behind her.

'It's only me.'

She clutched her chest, willing herself to calm down. 'Do you always move so quietly, Ross?'

'I suppose so. These casual shoes are more like slippers.' He held his hand out. 'Come on. Let's join the party.'

She took his hand without thinking, then felt embarrassed by her own reaction but tried not to show it by jerking hers away.

Cindy's house was only a few yards past their row of houses, thank goodness, and once they arrived, she could let go of Ross's hand without making a thing of it.

It was brightly lit inside and they stopped instinctively to peer through the window. To her surprise she could see several people standing chatting already.

'Where did she find them all?' he muttered.

'Do you know any of them? I don't. Oh yes, I do! Look! Euan's over there in the corner. I can't see Molly. But who are the others?'

'I don't know, but we're about to find out.' He rang the doorbell.

Someone shouted, 'Come in!'

Lara felt suddenly nervous. 'You go first.'

He looked at her in surprise, then grinned. 'Are you feeling shy? I'd have thought you'd be good at meeting people.'

'I am when it's business and I know what we'll be talking about. Just lead the way in, will you?'

As she shoved him forward, he grabbed her hand again and dragged her in with him, shouting cheerfully, 'Look who I picked up on the way here.'

Cindy came forward and the room seemed to settle into an expectant silence as she announced, 'This is Lara, who's just moved into the end house of the terrace, and Ross, who's moved in next door to her.'

She went round explaining who everyone was, which amounted to a couple who were waiting for their house to be finished, their daughter (highly pregnant) and son-in-law, another couple Cindy had met at the library, Euan and Avril, who used to be his secretary till she retired and was now a good friend of Cindy's.

'Avril helped me settle in and translated till I got used to the language differences. Euan's wife is just finishing for the day at the sales office and will be joining us shortly.'

Ross looked at her, surprised by this remark. 'Language differences? Isn't English your first language?'

'Yes. But although Americans and Brits are supposed to

speak the same language, there are quite a few differences, let me tell you, and some of them can be very confusing.'

Lara saw a chance to join in. 'It happens in Australia too. Someone I met emigrated in the seventies and was invited to a party. The hostess said to bring a plate and she did – an empty plate instead of a plate of food.'

They all chuckled. 'I like that sort of bring and share party,' Avril said. 'It's much easier on the hostess.'

The doorbell rang and a younger man came straight in, upon which Cindy flung herself into his arms. 'Tate, you made it! I'm so glad.'

He proved to be Cindy's youngest son and was as charming and socially confident as his mother.

Lara watched in surprise and not a little relief as, somehow, Cindy got people talking to complete strangers. Either she or her son made sure no one was left out while handing round platters of titbits, refilling glasses and laughing at jokes. She envied them this social ease, but at least she'd made a few contributions to the conversations. She took comfort in that.

It was a lovely evening, warm enough for them to spill out on to the patio, and the mood was relaxed enough that Lara soon forgot her nervousness and didn't feel obliged to 'perform' as she had when attending work-related functions.

When Ross excused himself and went home, she stayed on, chatting to the couple who would be moving here soon. She managed to slip into the conversation that Ross had been ill and was now convalescent, in case they thought he was stand-offish, and found that Cindy had already told them about that and his aunt dying recently.

'Poor man!' the pregnant woman whispered.

Lara blinked at that. She didn't think of Ross as 'poor'. He was not only attractive but nice with it. She could feel her cheeks getting warm at that thought and hoped no one had noticed.

The party started to wind down around seven and Cindy suggested going up to the hotel for a meal. No one seemed upset that Lara didn't want to come with them.

'Another time, perhaps,' she said. 'I went out for lunch today and I'm not really hungry. Besides, I have to watch what I eat or I put on weight.' That would serve as an excuse to cover her not spending a lot of money on food if she did go out with her neighbours another time.

Tate made his excuses at the same time and his mother gave him a big farewell hug, which he returned with enthusiasm.

Cindy watched him go, smiling proudly. She saw Lara watching her. 'He's such a good son, my Tate is, and I really like his wife. She couldn't come today because they have two small children and another on the way.'

Euan rang the hotel to book a table while Cindy bustled round, making sure the food was covered or put in the fridge.

Lara helped her with that, then went home and watched them walk past her kitchen window. The sight of Tate hugging his mother had made her feel a little sad. She couldn't remember Joel ever hugging her like that. Then she told herself not to be silly. Darcie often hugged her.

And she wasn't on *bad* terms with Joel, just . . . not close.

She checked but couldn't see any lights shining from next door. Ross must have gone straight to bed. It must be hard to get exhausted so easily. But he definitely looked better than he had a few days ago.

Once Cindy and the others were out of sight, Lara switched on the lights in her own house. No need to get anything to eat. She'd had an excellent lunch and Cindy had provided a generous supply of nibblies.

She smiled ruefully. She'd gone back to the super-frugal habits she'd developed as an impoverished student. Well, that's what you did when you had to make your money go a long way, wasn't it? Cut down on everything but the bare essentials.

All in all, things were going as well as could be expected, but oh, she couldn't help wishing that something bad would happen to John Crichton. She didn't know what, didn't want to him to be killed or anything, but she hoped something really bad would hurt him as he'd hurt others.

Donald had said there were several other people who'd been robbed of their savings. How could Crichton sleep at night?

Chapter Sixteen

At the moment John Crichton was definitely not a happy man. He was still feeling a little shaky after that heart incident and Sandra had decided they should move somewhere quiet to give him time to recover.

'No. I'd rather find a place to settle and get the travelling over with. I'll be happier in a proper house, one that's really our own, and I'm sure my health will improve there. Even a couple of days in this flat has made me feel caged.'

'Well, it's going to take time to organise the travel, John, unless you want to be picked up by the police at the airport. My contact suggests we move to a village in Austria where there's a quiet hotel. We can rent a suite for a couple of weeks.' She hesitated, then added, 'I know you're fretting, darling, but we really do have to stay off the radar.'

He couldn't argue with that, unfortunately.

She arranged the move with her usual efficiency but he hated the village on sight; it was so tourist-oriented and cutesy. It wasn't nearly as quiet as they'd hoped,

full of international visitors. And the suite might have
two bedrooms and a sitting room but none of them was
spacious. He didn't conceal his annoyance. 'Your contact
has let us down, Sandra. We should arrange things
ourselves from now on.'

'Do you know how to get false passports?'

'Well, no.'

'And I don't either.'

A group of very loud English people walked past just
then and he moved quickly back from the balcony, scowling
at her. 'I suppose I'm going to have to stay in hiding again
and not even poke my nose out of the door.'

She came to put her arms round him but he moved away.

'I'm sorry, John. Very sorry. He said it would be quiet
here but I agree with you. There are enough holidaymakers
around that we can't take the risk of you being seen and
recognised.'

His heart started to play up and he didn't want to take
another calm-down pill, which would make him dopey, so
he tried not to let it show. 'I'll go and have a rest, then. I'm
feeling exhausted.'

'Your heart's all right?'

'I'm just tired, dammit.'

He went into his bedroom and lay down, pretending
to be asleep. When his door opened and she peeped in, he
didn't stir, didn't want to talk to her till he'd got a few things
straight in his own mind and given his weary body a rest.

She closed the door and he decided to see if he could have
a nap. Then, as he began to relax, he heard her speaking
quietly to someone, presumably on the phone since no one
had come to the door of their suite. That brought him wide

awake and alert again. Who could she be phoning so soon after their arrival?

He slipped out of bed and stood near the door, but even from there he couldn't hear what she was saying because she was in her bedroom. The call went on for a long time, confidential murmuring sounds which made him wonder.

After it ended he lay down on the bed again, moving as quietly as he could and closing his eyes.

But he couldn't sleep and Sandra didn't come in to check on him again till much later.

When she did come, he yawned and pretended he'd had a nap. 'Did I hear you making a phone call earlier?'

She looked at him sharply, not her usual caring expression, then her face changed as if she'd donned a mask and she gave him one of her loving smiles. 'I was only calling room service to ask if they did dry cleaning. I need a couple of outfits freshening up.'

He didn't quibble about that, but it raised his suspicions a notch higher. The phone call had lasted far longer than would have been needed to ask a simple question like that.

So who had she been calling?

Worst of all, why was she lying to him?

The following morning, after they'd had breakfast in their room, Sandra said casually, 'I think it'd be easier if you gave me access to the money now, John. We can open a new account, a Swiss bank account, perhaps. My contact can help us with that and—'

'I don't think so, dear. I don't know this contact of yours, so I'd rather keep the money in my own hands for the time being. Anyway, I can deal with the money transfers myself. It's easy enough to do things online these days.'

She opened her mouth as if to protest, then snapped it shut again. 'Whatever. I'll go out for a stroll, then, if you don't mind.'

He felt worried about where she was going. Was she going to meet someone? After a moment's hesitation, he went out on to the balcony and stood watching her as she left the hotel.

She glanced back up at the rows of balconies, but he was standing behind a fat green artificial shrub that hid the barrier between one balcony and the next. He was pretty sure she hadn't seen him because she carried on walking. He was just about to go back inside when he saw her stop dead as a man hurried towards her.

John gasped in outrage as the man swept her into his arms and plonked a kiss on each cheek in turn. He looked more like an old friend than a helpful contact. A very good friend, too.

Pushing him away, she glanced again at the balconies before making her way rapidly out of the courtyard on to the street. As the man followed, she made a gesture with one hand that seemed to be a signal not to touch her.

She hadn't looked happy about the encounter, but her anxiety seemed to have all been about whether John had seen them.

Well, he didn't feel happy now himself. Her contact was too good-looking and was around her own age. The sight of the fellow looking full of energy had made him feel old and decrepit.

Was he credulous as well? Had he been taken in by a pair

of con artists? No, surely he couldn't have been mistaken in Sandra? No, no! They'd been so happy together.

Was he getting paranoid? Perhaps that was because of all the time he was spending shut in damned hotel rooms. Or was it because of something else? Had he now seen what was really going on?

He closed the door to the balcony and stood with his back to it, scowling at the small sitting room.

When they got to Brazil, he was going to buy a spacious house with a large garden you could walk round. He went into his bedroom and took out his mobile phone. He made a few adjustments to access the secret program and checked to see who had called or texted him.

His security guy had left a message. He read it carefully and grimaced, before sending a message asking for one or two other things to be checked.

He was much better with technology and modern devices than Sandra realised. Why had he kept that from her and pretended to need her help? He'd done it even before today's revelations.

Because he always liked to have something in reserve, that's why. Always. He'd learnt to be careful as a young man, learnt it the hard way, as you do. There was no one in the whole world whom he trusted absolutely now that his first wife was dead, though he'd come close to it with Sandra, more fool he.

Once he'd finished his calls, he reset the phone. That program would remain utterly silent, not even vibrating, let alone beeping, when a message arrived. The whole world seemed full of beeping machines these days.

As he sat down, weariness swept through him and he

fought a ridiculous urge to weep. He'd just contacted a rather special friend who had access to his lawyer. He'd asked to revert to his previous will, the one he'd drawn up before Sandra. He had, of course, made provision for that before he left. But now he'd added a new instruction for his friend, in case he died under suspicious circumstances.

He had to look on the bright side. He was rich beyond his wildest dreams and was going to spend the rest of his life in utter luxury. Sandra couldn't get to his money and if she proved untrustworthy, he could buy any help he needed elsewhere and pay her off, monthly payments that would stop if he died of anything other than natural causes.

It was at that stage in his cogitations he admitted to himself that he no longer trusted her and never would again.

That man she'd met had smiled at her as if he knew her in a personal way and was very fond of her. John had always been good at reading people's body language and his distance vision was still pretty good.

He did weep then. Briefly. Silently. Which showed what a sad case he was. Old age turned you into a weakling.

He'd been stupid as well as greedy, couldn't go back to the UK now. He was in too deep: a criminal. He didn't want to spend his final days in prison, so he had to find somewhere else to go and a way to make the best of the situation.

For that he still needed Sandra's help, unfortunately.

But he'd keep an eye on her at every step from now on. Oh yes.

Chapter Seventeen

Ross was woken on the Monday morning by a phone call from his tenant. He crossed the fingers of his free hand as he answered, hoping nothing had gone wrong with the house. He was counting on that money to build up his maintenance reserves for the old place.

'Hi, Tom. How's it going?'

'The filming is going really well. This house of yours is very photogenic. I'd just like to check with you that it's OK if we stay here for longer than we'd originally planned, say four extra weeks for sure and perhaps more?'

'Can you tell that'll be necessary at this early stage in the filming?'

Tom chuckled. 'This time I can. The powerful ones – may their names long be praised! – have just sold the rights to the first series internationally, so they've decided they want to make the second series two episodes longer and we are, of course, happy to oblige. We don't mind earning more money.'

'Congratulations.'

'I'm pretty stoked about it, I must admit. So, will it be all right for us to stay in your house for longer?'

'Fine by me. I have this place to live in and I don't mind earning extra money, either.'

'We're both happy, then. Oh, by the way, while I've got you on the line, did you know that someone was keeping watch on this house for the first day or two after you left? And they followed our van a few times, too.'

'One of your rivals?'

'Don't think so. If they'd wanted to find out more about what we're filming, they'd be keeping an eye on what we're doing at the house, not following our runabout into town. And why would they be spying on us, anyway? I've got the contract *and* I hold the rights to the series idea.'

'Oh. Did you get a glimpse of the person?'

'One of the camera crew did. There were two people, actually. A guy of about thirty or forty was driving the car and there was a woman in the back seat. He thought she'd be around the same age, though it can be harder to tell with women. There's nothing wrong with Hal's distance eyesight, believe me. If he sees a bird in the sky, he can tell you the shape of its wings, while the rest of us can see only a distant dot. And he's even quicker to spot a beautiful woman.'

Ross's heart sank at the word 'beautiful'. It had to be Nonie Jayne. She was the only beautiful woman he had ever known. But why would she have been watching his house? 'When exactly was this?'

'The day after we moved in and a couple of days after that. It hasn't happened again, so I didn't bother to phone you about it. Only, since I was speaking to you today, I thought I might just mention it.'

'I'm very glad you did. It was probably my ex.'

'One of those, eh?'

'What do you mean?'

'A stalker. Can't bear to let you go.'

'I sincerely hope not. I don't think she cares about anything except money, so she's probably checking whether the house is occupied. She's already tried to get her hands on some of my more valuable items, claiming I'd given them to her. As if I'd give away family heirlooms! She's made it plain that she'd expected far more than she got in the settlement. Um, would your guy recognise her again if I emailed you a photo?'

Tom chuckled. 'Do tigers wear stripy pyjamas? He hasn't forgotten her, told me a couple of times that she was as beautiful as it gets. But he also reckoned she was a predator, something about the eyes. I told you, that guy is an expert on women.'

Beautiful predator: that was as good a description of Nonie Jayne as any. 'Well, I'll email you the photo and you can show it to him, just to make sure I'm right. And can you please keep the security tight?'

'We have valuable equipment here so believe me, we're über-careful about security. I'll let you know if it's the same woman.'

'Thanks. Good luck with the filming.'

'Yeah. And thanks for being flexible. Bye.'

Ross sighed as he put the phone down. What the hell was his damned ex up to now? He looked round the room. There were a lot of valuable things here as well, if you added them up. Maybe he should put in a better security system. Would she remember where his aunt had lived after only one visit? Who knew.

He found a photo of Nonie Jayne and emailed it to Tom. She'd be easy to recognise. There were disadvantages as well as advantages to having such striking good looks.

As for security, he'd discuss it with Lara, who was a smart woman. She'd mentioned getting some extra bolts fitted to all her outer doors after she'd seen a figure wandering round near their houses. He should have done something about that more quickly but he'd thought she was worrying unnecessarily. After all, this was a very quiet place to live.

Now he was going to pay better attention to his surroundings, both inside and out.

Why was he so sure Nonie Jayne hadn't let go of him yet? Well, he wouldn't stake his life on it, but he thought it distinctly possible that she might be plotting something. She wasn't the smartest person on the planet but she was one of the stubbornest when she wanted something and could be very cunning. And she'd been furious about the divorce settlement.

He looked round. This place would be very easy to break into as it was now. You could approach it across the fields or golf course and leave the same way if you weren't carrying anything too heavy.

And at such an early stage of development there weren't many neighbours to see or hear what was going on.

He glanced at the kitchen clock. Lara would be round in a few minutes ready to start work.

As he put the kettle on, he promised himself they weren't

going to do anything else about selling his aunt's collection of ornaments until they'd made their houses more secure.

Lara came next door exactly on time, as usual, looking well rested and ready to start work – which was how Ross had felt until the phone call.

She took one look at him and asked, 'What's wrong?' She gestured to the table. 'Sit down and tell me.'

When he'd finished his tale she frowned and didn't speak for a moment or two. 'How can you be so sure this is your ex doing this?'

'I'm not a hundred per cent sure, but I do think it's possible. She has no morals, no *depth*, for lack of a better word, only a vast greed for money and possessions.'

'You have a very poor opinion of her morals.'

'Yes. And of my own judgement in marrying her. I was so happy with Diana, it never occurred to me that Nonie Jayne was putting on an act about loving me. We rushed into marriage but she didn't manage to keep the loving act up for long after we started living together.' He rolled his eyes. 'She's very grumpy in the early mornings. Never met anyone as bad. And she'll do anything to get hold of money – well, anything except work for it like the rest of us have to.'

'Does she know about this place?'

'She's been here once but I'm not sure she'll remember the address. I drove here and she spent most of the journey fiddling with her smartphone. She's definitely not into scenery and wildlife.'

'Hmm.' Lara sat drumming her fingers on the table for a moment or two, then cocked her head to one side.

'How about for a start, you suggest to Euan that he gets his security people to keep a better eye on all the houses. That won't cost you anything.'

'Why would he do that?'

'He won't want potential buyers to hear that these houses are easy to burgle and he's got a lot of building materials lying around.'

'Ah. Good idea.'

'But as I said before, you do need better locks and bolts on the outer doors, Ross.'

'I agree. And so do you. I'm sorry for not listening to you before.'

'We've both been busy.'

'Let's go out and buy some this morning.'

'We should talk to Cindy first. She might want to improve her security as well. It may be cheaper if we all work together.'

He chuckled. 'I can fit them and I promise not to charge you for doing it. I'm fairly handy around the house. I've had to be with an old house to maintain. Um, I hope you don't mind me asking, but how valuable is that silver of yours?'

'It's decent stuff, a few thousand pounds in all. I don't want to lose it for other reasons, though. I only kept things that were truly meaningful to me when I started working overseas. It'd hurt like hell to have those pieces stolen.'

He put his arm round her shoulders and gave her a quick hug. She seemed so very confident, but when you got to know her, you found out she had the usual human collection of weaknesses.

She hugged him back this time, looking at him almost

shyly as if unused to demonstrative behaviour. 'Stupid of me to care so much, isn't it?'

'No. Just proves you're normal. Anyway, who'd want to be with a person who had no weaknesses? A superwoman would give me an inferiority complex.'

'You always make me feel better about myself.'

'Do I? That's good, because you have the same effect on me.' He smiled warmly as he stepped away from her. 'Let's go and see Cindy straight away, then we'll call at the hotel to see Euan on our way out to buy some bolts.'

Cindy was in total agreement with them about the need to have better security, but she could afford to have a proper monitored system installed and her son had already arranged to have one fitted, so she didn't need Ross's help.

When they stopped at the hotel to let Euan know about the prowler, he expressed surprise but thanked them for the information. 'You can be sure I'll arrange for better patrols, especially now that we're building more houses. My main office should be OK because it's in the hotel and there's nothing valuable left in the sales office, but building supplies have to be left outside and often get targeted by thieves. The prowler might have been sussing out what was lying around.'

'It's sad when you can't even build new homes without such precautions,' Lara said.

'Tell me about it.'

Pleased with that response, Ross drove to a well-known hardware store on the outskirts of Swindon, a huge echoing cavern of a place which had everything they needed.

After loading their purchases in the car, he suggested nipping into the nearby shopping centre for some food supplies.

As they walked round, he couldn't help noticing how frugally Lara spent her money. She selected mainly things on special, then stopped to study the oddments on the clearance stand. He wished he could help her but he knew how fiercely independent she was, so didn't even offer to treat her to anything. At least the job he'd given her was a help.

She didn't mention her predicament and he admired how brave she was being about her losses and current situation.

He couldn't help thinking about their relationship again as he dropped her off and went into his own house for a midday meal. The more time he spent with Lara, the more he liked and admired her. He might be wary of rushing into a relationship with anyone, but he wasn't stupid enough to deny his feelings, either.

He was already sure that Lara wasn't like Nonie Jayne, but he was still getting to know her and still letting her get to know him. People of their age didn't confide in one another as freely as youngsters did. When he and Diana had met, they'd blurted out their deepest dreams and hopes without a worry about betraying their weaknesses.

What did Lara think of him? Did she see him as an idiot who'd married a rapacious woman for her looks? Or just as bad, did she consider him a weakling who kept having to rest and take naps?

Maybe he should try one of these other medical approaches to ME. He'd ask Lara who her friend had gone to for help. It wouldn't hurt to make enquiries.

But it might hurt to get his hopes up – and fail to make any further progress.

* * *

Nonie Jayne phoned the private investigator who'd been helping her intermittently to find out where things were at. When Peter's secretary answered, she asked to speak to him.

'Sorry, Ms Larson, but my employer is away on a case and won't be back for a week.'

'But he was in the middle of doing something for me!'

Silence, then, 'Just a moment. I'll check the files.'

Nonie Jayne tapped her fingers on the table, annoyed by this. She'd paid Peter Sangley well to help her and been assured that he'd be there for her any time.

'Ms Larson? I'm sorry but he's not left you any messages. What he has left is a reminder of how much you owe him.'

She ignored that. She never paid bills until the last minute. 'Well, perhaps *you* can help me. I'm trying to find my ex-husband and I know Peter had a lead. There was an old aunt Ross used to visit and he said he'd go there one night and see what he could find out. If you can just give me her address, I'll take it from there and—'

'I'm afraid I can't do that without Mr Sangley's authorisation.'

'But how am I going to find my ex if your company doesn't help?'

'I'm sorry but I can't go against the rules. Perhaps you could phone next week? Mr Sangley will be back then and you can speak to him yourself.'

Nonie Jayne slammed down the phone. She was sure Peter had said he was going to check out Ross's new address one evening.

Why had he not left a message? Then she remembered that she'd spoken quite sharply to him last time because he'd phoned her at some unearthly hour of the morning. Surely he hadn't taken a huff at that? When she spoke to him, she'd arrange to pay the darn bill. That ought to put him on side again.

She decided to mention the bill, so picked up the phone again. This time she got an answering service so had to leave a message on that, asking the secretary to phone her back ASAP.

The rest of the day passed and there was no return call, which annoyed her still further.

In fact, she was getting sick and tired of this country. People did everything at half-speed and wanted paying before they'd even finished a job. Should she go back to the States straight away?

No, Gil had said he could help her. She'd give him a try first. If he didn't move things forward and help her to get what she was due from Ross, she'd definitely leave the country and get on with her life.

She didn't usually act so carelessly but she had been feeling low ever since that arbitration meeting. The only person who seemed able to cheer her up was Gil and he was pushing her to do things she wasn't sure about.

Well, she could always change her mind, couldn't she? And leave the country if necessary. Flights to the States were always available.

On that thought she picked up her phone and rang Gil, who said he'd be happy to help and would be round in half an hour.

Gil arrived exactly twenty-seven minutes later and when the people at reception phoned up to let her know, she told them to send him up.

She gestured to him to sit down and didn't waste any time with greetings. 'You said you could help me. How exactly?'

He looked at her thoughtfully, then said, 'You seem like a woman who doesn't always approve of the stupidity of the law.'

'Tell me about it! Especially here in the UK. Which doesn't mean I like to break it, not exactly.'

'I agree with you absolutely, so I sometimes find ways to go round the formalities.'

'What exactly does that mean?'

'It means there are times when I take what I feel is owed to me.'

'Hmm.'

He grinned. 'Oh, come on. Stop pretending. We're in the same line of business, you and I, only I work with rich older women and you work with rich older men.'

She stared at him open-mouthed, not knowing what to say to that. Was it really so obvious what she was doing?

'I've recently been let down by a female I thought I had in the bag, so to speak. And it had cost me a fortune to set her up. Her niece turned up, took one look at me and whipped her aunt off for a holiday in Spain. If I help you to get hold of what's, um, *owed* to you and then sell it safely for you, we may both come out of the current dip in our finances a lot happier.'

'Hmm. And how will you benefit from that?'

'A few other things might fall into my hands at the same time.'

She didn't want to get involved in outright theft, but when he winked, she laughed and so did he. Oh, why pretend? She got sick and tired of pretending. 'All right. You're on, Gil. But you'd better find a safe way to do this because I'm not taking any risks.'

'Have you any idea where he is now?'

'Sort of. I think he may be living in his aunt's house while those film people are using his house. Unfortunately Ross doesn't have to share any of that inheritance with me. I visited her once with him and her house was full of valuable ornaments. Well, they looked valuable to me and I can usually tell.'

'Whereabouts was this house?'

'In some sort of retirement community or whatever they're called here.'

'What was her name?'

'Iris.'

'Surname?'

She shrugged. 'I didn't pay attention. There was no reason to at the time because I didn't intend to visit her again.'

'His full name?'

'Ross Quinton Welby.'

'Any idea where the retirement community is?'

'No. But it's not too far away from here because it only took us about half an hour to drive there, or maybe a little longer. Oh, and there was a golf course there *and* a hotel.'

'Should be easy enough to find. Leave it to me.' He stood up.

'Wait. I already found the names of a few retirement communities online and I tried phoning them but they wouldn't give me any information about residents on the phone.'

'Let me have a try. I'll need to get a friend to do it for

me. He's brilliant with computers. Let me phone him, then you and I will figure out how to spend a few quiet hours. You must be getting bored with hanging around.'

He gave her another of those winks and ran one fingertip down her arm, but she drew back at once. 'I'm *not* getting into bed with you.'

'Aren't you tired of sleeping with old men? Don't you want to just enjoy yourself for once?'

'Ross wasn't old. And he wasn't incapable of giving a woman pleasure.'

'Well, my ladies were old, and I like young, firm flesh now and then.' He shrugged. 'You and I will share a bed one day, I'm sure. I can wait.'

'I don't know you well enough.' She'd learnt years ago that if you gave in too soon, you lost your main bargaining chip. 'I think I'll go shopping to fill in a few hours.'

'Let me make a phone call, then I'll take you. I've got my car outside.'

'Oh. Well, all right. Thanks. That'd be a help.' It puzzled her that he was sticking so close, but she was fed up of staring at the TV screen and she did enjoy her little shopping trips. This man wasn't likely to buy her anything worthwhile, though, because he'd said he was short of money. Pity.

They strolled round the shopping mall, which proved to have only ordinary stores. She'd not be seen dead in such cheap, uninteresting clothes, so she didn't see anything she'd want to buy.

'I'll have to do some serious shopping in London before I go back to the States.' It was about time she started to prepare for her next search for a husband. Waiting around here was getting tedious and she still wasn't sure it was worth pursuing Ross.

Should she cut her losses and return to the States straight away? No. She might not get anything else out of Ross, but if she could figure out a way to get back at him she would, because he deserved it.

After a while, she and Gil found a nice café on the mezzanine level overlooking the main concourse and when they got chatting, she told him about Ross and the silver she'd taken. She hadn't thought he'd notice such small pieces.

Gil looked at her thoughtfully. 'They sound to have been quite rare pieces to me. If you're going to take an interest in silver, you really should get a list of hallmarks and learn about which ones are more valuable.'

'I'm not interested in silver, just in what it's worth.'

'Same difference.'

'Well, I prefer jewels anyway.' She had a few nice pieces stashed away in her other bank, in an account under her real name.

As she waited for her mocha surprise, idly watching people pass by below, she stiffened suddenly and leant forward. It couldn't be . . . but it was . . . 'What a bit of luck!'

Gil leant forward to look in the same direction. 'What are you staring at?'

'That guy in the striped polo shirt is Ross but I don't know who the dowdy female is.' From the way Ross was smiling at her, he was attracted. It made Nonie Jayne suddenly furious that he'd found someone else so quickly.

'Who is she?'

'How should I know?' She watched them go into a cheap café and sit there chatting.

She moved back to let the waitress put down her coffee, then leant forward again.

Gil grabbed her arm to get her attention. 'Do you know what his car is like?'

'Of course I do. Old. I tried to get him to change it for a newer model but he insisted on keeping it, said it was an old friend. If I were near it now, I'd run my keys along the side of it. That'd really upset him.'

Gil tapped her hand. 'Pay attention, Nonie Jayne. If we follow his car and he goes home, we'll know where he lives.'

'Oh. Sorry. Good idea.'

'Come on! Let's search the car park and wait nearby.'

She looked regretfully at the coffee, took a big gulp and left the rest before following Gil outside. He drove slowly along every row of parked cars but there was no sign of Ross's old rust heap.

'You're sure you'll recognise it?'

'Of course I will.'

'There's another small parking area to the side. Let's try that.' Gil turned into it.

At first she thought they'd failed to find it and was worrying that Ross would have left the shopping mall, but then, in the back row, she saw it.

She pointed. 'That's my ex's car. Have I time to ruin his paintwork?'

Gil held back a sigh. What an irritating woman she was! She might be beautiful but she hadn't been gifted with brains to match her face. Good thing he was used to pandering to foolish women. He spoke in the teasing tone that they seemed to love. 'Dear me, you are vindictive. But you don't want to do that. He might call the police. All we want today is to follow him and find out where he lives.'

'Pity.'

'You're going to have to crouch down in the back.'

'*What?*'

'And cover yourself right up.'

'But that'll mess up my hair.'

'The problem is, you're too beautiful, Nonie Jayne. People will notice your face and remember you. Wait a minute.' He got a ragged blanket out of the boot and held the passenger door open. 'Get into the back now and prepare to duck down if I give the word. And *do not* bob up again until I tell you it's clear.'

'This blanket smells of oil.'

'Do you want to find where your ex is living or not? If not, I'll drop you back at your hotel and go on my way.'

'Oh, very well.' She let him close the back door of the car.

'Get down!' Gil yelled almost immediately as he caught sight of the people she'd pointed out coming away from the shopping mall. He flicked a quick glance backwards to check that she'd pulled the blanket over herself and, thank goodness, she had.

He started the engine as the others got into Ross's car and followed them slowly out of the car park.

'What are you doing?' she called.

'I'm following them. Stay down.'

'Well, I hope they go straight back to wherever it is. This car needs cleaning out and it's uncomfortable crouching down. I'm going to get my clothes all crumpled.'

'Worth it, though, eh?'

Her only reply was a loud sigh, which sounded like a child being denied a treat.

'Try to find a more comfortable position and stay put. You said his aunt's house wasn't far away.'

A few minutes later, she said, 'I'm getting cramp. Can't I get up now? I'll bend my head down.'

'No. You'll spoil it if you bob up.'

'But I can't bear it a minute longer and—'

'Hang on. We're turning into a hotel car park. This might be it.'

He stopped the car near the side of the hotel and watched Ross Welby drive past it towards some houses. 'You can sit up now.'

She raised her head to peep at the hotel. 'Is he staying here?'

'No, but it's no use following him across to the houses or we'd give ourselves away. It says "Dead End" on the sign at the entrance to them, so it must be the only road. He won't be able to get away without us seeing him. Don't you recognise the hotel?'

'Of course not. I'd never stay in a dump like this.'

Stupid bitch. 'Right. We can't go any closer or he'll see us. You stay in the back.'

'I'm *not* staying down.' She got up to sit on the seat before he could say anything.

'Don't draw attention to yourself. I'm going to nip inside to get some information about this place.'

Bored, she took out her smartphone, but there were no messages and she didn't like to start doing something in case they had to set off suddenly. What was keeping Gil?

She began to worry that she'd rushed in. They'd found out where Ross was living now but what was Gil planning to do? She wasn't getting involved in any outright robberies, oh no! She didn't intend to wind up in prison. She shouldn't have given in to her temper, didn't often lose control.

Just as she was wondering whether to follow him inside the hotel, he came out carrying some leaflets.

She stared at the few houses that had been finished and jumped in shock when he spoke from right next to the car. She hadn't even heard him reach her.

'Surely you recognise it now?' he asked. 'And it's called a leisure village here, not a retirement community.'

'It looks vaguely familiar.' She stared, blinked hard, then reluctantly got out the spectacles she hated to wear and slipped them on.

'Why the hell didn't you put those on straight away?'

'Because I don't like wearing them.'

The first thing Nonie Jayne noticed was Ross, chatting to the dowdy female. Why were they taking so long to go inside the house? 'Look at him. Can't he do better than her?'

'Never mind that. Is this the place you visited?'

'Yes. But they've built more houses since then.'

When the two people didn't move inside, Gil asked, 'Which house is his? And keep those damned spectacles on till we've finished here.'

'Hey. Watch how you talk to a lady.'

Silence, then, 'Sorry, Nonie Jayne. I'm, er, a bit impatient. Which house?'

'Um. The end one of that row. Or was it the next one? No, the end one. Definitely.'

She remembered how dull her one and only visit here had been, but she also remembered something else and that kept her focused. 'I've never seen a house as full of ornaments as the old aunt's place was. I wonder if they're still there?'

'Tell me about them. Were they valuable?'

'Well, they were classy pieces, I'll give her that. I wouldn't have been ashamed to have them in my home, if I had a home, which I don't just now. I'm sure some of them would be worth a lot.'

'Did you recognise any brands of china? Any styles of silver?'

'No. Just that they were, you know, good quality. It always shows.'

'I'll need to find out if they're still there and if they are worth anything. We'll have to keep watch and find a time after dark when your ex is away to look inside, though. You can't be too careful.'

'He wouldn't notice if we stood on our heads next to him at the moment. He's still chatting up that ugly female and he looks besotted. Ah, they're going inside now. Thank goodness. It's so boring waiting around.'

As Ross and the woman started to move towards the end house, she suddenly tripped and he grabbed hold of her to stop her falling.

'See that, Gil! He can't keep his hands off her.'

'I think she's hurt her ankle.'

'They're going into his house now. She was probably just pretending to trip to get his attention.'

'Is that what you do?'

'I do whatever's necessary at the time. And what are you grinning at?'

'You. You're a case, Nonie Jayne!'

'I don't like your attitude.'

'You don't have to. It's money that's our shared interest, not friendship. Ah!'

They watched Ross come out, carry in some bags of shopping and shut the car up, then disappear into the end house once more.

Gil glanced at his watch. 'Look, we can come back after dark now that we know where he lives. If we can find a time when the car isn't there, the house is likely to be unoccupied. But if they don't draw all the curtains at night, I may be able to see what I need to by coming here very late and simply shining a torch in through a window or two.'

'Well, his aunt had so many ornaments that there's hardly anything else *to* see but them! And if we choose carefully even *he* won't notice that one or two are missing.'

'We need to be certain we're not observed going inside. I'll check whether the place would be easy to break into and whether the stuff is worth taking before I plan my move. At least I know which silver is valuable. Were there any other neighbours living in that row of houses?'

'How should I know?'

'Leave it to me. I'll find out.'

'Good.'

Nonie Jayne leant back, smiling. This was more like it. Before she went back to the States, she'd give herself the pleasure of taking some of her ex's more valuable ornaments, selling them with Gil's help and adding the money to her lifetime pot of gold.

Ross hadn't found out about her savings during the divorce proceedings, had he? No one knew her by her birth name these days, but she still had the documentation from it so could use it to keep her money safe in a bank.

It was lucky she'd met Gil, though. He was the key to getting away with this as long as there was something in it for him. But she had to tread carefully. He got annoyed very quickly and he didn't seem to care whether she flirted with him or not. Strange, that.

She'd keep a very careful eye on how things went and if it looked at all dangerous, she'd bail out quick smart.

Trust no one. It was the main thing her momma had taught her and had kept her out of trouble a few times.

She took off the spectacles and smiled at Gil. 'Now what?'

'Now we leave. We know which house your ex went into. I'll come back after dark and have a careful look round the houses. There are things lying around all over the place. I'm surprised they haven't had their building supplies taken.'

'Oh? And how do I know you won't just look after yourself?'

He chuckled. 'Don't sound so suspicious. I wasn't going to run off with the proceeds. Actually, one of the reasons I'm happy to help *you* with this is that I have another job I want you to help *me* with afterwards. It'd pay well.'

'I'm not breaking the law.' She saw his cynical look and added, 'This wouldn't be breaking the law for me because Ross *gave* me some things, said to take the ones I liked best. He's gone back on his word.'

'Yes, of course. Whatever you say. And what I want you to do won't upset the law either, because we won't get caught out. At least we won't if you do what I say, *exactly* what I say.'

'I'll consider it if the money sounds good.'

She gave him a trusting smile, one she'd practised for hours in front of the mirror until she got it right. He smiled right back. Men always did.

Chapter Eighteen

'For a while I thought that grey car was following us,' Ross said as he drew up outside their houses. 'I gave the driver several chances to pass me as we drove along and he didn't take any of them.' He shook his head, frowning. 'I wonder who he is.'

'But the car stopped at the hotel, so it can't have been following us.'

'Perhaps not. I may be getting paranoid about security, thanks to my ex.'

He looked up towards the hotel car park and frowned. 'Don't look now, but there's someone sitting in the back of the same car. Strange. There didn't seem to be anyone in it except the driver before. Let's stand here chatting for a minute or two and keep an eye on whoever it is.'

But the person was slumped down in the seat and they couldn't even tell whether it was a woman or a man from this distance.

'Oh, let's go inside,' Lara said and turned impatiently.

When she tripped, Ross was barely in time to stop her falling. 'Careful. The ground's rather uneven here. This is only a temporary surface till they've finished the major earthworks and put in permanent roads.'

'Thanks.' She let go of him, but when she put her weight on her right foot she grabbed him again, wincing. 'Ouch! I think I've twisted my ankle.'

'Let's get you inside and have a look at it.'

He forgot about the other car as he supported her into her house and helped her sit down on the armchair. The ankle was swelling a little. He moved it to and fro gently and she winced.

'I think it's just a slight sprain. Stay there and I'll find that packet of frozen peas you bought. If you wrap it round your ankle under a tea towel, it'll be just the thing to make the swelling go down.'

She sat waiting while he nipped outside and carried in the bags of shopping, then she flapped one hand at him. 'If you pass me the peas I'll be all right. You need to unpack your own purchases.'

'I didn't buy any frozen goods, so they can wait. You know, Lara, a person can be too independent. Sit back and let someone else look after you for a change.'

He noticed a little footstool and put it in front of her armchair. 'It'll help you keep your foot up.' But as he was helping her raise her injured foot, he muttered, 'Oh hell!' and kissed her.

As they drew apart she stared at him, breathing faster, just as he was.

He studied her face and relaxed. 'Don't pretend you didn't join in that kiss with some enthusiasm.'

'All right. I won't. You started it, though. I thought you said you were avoiding women.'

'Yeah. I was till I met you.' He stared earnestly into her eyes. 'Do you mind if we . . . well, get to know one another better?'

'No, not at all. If you're sure that's what you want. That was, um, a rather good kiss.'

'Don't sound so surprised. Other men must have kissed you.'

'Not for a year or two, so I *am* surprised, especially as you and I haven't known one another all that long.' She eased herself into a more comfortable position.

He spread his hands in a helpless gesture. 'How long does it take to be attracted to someone? Seconds. Minutes at most. And it seems to me you don't always get much choice about who you fancy.'

'I have to agree, but I'm a bit out of practice, so bear with me.'

He moved further away. 'And this isn't the time. Discussion to be continued.'

He cocked one eyebrow as if asking her to confirm that and she nodded.

'Good. But medical matters must come first. Let me get you that packet of peas.'

She chuckled and he looked at her enquiringly. 'What's so amusing?'

'Very romantic, frozen peas.'

'I'm not noted for my romantic skills, Lara, or so I've been told in no uncertain terms recently.'

'Good. Neither am I. We can brush up our skills together.'

He came back with the peas. 'Fine by me. That'll be fun. You know, you have a lovely smile. You should let it escape your control more often. Now, sit still and let's try a bit of frozen therapy on that ankle.'

'Spoilsport.'

He smiled as he put the peas on the ankle. It didn't seem to be a bad sprain, thank goodness. He looked up into her eyes and blew her a kiss. She was definitely relaxing with him and the change suited her, made her even more attractive to him.

He'd had one humourless wife and that had been hard going sometimes.

While Lara was sitting with her foot up, Ross got out the bolts they'd bought.

'Shall I start fitting these on the doors now?'

'If you have time, I'd be grateful. I'm not bad at simple do-it-yourself tasks these days but I'd rather the bolts looked neat. Why don't I make us both a sandwich?'

'That's a good idea, but you stay where you are and let me do it. I'm quite capable of making a sandwich. Or cooking a meal. I'll make you my special spaghetti with a variation on the theme of Bolognese sauce one night, if you like.'

'Sounds good. I'll look forward to it. In the meantime, ham sandwiches will do fine.'

By the time they'd eaten and he'd fitted the heavy duty bolts, the afternoon was half over and the peas were safely stowed away in the freezer.

She waved one hand. 'Go and fit your own bolts now.'

'Will you be all right?'

'Yes, of course I will. I'm quite used to looking after myself, Ross.'

'Too used to it, maybe.'

'Can you be too independent?'

'Yes. It makes sense in a two-people relationship to divide the jobs, even if you don't do that along gender lines.'

'Guy rarely did anything around the house.'

'No? Diana and I shared most things. I did more cooking, though. The food usually turned out better when I prepared meals.' He waggled his hands in the air, making her chuckle again. 'Some people have the cooking gene, some don't. These hands know how to do it.'

After a pause he added, 'From what you've told me, you and Guy stayed together till the kids went off to college, so it can't all have been bad.'

She shrugged. 'He was good company. Still is. But he didn't like me working away from home, even though *he* worked long hours and most of the weekends.'

It was her turn to pause before adding, 'So are you. Good company, I mean.'

'Then I hope you'll do me the honour of dining with me tonight.'

Her voice grew sharper. 'I can afford to feed myself. You don't need to keep feeding me.'

'All I'm intending to do is have pizzas delivered and sling a salad together. And anyway, you provided lunch.'

'So I did. All right. I accept. Sorry for being so touchy.'

'I'll come and help you round at about six.'

'I won't need helping. The ankle's a lot better already.'

He gave up trying to help her. 'OK. Six it is.'

The house didn't feel the same after he'd gone. She looked round and wondered what it was that made such a big difference.

Him.

He was a kind person . . . and very attractive . . . and he

made her laugh. When he was near, she was only too aware of his presence. Or, at the moment, aware of his absence.

She grew angry with herself for obsessing about what was happening between her and Ross. What was wrong with finding a man attractive? Even if nothing came of this long-term, it showed she was still able to function as a normal woman and it would be fun, was fun already.

But she hoped something would come of this. She really liked him as well as being physically attracted.

That felt good.

Had she changed? Perhaps. If so, it was for the better. Well, she hoped it was.

At four o'clock, Darcie rang to see how she was getting on and Lara had a nice chat with her daughter.

She hadn't intended to mention her little accident but it slipped out that she'd sprained her ankle slightly.

'Do you want me to come round and cook tea for you, Mum?'

'No, of course not. It's not that bad a sprain and I just have to rest it a bit. In any case, my neighbour has invited me to tea.'

'Oh, that's kind of her.'

Lara didn't contradict the assumption that it was a woman. She didn't want Darcie jumping to conclusions, or sharing those supposed conclusions with her father.

'How's the job going, Mum?'

'Very well. It's interesting doing the research and I'm setting up a sales website.'

'What are you calling it? I'll have to visit it online. They sound like the sort of ornaments I'd buy as presents.'

'Keep out of it, Darcie.'

'Out of what?'

'You know.'

'Well, I can't help taking an interest. I don't want this man taking you for a ride.'

'I'm a big girl now and have been for several decades. And Ross isn't the sort to take anyone for a ride.'

'Be careful, then.'

'I always am.' *Too careful*, she decided suddenly and changed the subject. 'Are you all well again?'

'Yes, Dad was right. The lurgy, whatever it was, only lasted a day or so.'

'Well, maybe I'll pop round at the weekend, then.'

'That'd be nice. Sunday morning would be best.'

'And once Minnie is used to me, maybe I can do a bit of babysitting, give you the occasional night out?'

'That'd be great, Mum.'

Lara put the phone down, but it rang again almost immediately.

'Donald Metcalf here.'

She could feel herself tensing up.

'Just keeping you in touch, Lara. That photo has gone out into the system. Nothing else come to mind about your former financial adviser?'

'I'm afraid not.'

'There have been no traces found of where he went yet, so we'll just have to hope he goes through a checkpoint and triggers an alarm. Facial recognition is still in its early days, though, so don't hold your breath. It's being installed as fast as possible.'

'Did no one else who was robbed have any information about him?'

'Unfortunately not. You're managing all right? Don't need confirmation that your money has been stolen for the social security people?'

'Thank you, no. I've found myself a job, so I can cope financially for the time being.'

'Good to hear. Don't forget – if you think of anything, any detail whatsoever, don't hesitate to share it with us.'

'I won't. And thank you for keeping in touch.'

As she put the phone down on the small scruffy table next to her armchair, she fought against the tears. And lost the struggle.

She tried to stay hopeful but it was so unfair!

At that moment someone knocked on the door and she hunted in vain for a tissue to wipe away the tears.

She got up slowly and carefully, but the door opened before she could get to it and Guy came in.

'Darcie said you'd hurt yourself. I wondered how you were managing.'

'I'm just fine, thank you. And who asked you to come in?'

'No one. I was worried about you and thought you might not be able to get to the door.'

'Guy, if I need your help I'll call you. Otherwise, we'll meet at Darcie's from time to time. Family situations we agreed on, nothing else.'

'Can't we even be friends?'

A shadow fell across the doorway and Ross hesitated on the threshold. 'I saw someone come in. Are you all right, Lara?' He looked at Guy suspiciously.

'I'm fine. Um, this is Guy, my ex. Guy, this is Ross, my next-door neighbour – and friend.'

The men gave stiff nods.

She hurried to fill the awkward silence. 'It seems my daughter was worried about me and contacted her father. I was just telling Guy that there's no need for him to worry about me. You're next door and able to help me if I need it.'

'It's my pleasure.' Ross smiled warmly at her.

Guy scowled at them both impartially. 'OK. I'll leave you to it, then.' At the door he spun round. 'Nearly forgot. I thought we might pick Minnie up on Sunday and take up where we left off last time. I'll pick you up again.'

He was gone before she could say anything and she let out a little growl of irritation.

'Sorry if I intruded.'

She looked at Ross and could feel that it was very different to how she'd been looking at Guy. '*You* are not intruding at all, Ross. Guy was, though. He just walked straight in.'

'Does he want to pick up with you again?'

'I don't know what he wants. I can't be rude to him because he gave me a car and I'm grateful for that. Though he can well afford it. But I can't read him like I used to, so I'm not quite sure what he wants. All I know is *I* don't want to get together with him again.'

'Good. As long as I wasn't interrupting anything.'

'I was relieved when you joined us. Why did you?'

He wriggled uncomfortably. 'I couldn't help wondering who he was when he simply walked in.'

'Well, now you know. And he'd better not walk in next time.'

'You're seeing him on Sunday, though?'

'We're taking Minnie out to the park, our granddaughter. It's part of the family getting together again. But I'm going to phone my daughter before then and tell her not to – to keep involving her father . . .' Her voice trailed away and she looked at him, wondering exactly how much she should say.

'Why not tell her you've already met a guy and are testing the water?'

Her face brightened. 'Yes. I will. If you don't mind.'

'Why should I? I'm testing the water too.' Another pregnant silence, then, 'I also came round because I found a website online that may be of interest. Want to come and see it and then you might as well stay for tea?'

She could perfectly well have got him to email her the URL but she didn't. She limped round to his house without too much trouble. 'See. My ankle is calming down already.'

'I don't know whether to be glad or sorry about that.'

'The website?' she prompted.

They studied it together, then shared a glass of wine.

It was all very . . . relaxing. She felt so comfortable with him.

She was sorry when the evening ended. Not sorry that he kissed her goodnight or that she dragged him back towards her for an extra kiss.

But that was enough progress to be going on with, enough changes to adjust to.

She felt better about going to bed now there were heavy bolts across the doors.

In fact, considering her financial predicament, she was feeling pretty good at the moment, far better than she had earlier on this afternoon.

And Ross seemed happy about their situation too.

Chapter Nineteen

John Crichton woke in the night and found it hard to get back to sleep. They'd been here in Austria for a couple of days now and already he was going quietly mad with boredom. Thank heavens for ebooks. He'd been able to download and read several. But you couldn't read all the time and anyway, he missed being outdoors. However expensive the ventilation systems they installed, the air never seemed as good inside buildings.

He got up and went into their suite's small living room, sitting down in the darkness rather than going back to bed. A change of position was often helpful for an older body, he'd found.

The lights went on suddenly, making him jump in shock because he hadn't heard Sandra get up.

'Are you all right, John?' Her voice was sharper than usual.

He turned to look at her. 'Just having trouble sleeping. I'll be glad to get the travel over with.'

'We'll hear about a date today.'

'You didn't say that when you came back.'

'Of course I did. You've just forgotten.'

That astonished him and a quick glance showed him she had that look on her face that he was beginning to recognise as a sign that she was either lying or not telling the complete truth. He took a few seconds to think about how to respond before he replied. 'Actually, I haven't, Sandra. And don't try to persuade me I have. I may be a fool and a criminal, but I don't have dementia.'

'No, no! Of course you don't. Sorry. I must have thought I'd told you.'

'Yes. That'll be it.' He got up and walked into his bedroom, suddenly out of patience with the way she had recently started watching his every move.

However, she followed him, so he turned round and stated in slow, careful words, 'I'd just like to make it plain that I know for certain I haven't got dementia, not even the beginnings of it, because firstly, it doesn't run in my family. Not a single close relative has ever had it. And secondly, when you and I were about to marry, just to be sure, I had a brain scan and got the all-clear.' He'd always planned the tiniest details of major steps well before he took them. Even now.

'But you keep changing your mind and not doing as you say you will.'

'About the money, you mean?'

'Frankly, yes.'

'I've found that I feel more secure when I'm the one controlling that, so I'll stick with looking after the finances myself.' He decided it was better to offer her a way out. 'My turn to be sorry. I should have told you. Don't worry.

I'll still pay for whatever we both need and I won't stint on your expenses.'

'Yes, you should have told me. Don't you trust me now, John?' She fumbled for a handkerchief and pressed it to her eyes.

He didn't let her continue and say something that might totally upset this increasingly wobbly apple cart. 'Sandra, this is not a time to discuss important things. No one thinks clearly at this hour of the night. Why don't you go back to bed? We'll discuss where we're up to in more detail tomorrow. And if your guy can't do what he promised in a timely fashion, I still have one or two contacts who will take over the task of helping us get away from Europe.'

'I'm sure he will do as promised.'

'That's good, then. Nothing to worry about. We'll both enjoy having our own home again, I'm sure. Once we reach our destination, I'll send you off to do the preliminary house-hunting.'

'Good. I'll enjoy that. In the meantime, do you want a cup of decaf? Or something to help you sleep?'

'No, thank you. You know I never take sleeping pills. You get back to bed.'

He was glad his health had stopped them sleeping together. He needed the quiet thinking time to work out what to do. His plans must change and quickly.

He smiled grimly as he snuggled down in bed. She had undoubtedly done all this for the money, but if he had his way, she was going to be very disappointed indeed.

He hoped she'd go out again tomorrow, as she had every other day. He needed to finalise one or two of his secret arrangements.

A sudden thought struck him. He'd better be careful of what he was eating and drinking from now on. Were all the horror stories of family treachery and doping elderly relatives that he'd read over the years clouding his judgement? Or were they helping him to avoid potential pitfalls?

Who knew? But having taken the step of stealing the money, he would now be forced to take some other steps, because he didn't intend to end his life in prison. It would be a big help if her contact did arrange their travel and new passports.

It was bad not being able to trust her, though.

What he'd done was bad, too. He was regretting it greatly now that the excitement had died down.

But what had really knocked his feet from under him was the medical diagnosis he'd been given. It had ruined what he'd planned, the very reason for committing a crime.

And yet, he was finding the strength to cope, even now. Mentally, he felt more like the young go-getter he'd once been, energised by what he had to do. He still had a chance to win something from his last campaign.

Sandra hadn't met this side of him before because he'd been a rather depressed and lethargic widower when she came to work for him. She'd helped him out of that, at least, so he owed her something. But not everything. No, not now.

Beware what you wish for, my girl! he thought. *I'm not going to fade away quietly.*

The next morning Sandra went out again to see her contact and John reset his phone. He had a long conversation this time, going over in detail what he wanted his only remaining friend to do for him.

'Are you sure, John?'

'Sadly, I'm very sure. It turns out I've not got long to live . . . and that Sandra hasn't been exactly honest with me . . . or faithful, even. I'll pay you to—'

'No need to pay me. We've been friends for a long time. I warned you about this but I'm sorry I was right, truly sorry.'

'Given my health situation, that doesn't matter.'

'It'll matter to those you've taken the money from.'

'Yes. Pity I didn't write a way of reimbursing them into the will. I can't worry about them now, got too many personal worries. But if you can do anything to give the money back, you'll have my blessing. You know where it is, now.'

'All right. Take care how you go.'

'Oh, I shall! I'll take great care.'

'I'll make sure the other will is the one that's used.'

'Thanks. Send me an advertising email to confirm it's been sorted out.'

The so-called advert registered on his phone a few hours later. He deleted it and if anyone checked his emails, it'd seem only to be spam.

Guy phoned Lara the following afternoon, just as she was debating what to have for tea.

'Want to come and help babysit Minnie for a couple of hours? Darcie's been invited to a colleague's birthday celebration after work and Carter has a late meeting. She wasn't going to her friend's party till I found out.'

'Oh! I'd intended to – but no, I can cancel that. I'd love to see Minnie again.'

'You'll have to drive yourself over this time because I'm about to pick up Minnie from childcare and take her home. You'll have to get Darcie to register you there as a trusted family member, then you can pick her up sometimes. I can get you a child safety seat. People leave them in cars they trade in occasionally and we keep one or two around to give customers with small children demo rides.'

'I'll do that. I'll set off at once. I'd rather use my own transport anyway.'

She rushed next door to tell Ross. 'I hope you don't mind cancelling tonight but I hardly know that baby and she doesn't know me, and it upsets me a lot.'

'Is Guy going to be there?'

His voice sounded tense, so she brought the possible problem into the open as she would have done at work. 'Yes, he is. But I don't have a thing going with him, Ross, and I wouldn't have, not ever again. You've no need to worry about him.' She watched his smile grow warmer as he took this in.

He took her hand and raised it to his lips, a gesture that she loved.

'No, of course not, Lara. Sorry. You go and have fun with your granddaughter. And hey, how about you and I take her out sometime? I was a hands-on father and I love littlies.'

'That'd be great. Just let me get to know her better first.'

'Pop in when you get back so that I can be sure you're home safely.'

'If I'm not too late. But don't stay up specially. I've no

idea how long this birthday session Darcie's attending will last. If there aren't any lights on in your house, I'll not bother you.'

Guy had brought Minnie home by the time Lara got to Darcie's and they spent a lovely hour playing with their granddaughter on the rug, then giving her tea and a bath.

After that Minnie obligingly fell asleep in Lara's arms and Guy took a photo of them both for her. She looked at it on his phone, her eyes filling with tears.

'What a lovely sunny nature she has! Will you email it to me, please?'

'Of course.'

'Shall I take her up to bed now, do you think, or will Darcie want to see her when she gets home?'

The phone rang just then and Guy answered it, waving her towards the stairs.

When she came down, he said, 'That was Darcie. Do we mind if she and Carter go out for a curry and come home a bit later?'

'I'm sure you've already said yes.'

'Well, of course I did. But if you can't stay, I'll be all right on my own.'

He had that slightly smug look on his face and she wondered if he'd suggested this to Darcie, but she didn't challenge him on that.

'I could phone for a takeaway for us if you like, Lara.'

'I have to admit I'm hungry. Oh, all right. I'll stay.'

'The boyfriend will wait up for you, I'm sure.'

'You don't know anything about him.' She sighed, thinking of Ross's health. 'He won't be able to stay awake even if he wants. He has ME, gets very tired. No wonder some people call it chronic fatigue syndrome.'

'Oh. I'm, er, sorry.'

Why should Guy care about Ross? She looked at him, letting her disbelief show, and he shrugged.

'I'd be sorry for anyone who had ME,' he admitted.

'That's more like the truth. But I will accept your offer of sending out for food as long as I pay my share. What sort shall we get?'

'We could follow our daughter's example. Do you still like curries, Lara?'

'Who do you think taught Darcie to like them? It was you who didn't like spicy food in those days.'

'I love it now.'

When their daughter came home, she was so grateful for the unexpected treat of an evening out that Lara's resentment at being conned into spending more time alone with Guy faded.

It had been the same as last time: she'd enjoyed his company but there had been none of the old chemistry between them, not as far as she was concerned, anyway.

They all chatted for a while and time passed so pleasantly that Lara was shocked to realise it was well after eleven o'clock. She said a quick goodbye and started off home.

Her happy mood vanished abruptly when there was suddenly a thump and the car started to drive erratically. She recognised the signs: flat tyre! Fortunately she was still in a residential area, with street lights and houses within screaming distance, so she felt pretty safe about changing the wheel.

Muttering in annoyance, she looked in the back of the car for the equipment she needed but found herself missing a jack. Why hadn't she checked that when she got the car?

No other vehicles had driven past at this late hour, so there was nothing for it but to phone for help. Only she hadn't joined a motoring organisation yet. She would do that tomorrow.

Who should she phone? She'd have preferred to call Ross, but he'd be asleep now. That left Darcie or Guy. They were closer anyway. Who should she phone? Her daughter needed her sleep so that was a no-brainer. It had to be Guy. He'd be free to rearrange his day if he was tired tomorrow and he was an expert at cars, anyway.

His voice was sleepy, but sharpened up again when she told him what had happened.

'I'll be there in ten minutes.'

He was there in eleven minutes. OK, she'd been watching time pass as she sat in the locked car keeping a wary eye on the street around her.

He helped her change the tyre quickly and efficiently.

'I'll get you a jack from work in case you get any more flat tyres. Bad luck, that. Some idiot must have dropped those sharp pieces of metal on the road.'

'Thanks, Guy. I'm grateful.'

'Do you want me to follow you home, just to make sure you get there all right?'

'No, thanks. Lightning rarely strikes twice in the same place. I'll drive back sedately.' She chuckled. 'After all, I can always phone and wake you up again if I break down.'

He hesitated, leaning slightly forward as if about to kiss

her cheek. Before he could touch her, she turned to open the car door. 'Goodnight and thanks again.'

'Yeah. See you soon.'

She looked at her watch as she set off. After midnight. She hoped Ross hadn't been watching out for her.

Chapter Twenty

Once Lara had left to visit her granddaughter, Ross sat down to watch the news on TV. He was sorry not to be spending the evening with her, as planned, but could understand how she felt. Family were so important. Look how his cousin Fiona had helped him rent out his house.

He yawned and closed his eyes 'just for a minute'.

When he woke, moonlight was streaming in through the rear windows. For a moment he felt disoriented. Then he realised where he was and looked at his watch. It was bright enough to see it clearly without switching on the lights.

Half past eleven. He got up, stretching the stiffness from his body. He glanced out of the kitchen window but Lara hadn't returned. What was keeping her so long?

He was about to put a light on when he heard something outside at the rear of the houses. Keeping perfectly still, he listened carefully. It sounded like . . . it was! Someone had trodden on the band of drainage pebbles that edged the back patios. But the sound hadn't come from outside his house; it had been further away, outside Lara's.

He was about to look out of the back window when it occurred to him that he'd see what was going on more clearly from a bedroom window, so he ran up the stairs and positioned himself behind the curtain of one.

He'd been right. There was a figure outside Lara's house. A man, it looked like. Even as he watched, the prowler slipped through the shadows to her back door and peered in through it. Was he about to break in?

Ross reached automatically for his phone but it wasn't in his pocket. Muttering in annoyance, he ran back downstairs and fumbled around the chair where he'd been sitting. No sign of it. Ah! There it was on the side table next to his half-full mug of cold coffee.

He picked up the phone and went into the kitchen area, where he'd be less visible. He rang the hotel, identified himself in a low voice and told the receptionist there was a prowler outside the end house of the row.

She said she'd alert the security guards urgently.

Then he waited, still keeping an eye on what was happening. To his surprise the prowler crept along the back patio and tried to peer into Ross's own house, shining a narrow torch beam downward first, then moving it up and down.

There was just enough time for Ross to bob down behind the breakfast bar, which had several objects standing on it. He didn't think he'd be seen if he kept still.

Before the man – it was definitely a man – could get a really good look at the house's contents, he jerked his head sideways as if he'd heard something. Switching off the torch, he started running away across the patio heading towards the lake.

Ross had heard something too, so he ran across to the window to see what had driven the prowler away. Two figures in black were jogging across from the hotel, making a lot of noise and shining powerful torches. These must be the security guards.

Not a clever way to investigate, he thought angrily. They'd not catch any prowlers that way. Or maybe they didn't want to get into a fight, just frighten intruders away.

Great! He'd be worried now about the prowler coming back, both on his own and Lara's behalf.

He went outside to speak to the security guys and they checked the rear of Lara's house as well as his. The windows hadn't been broken and of course there were no footprints on the paved patio, but there was a light scatter of pebbles on the far edge of his paved patio where the intruder had run away suddenly.

Why had the man targeted her house first? She didn't even have enough furniture, let alone valuables worth breaking in for.

Perhaps he'd intended to work his way along the row.

When the security guards left, they promised to walk past at regular intervals. A fat lot of good that would do if they were always so noisy and visible! Ross decided not to go to bed yet. He wanted to wait for Lara to return, tell her what had happened and warn her to be ultra-careful about keeping her house locked.

He paced to and fro, wondering what was keeping her so long. Were she and Guy getting on better than she'd expected? No. He trusted her and, anyway, there was always a slight edge to her voice when she spoke about her ex. Not as bad as when he spoke about his own ex, though.

Eventually, at about half past midnight, car headlights raked across the hotel car park and a vehicle moved past it to the narrow road that led to the leisure village.

Lara! At last.

Ross went out of the front door and stood waiting for her to get out.

She fairly bounced out of the vehicle, sounding annoyed. 'You didn't have to wait up for me!'

'I wanted to warn you that we've had a prowler.'

That stopped her in her tracks.

'Oh dear. This is the second time. Has he broken in?'

'No. Whoever it was prowled round the back of your house, though, shining a torch in the windows.'

'My house or all the houses?'

'He went to your house first and spent some time examining it, perhaps looking for an easy way in.'

'I bet he was disappointed in what he saw. I'm surprised he lingered.'

'That's not the point. Why would someone be targeting your house? With all due respect, your furniture is mostly only fit for the rubbish dump and you're not exactly loaded with valuables.'

'I agree. There are just the few pieces of silver I have on display. Maybe I should hide them, only I like to look at them. What did you do? Chase him away?'

'There was just one man, as far as I could see, but I'm so un-macho I didn't go out to tackle him because no one was in danger. I phoned the hotel to report it to the security guards and they walked across heavy-footed, with torches blazing, thus warning the prowler. He ran away, heading towards the lake.'

'Oh.'

'Your ex, do you think, trying to give you a fright?'

'No. He's not like that and besides, I had a flat tyre on the way back from Darcie's and I didn't have a jack, so I phoned Guy, who came and helped me.' She looked towards her house and couldn't help shivering at the thought of even going inside on her own.

Ross seemed to understand and put an arm round her shoulders. 'I'll come in with you, shall I? I'm fairly sure the prowler didn't get inside but it won't hurt to make sure everything's all right.'

'Would you mind?'

'Of course not. I'll just lock my front door and you can lock your car.'

When they were inside, he suggested she stay in the living area and he made sure the bolts were locked on the outer doors to prevent anyone getting away easily if they did find someone.

He didn't think this would happen, but could see how nervous she had become. 'We'd be two to one, remember,' he said gently.

He took the precaution of arming himself with a heavy knife sharpener. The steel rod felt nice and heavy in his hand. She followed his example, picking up a solid wooden rolling pin. Then he went up to start his exploration, not expecting any problems but knowing this would reassure her.

When he came down again, he saw how anxious she was

looking and said soothingly, 'There's no one here, Lara. I checked every cupboard big enough to hold a person.'

She put down the rolling pin. 'I can't thank you enough. It's silly of me to be so nervous, I know, but as a woman living on my own I've been targeted a couple of times.'

'Any sane person would be nervous if a prowler was spotted sussing out their home. Come here.' He dumped his makeshift weapon and held out his arms. She didn't hesitate to fling herself into them, cuddling close.

What a strange mixture of confidence and nervousness she was. But he was increasingly happy to hold her close. It felt so very right. It occurred to him suddenly that Nonie Jayne had never liked to linger in a cuddle, even before they were married. Why had he been so blind about her?

Lara shifted in his arms. 'You make me feel better just by being here.'

'Well, there's no need for us to stay apart, is there? You can come and sleep in my place, if you like, or I'll come and sleep here. I'm not putting the word on you for sex. We both have spare rooms.'

That made her look at him in obvious amusement. 'I know, Ross. One of the things I like most about you is how you deal with women. Even the way you talk shows it, or the way you make women smile when they're serving you in shops like the antiques centre.'

'Is that as big a compliment as I think?'

'Yes, it is. There are still a lot of male – yes, and female – chauvinists around. I've worked with some horrors of both genders as well as some lovely men and women.' She looked at him uncertainly. 'I'd prefer it if you slept here, but I think, given how many valuable items there are in your aunt's house, I'd better come next door.'

'You're right. I don't have a spare bed now, but there's a recliner armchair that I can use. It's very comfortable and I fall asleep on it regularly.'

'Are you sure? I'm not quite ready to seal our relationship by sleeping together.'

'I know, love. And I promised myself never to rush into a relationship again. Would it upset you if we started . . . courting?'

This old-fashioned term made her chuckle. She had a lovely gurgle of laughter, soft and musical.

'No. It wouldn't upset me at all. On both counts.'

She planted a kiss on his cheek, a very modest, gentle kiss and yet it made him feel oh so connected to her.

He felt safe to go on hoping something would come of their relationship.

Chapter Twenty-One

The following afternoon, just before her evening meal, Cindy walked along to the lake, making the most of the mild weather. She sat down at the far side on one of the simple wooden benches, enjoying the sight of a group of children splashing in the shallows. Sand had been dumped along the edge of a tiny bay and barriers installed across the deeper water to create a safe paddling area.

It was easy to get lost in thought in such a peaceful setting and she jumped in shock when a deep voice spoke to one side of her.

'Would you mind if I joined you on the bench?'

She looked up to see a silver-haired man standing next to her.

'I wouldn't have disturbed you but the other benches are occupied and I must admit, I love to watch children playing. Only one has to be so careful when dealing with children nowadays. Rightly so, of course.'

His voice was that of an educated Englishman. She

loved the way they spoke. 'Sure. Take a seat. There's plenty of room.'

'You're American from the sounds of it. Where from?'

'Florida these days, Baltimore originally.'

They got chatting and he seemed interested in the new leisure village, so she told him what a nice place it was to live in. This sort of conversation happened regularly as people came to look round with a view to buying a house, so she thought nothing of it until he mentioned Lara's name.

'I gather Lara Perryman has moved here. I know her ex-husband slightly and he mentioned it when I was looking at a car his company was selling.'

She looked sideways, surprised by this. 'You didn't think of getting an introduction to her to ask about the village?'

'I'd heard from someone else that she'd had some financial troubles and I didn't want to intrude. I was a mere acquaintance, not a friend. Is she – all right? Such a mean crime, from what Guy said!'

'She's coping. But you're right: it's hard to lose your retirement money. She was very upset, as you can imagine.'

'Yes. I heard there have been several people affected by the villain. Poor things.'

He looked at his watch and stood up, inclining his head in a farewell gesture. 'I have to meet someone at the hotel shortly. It's been a pleasure chatting to you, Cindy, and thank you for the information about this place. You make it sound very attractive. Maybe our paths will cross again.'

Nice man, she thought as he walked away. She didn't even bother to tell Lara about the encounter. Her neighbour's ex was bound to have met a lot of people, given that he sold cars, and would no doubt have mentioned the theft to one or two. He'd have done better to keep his mouth shut, in Cindy's opinion. He had given her a car, though, which said a lot about him.

She sighed as she strolled back. Word had got out round here about Lara's losses, so who knew how far the gossip had spread?

The man walked back up to the hotel. It had been easier than he'd expected to find out about Lara Perryman. He still felt angry when he thought how his long-time friend had cheated her and several other people.

If she'd been in real financial trouble, he'd have offered her some help, as he had one of the other victims. He was rich enough now that the money didn't matter to him. But she seemed to be coping all right.

Who'd have expected John Crichton to commit a crime? John, of all people!

But then, people could and did change suddenly. You just didn't expect it from someone you'd known since you'd both been at school together. And given that he'd worked for the government in intelligence, you'd think he of all people would have suspected that something was wrong with John.

He wondered where his former friend was now, whether he was feeling guilty about what he'd done.

Since Gil had told her he was going to be occupied scoping out Ross's house, Nonie Jayne told him she would treat herself to an early night.

'Well, you make sure you continue to stay in your room and don't invite anyone else in,' he said at once.

She lowered her lashes to hide the anger at this. She had no intention of staying in her suite on her own 24/7. She was tired of hotel rooms and wanted to be with other people. Even if she wasn't talking to them, she liked watching them.

She was very relieved that Gil was living in a cheaper place than this hotel. The more she got to know him, the more she felt she'd made a mistake linking up with him at all. Who did he think he was, bossing her around like that?

None of her husbands had barked orders at her, though Ross had called her stupid during a couple of their arguments. He was the stupid one, staying in that house that cost a fortune to maintain instead of selling it and investing the money, and so she'd told him several times. Not that Mr Stubborn had listened.

Gil insisted on taking her out to a café he knew for an evening meal. He said it was much cheaper than the hotel and the meals were good.

Unfortunately, it turned out to be a dreadful place serving fattening, unhealthy food, the sort she'd never put into her mouth willingly. He'd even swapped plates with her and finished off what she'd left, which was most of it. Talk about shovelling food into his mouth. He had the manners of an ape in the jungle!

As they were coming back into the hotel, she noticed a couple of men sitting in the bar area, each alone. They each glanced up with *that look* that said they'd rather be chatting to someone than staring at a newspaper.

She waited ten minutes after Gil left her going into her room, then checked her appearance in the mirror one final time and made her way down to the bar.

The younger of the two men was no longer there, but the older one was still sitting nursing a glass of wine and watching the other customers, his newspaper lying neglected by his side. He had beautifully cut silver hair and what she'd call a civilised expression on his face.

She saw the moment he noticed her as she stood in the doorway. He studied her openly as she sauntered across to the bar and ordered a glass of house champagne. She didn't mind. The day men stopped admiring her would be a very sad one.

Edward watched the woman come in, shocked at how much she resembled his first wife. Only she was even more beautiful.

He made no secret of the fact that he was watching her, wanted to see how she reacted.

She studied him quickly, then looked for somewhere to sit. Was it his imagination or had she chosen a place where she'd not be noticed from the hotel entrance?

He found her attractive. It was at times like this that he regretted being old, though his body still functioned perfectly well where women were concerned.

He beckoned the bar attendant across and asked if the lady who'd just come in seemed to be meeting someone.

'I don't think so, sir. She's staying at the hotel.'

'Thank you.' He slipped the man a tip.

Maybe he was an old fool, but he'd welcome someone to chat to. Welcome more than that, if possible.

Careful not to react, she chose a table from which she could see everyone who came into the hotel, in case Gil returned, and when the bar attendant brought her drink across, she thanked him and took a tiny, leisurely sip. Champagne was fattening but you had to drink something if you wanted to sit in a bar, and ordering lemonade, which she much preferred, would have made her look a childish fool, not a sophisticated woman.

The old guy raised his glass to her and she didn't have to pretend to look surprised. She *was* surprised. It was usually she who found an excuse for making contact with men of that age.

She raised her glass in reply and gave him a half-smile, even more surprised when he immediately got up and walked across to her table.

'Would you like some company, my dear?'

His clothes were expensive. She could always tell. 'That would be nice, but I won't be staying for long.'

He sat down. 'I won't be staying long, either. I'm waiting for my chauffeur to bring my car. But it's always nice to have a chat, so tell me about yourself. I'm Edward, by the way. Edward Charsley.'

Him having a chauffeur was an excellent start. 'I'm Nonie Jayne, newly divorced and waiting for the decree absolute, so there isn't much to talk about in my life at the moment. I don't even have a permanent place to live yet.'

'You're American by your accent, the second American lady I've met today, strangely enough. Where are you from?'

'All over the place really. Since I'm in a boring patch of my life I'd much rather hear about you, Edward. What are you doing in Wiltshire?'

'I've been visiting some friends and then I went to see Avebury, which is much nicer than Stonehenge and you can actually touch the big stones.'

She had no idea what he was talking about but she tried to look interested. 'Must have been nice. Are you retired?'

'Sort of. I used to own a building company. But I sold it a while ago.'

'What did your company build?'

'Commercial developments. Much simpler than the residential stuff but rather boring to outsiders. I'm too old for all those hassles nowadays and I don't need the money, but I still like to dabble in this and that.'

She said it without thinking, because he really did have a youthful expression on his face. 'You're not all that old.'

He grinned. 'I'm seventy-five, which is old in body, but I'm still ticking along nicely healthwise and here is where it counts most.' He tapped his forehead, then leant back and stared at her assessingly. 'What's a beautiful woman like you doing with only an old man to talk to, anyway? I'd have thought the younger guys would be queuing up to take you out.'

She shrugged. 'Let them queue. I find most younger men rather boring.'

His grin became broader still. 'And not as rich usually, eh?'

She stared at him open-mouthed. Should she pretend she didn't understand the implications of that?

While she was still hesitating about how to answer, he added, 'I'd rather we spoke frankly, Nonie Jayne. It doesn't offend me, you know, if a woman as lovely as you chooses to make a *practical* use of her good looks.'

It took her only seconds to decide that he really meant that. She was starting to like him and didn't even try to hold back a genuine smile. 'My body is the only capital I was born with, so yes, I've used it to attract men with money. I've never *sold* it though.'

'You're too classy-looking for me even to think that.'

His remark pleased her. It was what she aimed at: a classy look.

'And I'd guess you're between men now, if you've just divorced someone.' He took out a card and slipped it into her hand. 'Give me a call when you come to London. I'll prove that I'm not boring – or too old – and we'll see if we continue to get on well.'

She picked up the card. 'All right. I've certainly enjoyed your company tonight. I'll be in London in a few days, probably.'

'I'll be there for a few days . . . probably. No longer. Let's see if we can coincide.'

She was good at reading between the lines. What he really meant was if she was interested, she should join him quickly. And she was interested – but she'd do her research properly this time before making a move.

He got up, gesturing towards the hotel entrance, where a man wearing a chauffeur's cap was standing waiting. 'Unfortunately something came up this afternoon and my driver had to collect me tonight or I'd stay with you longer. I do hope we meet again, Nonie Jayne.'

He walked out, not looking back.

She sat thinking this meeting over, staring at the business card till she'd learnt the phone number on it by heart, then putting it safely in her purse. Unusual sort of card, which only carried his first name and a phone number, but she remembered his surname.

At a guess, he only gave this type of card to a few personal friends. If she was right, that was promising.

She didn't finish the glass of champagne; she never did.

It was getting late and no one else of interest was left in the bar, so she returned to her room.

It must be her lucky night. Edward smelt of money. She could usually tell. She bet he'd be good company, too, given the way his eyes had twinkled and he'd teased her. It made a refreshing change that he hadn't wanted her to pretend about her way of life. She was sick of pretending all the time.

Did she want to find herself another Englishman to link up with? Maybe. If she found one rich enough.

Did she want to find herself an older man again? She most certainly did. They were much easier to handle than men of her own age, as her marriage to Ross had proved.

Though come to think of it, she wasn't sure anyone could handle Edward Charsley, who seemed powerful; she couldn't work out why. He had intrigued her, with those young eyes in a lined, older face.

She would go up to London and stay on in England for a while if it seemed likely to be profitable. And she'd ditch her anger, along with Gil.

Let's face it, money was the only thing that stayed your friend, so it didn't matter which country she was in if she had access to it.

Half an hour later Nonie Jayne looked up in surprise as someone turned the key in the lock and Gil slipped into her hotel room, interrupting her nightly beauty routine. 'How the hell did you get a key to this room?'

'I waited till the clerk had left the reception area and slipped behind the counter. You could see the spare keys in the pigeonholes.'

'That's pretty poor security.'

'Isn't it? And you didn't put the bar on the door, either.
Poor security on your part, too. Or were you expecting
someone? You'd better not have been.'

She stared down her nose at him. 'Of course I wasn't.
It's just that I'm used to superior hotels which are much
safer than this one.' And she'd been thinking about
Edward, wishing his business card gave more information
about his current business interests so that she could look
him up on her smartphone. Pity she'd forgotten to lock
the door fully.

'Never mind that. Don't you want to know how I got
on tonight? And how about a glass of something while
we chat?'

'Hotel mini-bars are too expensive.'

'Lighten up. One drink won't break your bank. After
all, I paid for your tea.'

She declined to join him in a drink and sat scowling while
he emptied the small bottle of whisky into a water glass.

'There was no car outside that house, so I had a good look
round through the back windows of the end two houses.'

'Did you see the ornaments?'

'A few, mostly some rather nice antique silver. The place
is a mess inside, though. They've probably started clearing
it out already and got rid of the valuable furniture. But
the house next door had a good few ornaments as well,
so if we hit them both, we could make a decent profit.'
He let out a harsh caw of laughter. 'I walked all round
the finished houses at a distance first, checking, and there
are definitely no security systems monitoring the area, just
one covering the road leading across to it. But someone

must have seen me because two guys in security uniforms suddenly came running from the hotel.' He let out a scornful grunt. 'They made sure I saw them coming and had time to get away, so I doubt they're into capturing criminals who might fight back. A lot of private security officers are like that: cowards. I'll be more careful next time, though, because I don't want them or anyone else interrupting me.'

'And when will that be?'

'Tomorrow. We'll go there in the middle of the night and I'll take special glass-cutting equipment with me to deal with the windows. You can wait outside with a couple of extra bags to carry what we find.'

She slapped her hand down on the low table. 'No way. I've already told you: I'm *not* getting involved in any burglaries.' It was one thing to take what she was rightfully owed from Ross as a farewell present and quite another to do a burglary of this sort. And anyway, she'd known Ross wouldn't prosecute her even if he did catch her. He was too soft.

Gil glared at her, so she glared right back.

'You're the one who put me on to this, Nonie Jayne. You *are* involved.'

'Well, I made it plain from the start that I wasn't taking part in the action.'

'You'll help me out, my girl, if you want your share. And if you try to back out now, just as we're getting it nicely set up, I'll make sure the police find something incriminating among your things afterwards. I'm good at getting in and out of places, as you've already seen. You'll not even know I've dumped a stolen piece on you till they find it.'

She stared at him with her pitiful expression and summoned up a few tears.

He laughed, and not a nice laugh, either. 'Save your false tears for someone stupid enough to believe them.' Then he put on an unconvincing fake smile and said in a smarmy voice, 'But let's not quarrel, eh? It's much nicer to seal a bargain like ours the usual way.'

He moved towards her, arms outstretched, and she had the knife she kept hidden in the side of her purse out in an instant. 'Keep your distance.'

'I was only going to kiss you. You are a rather tempting piece of goods.'

'No, thank you. I don't do casual sex.' She didn't want to risk catching anything.

'I'd give you a great time.'

'I said no and I meant it. I save myself for marriage.'

'Marriages, you mean.' He stepped back. 'Very well. We won't go to bed together.'

She heard the unspoken 'yet' and shivered.

'But I *shall* need your help to pull this off. I can't carry all the goodies myself.'

She sighed and sagged back in her chair, still keeping the knife visible. 'All right. I'll do what you want. But you'd better play fair with me.'

He laughed loudly, picked up the glass and gulped down the rest of the whisky. As he moved towards the door, he pulled up the hood of his light jacket so that his face was mostly hidden. 'Very sensible of you. But remember that I'll be keeping watch on the hotel from early morning onwards tomorrow. If you try to skip out on me, I'll follow you and make sure you pay for it one way or another. You'd need a taxi to get away and no taxi driver is going to care about protecting you if I stop him and claim you're my unfaithful wife who's robbed me.'

He paused to let that sink in, then added, 'Look, Nonie, I need you to—'

'Nonie Jayne!' She never allowed anyone to shorten her name. It was special, her name was. There weren't many people called that. She'd chosen it with care.

'Nonie bloody Jayne, then. I'm definitely going to need help carrying the things we take if we're to make this job pay well for both of us. There won't be time for me to come and go a few times. And tomorrow, put on running shoes or whatever you call them in the States . . . right? Not those stupid high heels you totter around in.'

'I'll be there. I just said so, didn't I? Only, what if Ross is in his house?'

'If he's around, I'll make sure he's in no condition to stop us.'

She looked at him in horror.

He rolled his eyes. 'I meant I'd tie him up. I'm not into murder, you fool.'

'But he'd still recognise me.'

'I just told you, you'll be waiting for me outside, you stupid bitch. He'll never even see you if you do exactly as I say. I've got it all planned.'

She didn't reply, waited till he'd left, then put the bar on her door and leant against it. His last words had confirmed that he was a violent man, whatever he claimed. What *had* she been thinking of, hooking up with him?

She wasn't putting up with this. He'd find out she meant what she said about not doing violence *or* committing crimes.

Besides, if he succeeded in forcing her to help him once, he would undoubtedly try to make her do his bidding in other things afterwards. She'd seen it happen to other women with thugs like him.

No, thank you. There had to be a way out of this. Had to. But what?

Chapter Twenty-Two

When Lara woke up, it took her only a minute to realise she was in the house next door, lying in Ross's bed. He wasn't there with her, of course, but his possessions were scattered around and it felt as if he had just slipped out for a moment.

And that wasn't a bad feeling. Definitely not.

The room was flooded with light and she could almost catch a sunbeam in her hand, it was slanting so close to her. She couldn't bear to stay in bed. Mornings as beautiful as this weren't plentiful anywhere in the world. It would be foolish to waste this chance to enjoy one.

She glanced at her watch, amazed that it was only seven o'clock. She didn't usually get up this early, especially when she hadn't gone to bed till the small hours. But she felt refreshed and ready to go, better than she had for ages, so flung back the covers and got dressed.

Downstairs, she found Ross also awake. The recliner armchair he'd slept on was upright again and he was sitting on it sipping a cup of what smelt like tea.

He smiled at her, his head haloed in sunshine. 'So you couldn't sleep either, Lara?'

She waved one hand towards the rear windows. 'It's far too beautiful to stay in bed. All right if I get a cup of tea?'

'Of course it is. Help yourself. The kettle's boiled recently and I left plenty of water in it.'

'Thank you.' She looked out of the kitchen window. 'We're not the only early risers, it seems. There's a luxury car just turned up at the hotel. Someone must be leaving early.'

'Off to make a business deal or catch a plane, I suppose. Who cares about them? I'd rather enjoy your company. Now that you're awake, maybe we can sit out on the patio to drink our cuppas?'

'Sounds good. I'll nip next door and get my cardigan first. I can't think how I forgot it last night. The English sun won't be warm yet and I'm still more used to Australian temperatures.'

When she got back, he was in the kitchen pouring boiling water into a mug for her.

As they waited for her tea to brew, they stood side by side watching the hotel, something you couldn't help doing whenever you were at the front of the house. No one else was around at this hour, except that one car, presumably waiting for a client.

When her tea was ready, Ross threw the soggy teabag away, picked up the biscuit tin and led the way outside to the rear patio. She was about to follow him when she saw the driver get back into the car and leave the hotel.

'How strange!' she said as she sat down outside. 'That car went away again but nobody had got into it.'

'That *is* weird. Oh well. Nothing to do with us. Look at that view!'

By moving their chairs further away from the house they could see the lake to one side of the leisure village, which was a very pretty outlook. Already there were walkers striding round it.

They were both silent for a while, then he said suddenly, 'I can't believe how well I slept last night. Even though it wasn't for a long time, it was very refreshing.'

'Mine was, too.'

'Perhaps it was because I knew you were near.'

'Perhaps that worked for both of us. Who knows?'

He held out his hand and she put hers into it, then they sat there quietly, enjoying the clean-washed brightness of the early morning sunshine without the need for meaningless chat – and also enjoying the warmth of hand holding hand and heart reaching tentatively out to heart.

After Gil had left her at her hotel room, Nonie Jayne didn't go to bed but sat on the uncomfortable upright chair, thinking hard. But however much she searched for a solution, she couldn't see an easy way to get herself out of this situation; well, not in the short time before Gil intended to force her to help him.

She could call a taxi, but what if he was already watching the hotel and saw her leave in it? She wouldn't put it past him to follow her and catch her as she got out of it. He might hurt her, damage her looks in some way, which would be disastrous.

She got up to stare at herself in the mirror, something she often did, studying her appearance. Well, she had to protect her looks because she depended on them for a living, if you could call marriage a living. She was approaching the big four zero now and could see the signs the years were already writing on her skin, however carefully she looked after it.

With a sigh, she began pacing to and fro, which usually helped her to work out a problem. Only there was so little space between pieces of furniture, she couldn't step out freely and didn't dare go out to walk around the public parts of the hotel. Well, how strange would that look in the middle of the night?

In the end she could see only one way of getting help quickly and took out the business card Edward had given her. She would have to trust her instincts, which said he was trustworthy. And rich.

She'd been too angry to take proper care when she met Gil, but she wasn't blind with anger now, so at least this situation was more hopeful. Wasn't it?

She was afraid, though. Very. Gil seemed full of violence, like a volcano about to erupt.

Taking a deep breath, she called the number on the card and listened as the phone rang . . . and rang . . . Just as she thought it must be about to ring out, a sleepy voice said, 'This had better be important.'

'Edward? Is that you? You gave me your card tonight. I'm—'

'—Nonie Jayne.'

'Yes.'

'What the hell are you calling me for at this hour?'

'I'm in trouble.'

Silence, then he said in a more alert-sounding voice, 'What sort of trouble?'

'Nothing I want to go into details about on the phone,

only I've done something stupid and . . . and this man is threatening me, trying to make me help him commit a burglary . . . and perhaps worse.'

'Oh? And why did you call *me* about this?'

'We got on so well and you seemed kind. I thought you might help me escape. I'm not clever, Edward, and I have my faults, I know that, but I've never committed a crime before and I don't want to do it now.'

'Go on.'

'I don't know how to get away from the hotel, even, because he's waiting out there. He'll follow me, I know he will. And he's vicious.' She was sobbing for real suddenly.

It was a moment before he spoke again and his voice was gentler. 'Stop crying and listen!'

She gulped to a halt.

'Get your things packed, then pay your bill. You can afford to pay it?'

'Of course I can!'

'Good. So pay the bill and I'll send someone in a car to pick you up. Just hold on for a minute.'

She heard his voice muttering, maybe on another phone, but couldn't make out the words. This seemed to go on for ages, but at last he came back to her.

'My chauffeur's partner will pick you up. He's in the same business, luxury cars. The only problem is it'll take him a few hours to get to you. Will you be all right till then?'

'Yes. I can yell for help if I stay in the hotel and it'll be light when the car arrives, won't it? That'll feel much safer.'

'Good. The driver is called Jim. Wait in your room till the clerk at reception calls to say Jim has arrived to pick you up, then go down and get into the car.'

She hesitated, not entirely reassured. 'Anyone could say they'd come to pick me up. Jim's such a common name.'

He grunted. 'Not just anyone will have been sent by me, will he? If it makes you feel better, I'll tell him to call himself Edward Jim for the purpose of picking you up. No one else will be likely to use such an awkward double name.'

'Yes, Edward Jim sounds better. Um – will it be a big car? Only I have a lot of luggage.'

'Yes. It's a big car.' He chuckled suddenly, as if genuinely amused by her question.

'What are you laughing at?'

'You, honey. But in a nice way.'

'Hmm.' People did sometimes laugh at her and she could rarely work out why. She'd learnt to fix a half-smile on her face and wait till they got over it. Now she didn't need to smile, just wait for a moment then ask, 'Where will he be taking me?'

'He'll bring you to my flat in London. I may or may not be here, but my housekeeper will have instructions to look after you. She's called Mrs Bryant and she rules the place with a rod of iron, so don't get on the wrong side of her.'

The thought of a bossy housekeeper was reassuring, she didn't know why. 'Oh, good. I like London. There are so many lovely shops.'

He chuckled again. 'Yes, there are. Goodbye, then.'

'Just a minute. Gil said he'd be watching the hotel, so perhaps you should tell the driver to watch out for him.'

'Yep. I'll do that.'

'Bye.' She put the phone down and nodded happily at her reflection in the mirror, then began to check her luggage. She had most of her clothes with her, since she'd not found anywhere to live yet. She'd hung some up to stop them creasing, so had to repack them again now, which helped take her mind off her worries.

She couldn't sleep, kept glancing at her watch and when it started to grow light, she phoned down to reception to warn the guy there that she'd been called away and would need a luggage trolley sending up once her car arrived. Oh, and she needed to sort out payment for her stay right now, but she wasn't coming down to reception till her car arrived, so if they needed a personal signature, they'd have to come up to her room for it.

'To your room? But all the payment equipment is down here, madam.'

She had her story ready. 'Well, my ex is stalking me and I'm frightened he'll hurt me if I hang around in the public areas of the hotel. I'm sure *you* won't want to get into a fight with him. He can be very vicious.'

'Oh. You're right. I definitely don't want that. Um, look, I think I'd better call Mr Santiago, the owner. He'll know how to sort this out. He won't let anyone hurt you, I'm sure.'

'Just the regular security guy will do. Someone I trust is coming soon to pick me up.'

'Mr Santiago lives nearby, madam. I'm sure he won't be long.'

The clerk cut her off and she dumped the phone down harder than she should have done. She hadn't wanted a fuss made, didn't want to attract Gil's attention if he was watching the hotel, as he'd threatened.

Why would no one do what she wanted? Ever since she'd moved to Wiltshire things had gone wrong for her.

She hoped desperately that everything would work out

well in London and that Edward was as kind as he seemed – and as rich. Kind was not much good without the money to do what was needed to live a comfortable life.

As the minutes slowly passed, she admitted to herself that she was feeling more frightened than she could remember for a long time. Gil was a dreadful man. Who knew what he'd do to her if he didn't get his own way in this.

She'd been such a fool!

Euan put down the phone and got out of bed. 'There's some woman at the hotel who's afraid of her ex and has asked for a security guy to escort her out of the hotel. She's afraid of going out on her own to the car that will be coming for her. The night clerk called me to ask if I would go and take charge.'

'In other words, he's worried about the situation.'

'Yeah. But he's only young and I don't want things to go pear-shaped, so I will go and keep an eye on what's happening. Sorry you got woken up, Molly love. Will you be all right if I leave you?'

She looked at the clock and threw her covers back. 'I'll never get to sleep again. It's too near morning and it's starting to get light. I'll come with you and we'll have breakfast together at the hotel once it's all sorted out. We can always freshen up later in our private room there.'

Less than five minutes later they left the house. 'I've never met a woman who can get ready so quickly,' he teased.

'I probably look a mess, but who cares? I'm curious. Who is it making a fuss?'

'Some American female.'

When they reached the hotel, he told the desk clerk to

phone the worried guest to let her know they were on their way up to see her. He'd already asked Molly to come with him to make sure the woman felt safe speaking to him.

He blinked in shock at the person who opened the door to him, momentarily bereft of speech. He didn't think he'd ever seen a woman as beautiful as this in real life. 'Ms Larson? I'm Euan Santiago, the owner of the hotel, and this is my wife, Molly. I'm sorry to hear you're, um, feeling insecure.'

She scowled at them both and he thought her beauty seemed to fade a little as she did so.

'I didn't want a fuss made, Mr Santiago. I just wanted to slip out of the hotel quietly without alerting anyone who might be watching and without being followed.'

'Is your ex that dangerous?'

She shrugged. 'I think he is and he's been making serious threats about what he'll do if I don't, er, go back to him. It's better to be careful than sorry, so I need to get well away, I think. You could have left it to your security guy to see me out, though.'

'I prefer to keep an eye on such a delicate situation myself. Anyway, the security guy won't be inside the hotel just now. He'll be doing a tour of the grounds and checking a few places out.'

'Fine security that is!'

'That's why I came myself. Would you like to wait for your car downstairs in the bar area? You can pay your bill first, then my wife and I will sit with you, so you'll be perfectly safe.'

She paused to consider this, head on one side, then nodded. 'All right. I'd welcome a cup of decent coffee, too, if there's one going.' She scowled at the in-room refreshment bar.

'Not happy with the in-room coffee?' Molly asked.

'I've had worse, but yours isn't exactly a pleasure to drink.'

'I'll check that out later. It seemed all right when we chose it.'

The guest merely shrugged.

Chapter Twenty-Three

Nonie Jayne could have done without all this fuss. The conversation in the bar area was awkward and she left it mostly to the Santiagos, but at least this coffee was excellent and she felt safe with them. She sat where she could see the entrance but not be seen from outside the hotel.

When a big car pulled up at the front, the driver got out but stopped to shade his eyes and stare across the car park before coming inside.

He looked round the reception area and his gaze settled on Nonie Jayne. 'Ms Larson?'

'How did you recognise me?'

'I was told you were beautiful. I'm Edward Jim.'

'Oh. That's all right, then.' Pleased by this compliment, she pointed to the pile of suitcases on the trolley. 'That's my luggage.'

To her surprise, he didn't attempt to touch it.

'Look, Ms Larson, Mr Charsley told me to keep my eyes open as I drove and I had a feeling someone was following me from a few miles back. It started when I turned off the main road. We were on narrow country lanes and this little grey car stuck right on my tail in a way that puzzled me. If I went fast so did he. If I slowed down, he did the same. Once I pulled into a passing space and he stopped nearby, which made me certain I wasn't mistaken about him following me.'

He shook his head, looking worried. 'When I reached the hotel entrance, I didn't signal but braked at the last minute to turn off. Sure enough he braked hard too, then followed me into the car park, though he stopped under a tree at the far end. Would you please look out of the window and see if you recognise the car, Ms Larson?'

She did as he asked and jerked back almost immediately. 'Oh no! That's his car! It must be him inside it. He'll know it's me leaving when we load all the luggage into your limo and I bet he'll follow us. And he's a violent man.'

There was silence, then Molly snapped her fingers as she got an idea. 'How about this? Euan and I could take you and your luggage away from the hotel in the delivery van, which is plenty big enough for all your suitcases. It's parked behind the hotel so the man in that car won't be able to see you go out to it. And if you sit in the back of our van, he won't see you leave, either, especially if I get into the passenger seat at the front of the hotel.'

Nonie Jayne nodded vigorously. 'Good idea. Let's do it.'

'We'll transfer you to your hired car somewhere away from the hotel, once we're sure we're not being followed.'

The driver nodded slowly and thoughtfully. 'Yes, that's a great idea. We could stay in touch by phone and if anything goes wrong, make new arrangements. I'll leave first and wait nearby to make doubly sure he doesn't follow either me or you, shall I?'

Since Euan knew the area better than Molly, he took over. 'How about we meet at The Blackbird pub? It's in a nearby village, not visible from the main road.'

He and Jim got together and put the information into the satnav on the driver's smartphone, then Jim left the hotel and drove off.

Euan kept watch from inside the hotel, calling to the others. 'The grey car has stayed at the far side of the car park. Either he wasn't following the big car or he was only doing it to look for you.'

Nonie Jayne let out her breath in a long whoosh. 'I recognise the car so he's come after me. That's scary.'

'Come through to the rear, Ms Larson, and we'll load you and your luggage into the delivery van. After that I'll bring it round to the front and Molly can get into it openly. That should fool him.'

Nonie Jayne didn't enjoy having to sit on a lumpy old cushion among her luggage in the rear of the van. It reminded her too much of when she was a child and the family was doing a midnight flit because of unpaid rent. But she didn't protest. All she wanted at the moment was to get away from Gil.

After that, she'd see how things went with Edward. Or else go home to the States.

She sat clutching a hand loop on the side of the van, hardly daring to breathe till they'd picked up Molly openly near the front entrance and driven away from the hotel.

Then she asked, 'Did he follow us? I can't see out behind us from here.'

'No, he didn't follow. He's still waiting in the car park. You'd better stay where you are, though. After we meet your driver, you can travel in more comfort.'

'Sure. And thanks for this.'

She hadn't a clue where they were now but she trusted the Santiagos.

How had she got into this mess? She usually managed things better than this, planned ahead, had fallback plans.

It just proved you shouldn't get angry when you were dealing with either money or ex-husbands. Or greedy.

She would engrave that on her heart from now on.

Gil stayed where he was at the far corner of the hotel car park and watched the luxury car he'd been following pull up at the hotel. It was just the sort of vehicle he'd have expected Nonie Jayne to hire to get away in. He wasn't going to let her do that, though, because *she* was his prime target.

Unless he'd guessed badly, from what she'd let drop and the way she dressed, he was sure she had a big chunk of money stashed away somewhere. He meant to get hold of it, one way or another.

Beauty like hers could be useful to him later in scams, as well. She'd dazzle most men, distract them and leave them vulnerable. This was it, his big chance in life.

There was only the driver in the limo, so it wasn't bringing someone here, that was certain. The driver came out after a few minutes on his own, not looking happy. There must have been some mistake about his booking.

One thing was certain, Gil decided as he watched the car pull away: Nonie Jayne hadn't gone off with this fellow. She couldn't have sneaked out because the car had been in full view the whole time and besides, she'd mentioned having several suitcases to lug around as well, since she was between homes.

No, he'd been mistaken in his suspicions about this luxury car.

He settled down again to keep watch, feeling more relaxed about the situation. He'd go inside openly later in the morning and ask to see her.

Five minutes later he jerked upright, on high alert again, as a van pulled out from behind the hotel. This one had a sign on it: *Penny Lake Hotel*. It stopped in front of the building and a woman came hurrying out, carrying a shopping bag, and got into the passenger seat. Not Nonie Jayne.

Still no sign of her leaving, then. Perhaps she'd taken heed of his warning.

He wriggled down into a more comfortable position. It was going to be a long, boring morning but he had to keep an eye on the hotel to make sure she didn't try to leave. Luckily he could use his binoculars to keep watch on the row of houses as well from here.

Not his favourite sort of robbery, this; too much hanging around in daylight. But it'd bring him in something to tide him over till he got hold of Nonie Jayne's money.

As the morning crawled past with nothing happening, he began to feel a bit uneasy and wondered if he was right about all this. He'd been wrong before and it had landed him behind bars.

Well, you had to try, didn't you? Nothing ventured, nothing gained. If he was wrong and she didn't have money stashed away, he'd use her in other ways.

He'd seen a film once where a guy used a beautiful woman to trick money out of older men. He'd never forgotten it.

He glanced at his watch from time to time. Not yet.

His stomach rumbled and he was thirsty.

He hated waiting around.

John Crichton scowled at Sandra when she returned to the hotel empty-handed. 'Is your contact ever going to come up with the goods?'

'I'm really sorry but he's working on it as fast as he can, dear.'

'Well, I'm fed up to the teeth of waiting around, *dear*.'

She gave him a wounded look. 'He's doing his best. After all, you'd have had to wait around for even longer if you'd been able to have the plastic surgery.'

'Well, that would have been worth it. Only I couldn't have it and my time on earth is more limited than I'd expected, so it's not worth hanging about. If the travel arrangements don't get sorted out quickly, I'll get in touch with a guy I know instead. He can arrange anything, anywhere.'

'No, don't do that, John. I'm sure my contact will have it all sorted out by tomorrow.'

It took a big effort not to snap at her again. Everything was an effort these days.

He went to bed early because he felt exhausted, but slept only intermittently. Well, that had one good result at least – it gave him time to develop his final plans. Strange how he often got ideas during the long watches of a wakeful night.

As they were having breakfast together the following morning, he complained about how badly he'd slept. Later on, he yawned a lot and when Sandra suggested he have a nap, he pretended to be reluctant, then finally agreed.

Sure enough, she peeped in a short time later to check that he was asleep, then she closed the door fully. He got quietly out of bed and went to stand by the window, which he'd left slightly open. As usual she had gone to stand by her window to make the call. She was a fanatic about fresh air and always left the windows open when she could.

Bingo! His plan had worked and he could hear most of what she was saying. She sounded angry and after a while she didn't even try to keep her voice low.

Careless of you, Sandra, he thought and leant against the wall next to the opening, wishing he could also hear what the other person was saying.

'No, Dirk, it has to be today or he'll arrange it himself.'

She was quiet, making little noises as if to encourage this Dirk person to continue, then said grudgingly, 'Yes, that's possible. Go on . . . Hmm.'

A longer silence, then, 'Are you sure that's going to be safe for us?'

More silence, then, 'Well, it's a small risk. Very tiny, really, so we'll do it. No, Dirk, it's that or I'll have to do things his way, which may not suit us half as well. For our plan to work, I need to be in charge, so that we can do what's been arranged at the other end.'

Startled, John wondered whether they were planning to kill him. Had this man always been in the background of her life? Had she been seeing him when she was supposed to be visiting her family in Spain?

When he heard her end the call, he lay down on the bed and feigned sleep. His heart was pounding again. It was getting increasingly unreliable. Had that specialist been telling him the truth about how long he was likely to live? Or was he closer to extinction than he'd thought?

Sometimes he wished his damned heart would just give up trying to beat and put him out of his misery once and for all, but so far it had always steadied again.

So he'd put himself out of his misery, one way or another.

Late that afternoon Sandra said she had to go out.

'Oh? Where?'

'To meet my contact, of course. He rang while you were asleep. With a bit of luck, he'll have booked our flight and have the tickets ready, then we can start our new life.'

'Paper tickets, remember. I want to *see* where we're going.' He didn't trust electronic sign-ins.

'Yes, I told him.' She came to kiss his cheek and cuddle against him for a moment or two. He forced himself to put his arms round her. He didn't want to, though. Now that he knew she didn't care about him, only his money, he wished he could get rid of her this very minute.

He would have thrown her out, only he was determined to pay her back, if it was the last thing he ever did.

'Poor darling. No wonder you're getting cabin fever, stuck in this hotel.'

'Not my favourite way of spending time, I must admit.'

'Fingers and toes crossed that I bring back good news.'

He really did fall asleep as he waited for her to return. It annoyed him that he needed so many naps.

A lot of things annoyed him these days.

When she got back she had a triumphant expression on her face. She fished in her handbag and waved an envelope at him. 'Ta-da!'

'Is that what I think it is?'

'See for yourself.' She held the envelope away from his outstretched hand. 'Just a minute. There's something I have to explain. First, he didn't want us to have an electronic book-in, either, because he's going to dispose of the computer he used.'

'Whatever.'

'Secondly, there's one snag about doing this quickly, John. It turned out we could either go economy class and travel non-stop or go business class and have a lot longer flight, because there's at least one stop en route, sometimes two. My contact thought we'd be more noticeable in business class anyway: smaller group, more service offered on board and so on. They really fuss over you. Anyway, there weren't any business class seats available for over a week, so because you were in such a hurry, he booked us economy class. Is that all right?'

'I suppose so. How long is the non-stop flight?'

'Only about fourteen hours.'

'Not fun, but I can cope. When exactly do we fly out?'

'Day after tomorrow. From Paris. We can fly to Paris early that morning. Easy-peasy.'

'That'll work. I'd rather leave early. I hate hanging round all day waiting for a late flight.' He closed his eyes for a moment, mentally shrugging. What did it matter what sort of seats they booked? He might or might not get on that plane, still wasn't sure how his plans would work out.

He usually fell asleep on planes anyway. He could put up with a little discomfort. It wasn't as if he was a tall man.

When he opened his eyes again, she was looking at him anxiously. 'It was the right choice, Sandra. You look after the actual tickets, but I'll write down the travel times on this hotel notepad so that I don't have to keep asking you about the details.'

'All right. Tomorrow I'll pack for you.'

'No need. I'm only travelling light and I'll be buying warm-weather clothes there, so I'm not taking everything with me. It won't take me more than a few minutes to pack. Just write the times down.'

'OK.' She did that, then came to sit opposite him, leaning back in the chair. 'I'm hungry now. Have you thought what to eat this evening? Do you want to go down to the hotel dining room or have room service?'

'I'd prefer to eat here. Something light. I'm not particularly hungry.'

'Shall I choose?'

'Yes, please.'

They spent a quiet evening, allegedly watching a film on the TV, though John couldn't have said what it was about and he knew he'd dozed off at one point.

He went to bed after it ended, praying that he could keep up the pretence of being a loving husband for long enough to get her where he wanted her.

His current plans were in a shorter time frame than he'd first expected because he felt . . . well, fragile was the only word for it. During last night's tossing and turning, he'd fully taken on board that he didn't have long to live now and accepted it.

Sandra would go out tomorrow, as she did every day, and then he'd email his final request to his friend. Shouldn't be too hard for Edward to make these last arrangements. He'd already agreed to suss things out.

Edward had said the other arrangements would work as John wanted, since they'd be flying out from Paris. The authorities would be only too happy to cooperate.

Of course they would. The most unhappy person would be Sandra. John didn't care about her now.

Chapter Twenty-Four

Lara and Ross spent another quietly busy day. He left her working in her own house, finalising the website for selling his inherited ornaments. She'd started entering stock and had showed him how it appeared on the screen. She had all sorts of talents, seemed to think this was easy stuff.

They left their front and back doors open so that they could nip from one house to the other easily as needed, to confer about some of the special items, but he mostly stayed in his own place. His main job today was washing and dusting the various items as necessary, then photographing them and emailing the photos to her. He knew he was a capable photographer but her praise about the results pleased him greatly.

When she hadn't come next door for food by one o'clock, however, he took it upon himself to interrupt her. 'I insist you take a break now, Lara, and join me in a simple meal. I've only got salad, cheese and crispbreads, but it's a rather good vintage cheddar.'

She smiled and stretched. 'Sorry. I don't always remember to eat when I'm busy.'

'Forgetting to eat is something I never used to do. I enjoyed my food too much. There was a time, though, just after Nonie Jayne and I broke up, when I didn't have much appetite at all and I lost quite a bit of weight.'

'Yet you're the one who reminded me to eat today.'

He stared at her. 'Yes, I did, didn't I? And I remembered because *I* was hungry. You know what, I've suddenly realised that I'm starting to enjoy my food again.'

'There you are! It has to be a sign of you getting better.'

He beamed at her and plonked a kiss on her cheek. 'You're not only a pleasure to be with, you're good for my morale, Lara.'

'Well, you're good for me, too.'

When he kissed her properly, she welcomed it, kissing him back with enthusiasm, then they went next door hand in hand, smiling.

After they'd finished eating, she said, 'Let's sit down in your lovely comfortable chairs for a few minutes and chat.'

'Good idea. These are great chairs, aren't they?' He snuggled down and she followed suit.

Lara was woken half an hour later by the vibration of her phone, which was still attached to her belt. She found a message from a friend, giving some information she'd asked for: the name of the doctor who'd treated Rowena's ME differently and successfully. *Not cheap but worth it!* the message ended.

She sat staring at the words. Ross didn't seem to be short of money, but would he give this a try? She hoped so. Rowena was no one's fool and if *she* recommended this doctor, Lara was sure he wouldn't be 'selling snake oil', as Ross's doctor had apparently said about all alternative ways of treating ME.

She'd have to wait for the right moment to broach this to Ross and try to persuade him to have a go. What had he got to lose, after all? The treatment was very gentle and carefully worked out.

She looked sideways but he hadn't stirred, so she tiptoed out and went back to work. A nap was unusual for her, but it seemed to have re-energised her today.

As she was walking back into her own house, however, she shivered suddenly, feeling as if someone was staring at her. She stopped and spun round, scanning the grounds of the hotel and the other buildings in the village.

Two men were working on a detached house that was nearly finished, but they weren't looking in her direction. They were holding an animated conversation as they went in and out, and were carrying what looked like equipment for electrical wiring and things like plug sockets.

She couldn't see anyone else nearby, though there were a few cars in the hotel car park, as usual.

Ah, she was just imagining things, she told herself and continued into her house. She tried to dismiss what she'd felt, but didn't manage that. You could sometimes tell when you were being watched and just let anyone try to tell her different. She'd definitely had that shivery spine feeling today.

She started work but found it hard to concentrate. Why would anyone be keeping watch on them? Was it to do with the prowler? Hadn't it been enough to chase him away? Was he still planning a burglary?

Well, if anyone tried to steal the few things she had left, she'd use the methods she'd been taught in a self-defence course. She'd thought it a waste of time, but she'd proved to be quite good at it. Now, with so few people nearby, the memory of it gave her more confidence.

Ross joined her a couple of hours later as she was about to make a cup of tea. He paused to look over his shoulder before coming into the house and joining her in the kitchen. 'I timed that well, didn't I? You're obviously about to take a break. I was going to invite you round for a coffee.'

'I'll make you one, though it won't be fancy.' She stopped with the spoon in mid-air because he was peering out of the window now, still looking towards the hotel car park.

'What's the matter, Ross?'

'I know it sounds silly but I felt as though someone was watching me.'

'Wow! I had exactly the same feeling as I walked across, only I couldn't see anyone.'

'Neither can I. I think we'd better be very careful indeed for the next night or two, though. Will you be all right this afternoon if I nip out and buy some security equipment? I want to be able to make a very loud noise if anyone tries to break into the houses. And it wouldn't hurt to have a couple of powerful torches to hand.'

'I'll be fine, Ross, but make sure you lock up your house properly before you go.' She opened the jar of coffee but he held one hand over his mug.

'Hold that coffee till I get back. I'll only be half an hour at most.'

'All right.' She made herself a cup of drinking chocolate, checked again that both front and back doors were locked, and went back to work.

Over an hour later, she nipped downstairs again to put the kettle on for Ross, wondering what was keeping him.

While she was getting the milk out of the fridge, her phone rang. She looked at the caller ID and it was Donald Metcalf, so she answered it immediately. She never knew whether to be pleased or annoyed by his phone calls, which seemed mainly to report a lack of progress.

'Hi, Lara. Have you a minute?'

'Yes, Donald.'

'I wondered if you knew anything about Sandra, your ex-financial adviser's wife?'

'Not really, no. I only ever met her at the office and she didn't start there till two – or was it three? – years ago. She was always pleasant enough, but not chatty. Why do you ask?'

'We've been trying to trace her – you know, previous job, family history, education and so on. Only we can't find any verifiable records.'

'But she must have had the necessary paperwork to get married to John!'

'She had some paperwork, but when you look more closely, the details appear to have been generated out of nowhere.'

'Good heavens! And she appeared so friendly and – and *mumsy*.'

'Mumsy?'

'Yes, like everyone's favourite aunt. Sorry. It's one of my grandma's words.'

'Well, we can't even find the exact date at which she started working for Crichton, because they destroyed their records before they left.'

'Ah. I may be able to help you there. I'm pretty obsessive about keeping a paper log of what I do. I even keep the scribbled-down names of the people I've dealt with on the phone.'

'Could you check that now, do you think, and get back to me as soon as possible?'

'Yes, of course. I have a deep personal interest in tracking those two down.'

'I bet you do. So do we. I think this information may lead us to something.'

'I sincerely hope so. I'll text the info to you. Shouldn't take me long.'

She went upstairs to the room she was using to store things she didn't need at this stage and checked her business diaries from previous years. She'd been trying to persuade herself to throw them away and was glad now that she hadn't. It just went to show you never knew what you'd need.

It took her only a few minutes to find the date Sandra had first appeared as the secretary at Crichton's place of business and she sent it to Donald immediately.

After that, she didn't think about why he might want it because she was concentrating on the website. She was going to activate some of it tonight, to see how it went. She'd get Ross to pretend to be a customer for her and 'buy' an item.

When Nonie Jayne arrived at Edward's house, the housekeeper had studied her thoroughly, then nodded and said, 'Do call me Freda.'

Mrs Bryant was a stern-looking woman, slightly overweight but tending towards muscular rather than fat, and somehow she radiated power, just as Edward did. Strange, that. It felt like calling the Queen of England 'Lizzie' to call this woman by her first name, but the invitation felt like a command.

The driver carried in the luggage and deposited it in a luxurious bedroom with an en suite shower room.

Freda saw him out, then came to find her employer's guest again. 'Now, how about something to eat? Edward won't be back for a while, so it'll just be you.' Another stare, then, 'I'd guess you watch your weight carefully. You'd better tell me exactly what sort of meals you want.'

'You mean I can choose?' People usually insisted on piling her plate high.

A near smile creased Freda's face for a moment. 'Of course you can. Easiest way. Save me wasting time on preparing food that you're just going to stir around the plate and then I'd have to throw it away. I can't abide waste.'

'I'm not a big eater, I must admit.'

They came to an agreement about salads, grilled fish or chicken, and berries or other low-calorie fruit for dessert, then Freda asked if she wanted to rest after such a disturbed night.

'What time will Edward be coming back today?'

'I never know, but I'd guess not till much later, perhaps not at all. He's dealing with some rather important business for a friend, so you might as well have a rest, sit and watch TV or go out for a walk. I'll be here all day to let you in again.'

'I think I'd rather stay here till I'm sure it's safe. I'll have a lie-down, though. I didn't sleep last night. But I'd be grateful if you'd let me know when Edward returns.'

'I can do that.' She indicated an intercom. 'Just press that red button if you want to speak to me or you need anything.'

Nonie Jayne got out her toiletries and a couple of outfits, which she hung in the wardrobe so they'd lose their creases, but as she didn't know what was likely to happen to her till she'd spoken to Edward, she left the unpacking at that.

She took her time about studying herself in the mirror. The tiredness showed. 'Well, Nonie Jayne, what have you got yourself into now?'

With a shrug she lay down and let herself rest. You always looked better when you were relaxed. And she wanted to look her best tonight.

Unusually for her, she fell asleep and didn't wake up until the intercom sounded. 'Hello.'

'Edward's just phoned. He'll be back shortly and see you for dinner at six.'

'Fine. Thanks for letting me know.'

She went to take a leisurely bath, then got ready to dazzle him.

She hoped she was doing the right thing.

Edward was rather unpredictable compared to most men she'd met. She couldn't work out whether that was good or bad.

He was waiting for her in the beautiful sitting room, dressed casually but in clothes that must have cost a fortune.

'Thank you for saving me, Edward.'

'My pleasure. I'm only going to ask one thing of you in return.'

She tensed up. Oh no! Had she misjudged him?

'I want you always to tell me the truth, whether it's about your past life or about everything else.' He grinned. 'The whole truth. I'm a man who enjoys such tales, and I *don't* enjoy boring or predictable people. Nor am I burdened by useless morals or rules for living. If I have any rule at all, it's to hurt no one, unless they try to hurt me first or they deserve punishing.'

She stared at him, head on one side, letting his words sink in. 'You mean that, don't you?'

'I always mean what I say when talking to friends, Nonie Jayne. Always. And I'm hoping you and I will become good friends.'

She abandoned the attempt to speak elegantly and let the traces of her original accent show. 'Well, it'll be a relief to stop pretending, I must say.'

'Attagirl! Is that how you speak naturally? Good. I like it better.'

'I'm glad.'

'There's just one other thing before we start chatting: a friend of mine is in trouble and needs help so if I get a phone call, I'll need to answer it immediately. He doesn't have long to live, so it'll probably be the last thing he asks of me.'

'Do you always help people?'

'Only when they're close friends or when I find them amusing.'

She frowned. 'I'd guess that means you find me amusing.'

'I'm afraid I do. In a nice way.'

She risked telling him the truth. 'I don't always understand why people laugh at me and I haven't got a good sense of humour, so I don't know if I can amuse you on purpose.'

'Don't even try. Just be yourself. Sometimes it's life and how people behave that make me laugh, not silly and usually predictable jokes. Now, let's go and sit down to dinner. You can start by telling me how you met your first husband and nudged him into marrying you.'

Why not? She had very little to lose, couldn't see Edward as a potential husband anyway, because he was far too clever for her. But it'd be nice to have him as a friend. She didn't really have any close friends and sometimes wished she had.

'Well . . .'

Just after Freda had served dessert, which included a dish of berries without cream for the guest, Edward's phone rang. He had it on the table beside him so was able to answer it immediately.

He did more listening than speaking, but ended up saying, 'Yes, I can do that. I'm sorry it's come to this, John. I've enjoyed our friendship.'

He put the phone down and stared at it so sadly for a moment or two that Nonie Jayne couldn't help asking, 'Bad news?'

'I'm afraid so. That was the friend I told you about and he's definitely dying. He needs my help about some unfinished business. Will you excuse me for a while, my dear? When you've finished your meal, please wait for me in the sitting room. It'll only take me an hour or so to get things started.'

And he was gone without pausing for her answer.

Nonie Jayne ate a few berries for their anti-oxidant

content. So good for the skin. Then she picked up her fizzy water and wandered into the next room, taking her time to stroll round it and study the beautiful things there, including looking at the makers' marks underneath the ornaments. The paintings all seemed to be originals.

There wasn't a clutter of things like her ex had had in that stupid old house, but each object was displayed elegantly to give the maximum pleasure.

She loved the room. Edward had exquisite taste.

Chapter Twenty-Five

Donald picked up the phone and whistled softly as he looked at the caller ID. 'Long time since you've called this number, Edward. I thought you'd retired.'

'Semi-retired. I've done odd jobs for certain people here and there over the past few years. Now, please listen carefully, my friend, because this is very important to me. I'm guessing that it'll be important to you as well, but you won't have time to check my facts if you want to be sure of catching your man, so you'll have to trust me. It'll need very speedy action.'

'Go on.'

'You're looking for John Crichton, I gather.'

'Yes. You have news of him?'

'Better than that. I have a message from him for you. This is what he wants you to do . . .'

There was dead silence when he'd finished explaining.

'Are you sure? I can't understand why he'd do this.'

'He's found out that he's got heart problems and is

dying, plus he's been betrayed by the woman he loved.'

'You're quite sure this isn't a farrago of lies to divert our attention.'

'I'm utterly certain. I've known him since we met at university. I'd stake my life on the truth of it. John went astray for a while and that upset me greatly, but he's come back into the good guys' fold – as much as he can, given the circumstances.'

Donald whistled softly. 'Then it's a gift from the gods.'

'A gift from John, rather. Let's say he's settling certain debts before he leaves the stage. Can you sort it out for him?'

'Can I ever! We'll have over a day to arrange it, after all.'

'I'll tell him you've agreed.'

'It might help if you gave us his phone number, Edward.'

'No. Sorry, but I've given him my word that I'll allow him to do this the way he wants.'

A few moments of silence, then, 'Very well. I'll get on to it straight away.'

'Um. One more thing. I'd be grateful if you let me know how it works out . . . afterwards. As soon as you can after it happens, anyway. That's all the payment I shall need. He used to be a good friend, close as a brother.'

'Yes, of course.'

Edward ended the call, then walked slowly and heavily back into the sitting room.

She took one look at him and asked gently, 'More bad news?'

'Same bad news, next stage confirmed. Look, I've enjoyed your company tonight, Nonie Jayne, but I think I'd like to go to bed now. And I'll not be available for most of tomorrow. Would you like to go shopping?'

'I'm saving my money at the moment.'

'I'll leave you something to spend, to make up for being such a bad host. I do want you to stay.'

She looked at him, then walked across to stand on tiptoe and kiss his cheek. 'Thank you. I'd like to stay. I hope you get better news tomorrow.'

'Yes, well, that's a nice thought, my dear, but not possible.'

He watched her go, heard her bedroom door close, then poured himself a large cognac and raised the glass to his friend before taking a sip.

He wondered how John was feeling tonight, hoped that whatever had been arranged happened quickly.

When John got up on the morning they were leaving for Paris, he found it a struggle to appear anything like normal. He didn't fool Sandra, of course. He shouldn't even have tried.

'Are you well enough to fly?' she asked, watching as he tried to force down a few bites of croissant.

'I'm not looking forward to it, but I don't think my health will improve till we get to our destination, so I don't want to cancel.'

'You're probably right. How about I book you a wheelchair for getting you across the airports?'

'Why didn't I think of that? Good idea.'

'It's fortunate that we can fly straight to Charles de Gaulle Airport from here and then on to Buenos Aires.'

'Yes, isn't it?'

John was grateful for the wheelchair, couldn't have managed without it.

Once they'd taken their seats on the first plane, he leant back and closed his eyes. After a few moments he realised she was speaking to him.

'Are you all right, dear?'

He forced a smile – well, as near to a smile as he could manage. 'Yes. Don't fuss, Sandra. I'm conserving my energy.'

He closed his eyes for the rest of the short flight to avoid having to chat to her, terrified that he'd give something away.

He shuddered as he was wheeled across Charles de Gaulle Airport. He'd never liked places like this. It was so crowded and voices echoed round them in so many different languages and accents that it made his head spin.

It seemed an appropriate sort of place for today's events to play out, though. He was feeling increasingly detached from his surroundings in one sense.

And from her.

They were directed to a landing gate right at the end of one concourse, which made people around him grumble that planes to South America didn't usually set off from here.

'Sorry, sir, we had an emergency elsewhere,' an official told him.

'This is a long walk,' Sandra muttered. 'Are you sure you're all right to continue, John?'

'Yes.'

'I could ask the attendant to—'

'Just leave it. I'm fine. He doesn't understand much English anyway.'

Indeed, the man pushing the wheelchair had only responded in monosyllables and seemed in a dour mood. People like him were usually more helpful, hoping for a tip.

Oh, what did it matter? *Just get it over*, John thought to himself. *Just get it over and done with*.

When they reached the check-in point, he thought there seemed to be more staff in attendance than usual and several gendarmes were standing by, but none of them seemed to be looking at them.

Had his friend not succeeded in passing on the information? If he hadn't, John didn't know what he'd do about the situation.

The attendant pushed his wheelchair to a shorter queue of other people needing assistance at the far end and started chatting to an official in some language John didn't recognise.

Slowly they edged towards the head of the queue, where people turned to one side and went behind a partition. For the first time they caught a glimpse of what they were queuing to do. Not just to get on to the plane.

Thank you, Edward! he thought.

He heard Sandra gasp behind him and move closer. She gripped his shoulder tightly and bent down to whisper, 'It's one of the new facial recognition systems! I didn't think there were any in operation for this route. Quick! Pretend to be taken ill. We'll have to find another way to get there. We'll probably be on record, so we can't risk doing this.'

He grabbed her hand and tried to keep her from pulling away. 'We destroyed all the photos. We can't be on their records.'

'I'm not risking it.' She raised her voice to a shout and clutched her stomach. 'I feel bad! I'm going to be sick. Where's the nearest restroom?'

John wasn't strong enough to keep hold of her and she pulled away from him. He watched her start pushing her way towards the exit, but she had only taken a couple of steps when another official moved forward to intercept her.

People were staring at them. *Let them stare.* He didn't care about anything, except making sure she didn't escape.

'Please, *madame*, follow your husband.'

To John's relief, the official was strong enough to stop her getting away and she soon stopped struggling.

The attendant had pushed John towards the facial recognition equipment by now and there a woman took over, explaining how to look at the machine.

He did as they asked, didn't care any more, could hear Sandra still making a fuss nearby.

As he stared at the screen, the equipment suddenly started making a harsh beeping noise and he found he now had two armed men standing by him.

'Monsieur Crichton, is it not?' one asked.

'Yes.' He turned to point towards Sandra. 'And that's my wife. Don't – let her – get away.'

The last thing he was aware of was her yelling, 'Damn you, John Crichton!'

He was, indeed, damned.

Then it seemed as if everything in his body was sagging, crumbling, and the world around him was fading.

He hoped he had done something towards atoning for his sins, he really did.

Then a huge wave of blackness swallowed him and he gave himself up to it gladly.

* * *

On the morning of the day of reckoning for his friend, Edward couldn't settle. He had breakfast with Nonie Jayne, who didn't bother him with empty chatter. He hadn't expected her to be this sensitive. She'd surprised him a few times. He liked her more now she'd stopped pretending, far more than he'd expected to.

'Thank you for a peaceful meal, my dear,' he said.

'I can see how sad you are, Edward. You'll tell me if there's anything I can do to help?'

'I will. But the next act of this farce is out of my hands, I'm afraid.' He glanced involuntarily at the clock.

'It's happening today?'

'Yes. All I can do is wait for news. Now, let's talk about something more cheerful. Did you enjoy the shopping yesterday? I forgot to ask you.'

'I enjoyed walking round the shops, but I didn't buy anything apart from a couple of magazines. Here.' She held out the envelope containing the money.

'Keep it.'

'You don't need to buy me, Edward. I value your friendship more than your money.' She pushed the envelope into his hands.

'I think we might be on our way towards becoming good friends.' He put the envelope into his pocket and pushed his chair back. 'Nothing will happen until later. What would you like to do in the meantime?'

'I can sit and read, here or in my room, whichever you'd prefer. You don't need to entertain me.'

'I have some business to sort out this morning. It'd be good if you joined me for lunch, then sat with me this afternoon. Will you do that? I'll read the newspaper and you can read or watch TV or do whatever else you like. Several of today's newspapers will be around, if you want to read them. Just ask Freda.'

She smiled. 'I'll watch TV this morning in my room, then sit with you and read this afternoon. As long as you don't make snide remarks about what I'm reading.'

'Oh? What do you read?'

She gazed at him defiantly. 'Romances. I like the happy endings.'

'Not had much romance in your own life, eh, Nonie Jayne?'

'No.'

'Well, I'll do my best not to give you an unhappy time here and you can read whatever you like in front of me. I prefer fantasy novels myself. Imaginary planets, nothing to do with this world. I won't laugh at your books if you don't laugh at mine.'

She held out her hand and he clasped it in his for a minute. 'It's a deal.'

The call he'd been waiting for didn't come through until that evening. Edward took a deep breath and picked his personal phone up when it rang.

'Donald Metcalf here.'

'Just a minute. I'll go into the next room.' He walked into his home office. 'Right. You can talk freely now.'

'Your friend was stopped at Charles de Gaulle Airport this morning, thanks to the information you gave us. His wife was with him and was also stopped.'

'Good. It's what he wanted. How is he?'

One of those short silences that said there was difficult news to come. 'Just tell me, Donald.'

'I'm afraid Crichton died at the scene. He had a heart attack. There was no struggle of any sort; it just happened, and quickly, too.'

'Better that way. He was expecting it to happen soon.'

When the call ended, Edward sat staring into space for a long time. There were still things to be done, because John had made his wishes very clear. But not till tomorrow.

It took Edward a few minutes to pull himself together, then he went back to join Nonie Jayne.

She looked across at him, her eyes assessing.

'Do you ever drink?' he asked.

'Sometimes. But not more than half a glass.'

'Join me in some fine old cognac and we'll drink to my friend, who died today.'

'Oh. I'm sorry.'

'It was better that way, given the circumstances, but it still hurts to lose him. I've known him since we were schoolboys together. Let's sit on the couch. I need to hold your hand.'

He didn't bother with the cognac, after all, because he needed her human warmth more. He sat down next to her and put one arm round her shoulders.

She put her nearest hand into his.

'You feel young and full of life.'

'You're not young, but you seem full of life too, Edward.'

'Not tonight. And I have a rather difficult job to do tomorrow for my friend. Will you come with me? I need to do this in person.'

'If that's what you want.'

'I do. Very much.' He looked at her. 'Going to stay around here for a while?'

She took a moment to answer, studying his face, then nodded. 'If I'm invited, I'd love to. I enjoy your company, Edward. And I'm not just saying that. I don't have to pretend with you, which is so rare.'

'Well, one good thing came out of all this, then. I'd been feeling a bit lonely. And I'm too old to pretend.'

He didn't speak for a while, just sat and cuddled her.

It helped, he thought. A little. It was always hard to lose someone.

And he couldn't help thinking he might find her useful if he did any more of these little fact-finding jobs for the government. Who'd suspect an old fool with a younger woman on his arm from being anything but what he appeared?

In the meantime, she was there for him, and whatever happened between them in the future, he was grateful for that today.

Chapter Twenty-Six

When he eventually judged it a suitable time to go into the hotel and ask to see Ms Larson, Gil was furious to be told that she had checked out.

'When?'

'I'm afraid I can't give you any details, sir.'

He went into the bar and was told it was only open to residents, so returned to his car, feeling ravenously hungry now.

When a security guy stopped for the second time to study his vehicle and note down the number, he decided it'd be prudent to leave the car park. Good thing this vehicle wasn't registered to him. He grinned. Wouldn't the owner be surprised when she returned from her holidays to find it missing?

There was a small lake nearby. He'd go to the nearest village and buy something to eat, then park there and stay till dark.

He couldn't decide whether Nonie Jayne was still at the

hotel, in hiding, and the man at the desk was lying for her or whether she'd got away somehow. Stupid bitch!

He'd have to give up on her, dammit, but one thing he was not giving up on was getting hold of something he could sell. After all, he had his special tools with him. If only the owner of that end house would just go out, it should be a piece of cake to break in and snatch a few things. Those silver pieces he'd seen through the window ought to bring in enough to tide him over for a while.

He couldn't see half as much of what was going on in that new development near the hotel from the car park of Penny Lake – stupid name for a lake – so he went to sit on a bench which had a better view. As it was starting to get dark, he saw there was no one nearby and used his binoculars a few times to check the houses.

'Aha!' His luck had changed. The third time he checked, he was just in time to see the car that had been parked outside the end house pulling out. He hadn't been able to see it till it moved. It drove across towards the hotel but he couldn't see where it went then from where he was sitting. Out of the development, he hoped. He got up and ran towards his car for his tools.

He'd have to do the job quickly, though. Who knew when the car would return.

He flung off his jacket and closed the boot. He was dressed as a jogger now – well, more or less – with a knapsack on his back.

He started running round the lake. Unfortunately he had to slow down when he started to puff and pant.

'Got to pace yourself,' another jogger called out

cheerfully as he loomed out of the darkness under one of the lamps along the path and carried on past.

'Yes. I'm finding that out.'

The man continued to jog round the lake, but Gil stopped for a moment, chest heaving. Damn! He hadn't been able to jog with his hood up, because it would have looked wrong. The fellow might remember his face, though.

To his relief, Gil managed to find a place among the heaps of building materials near the unfinished new-build house to check the situation out. He was delighted to see that there were no lights on in the end house now, except the one in the kitchen. He circled round to the rear patio carefully, able to see through the window and check that there was actually no one in the kitchen.

Taking care to make very little noise, he fiddled with the lock on the back door, cursing when he realised the sods had put bolts in place. Well, that wasn't going to stop him. He used his cutting tool to get access via the smaller window next to the door, and a fiddly job it was too.

He was just climbing into the house when noise burst out around him, nearly deafening him, it was screeching so loudly.

An alarm system. Damn them!

He tried to get out again quickly but his sleeve got caught on a piece of glass and the sharp edge slashed his arm. Blood poured out and he felt sick, couldn't move for a moment or two.

When Ross set up the alarm system, he needed Lara's help to finish the job, since the instructions which came with it were rather confusing. He watched ruefully as she quickly solved the problem. 'Not the best person at electronic stuff, am I? I think you're far more skilful than I am.'

'I've had to be. I've been on my own for a while. Though there's not as much fixing needed in rented accommodation so I have only patchy skills.'

Then there was a problem with the website which further delayed them and it was getting dark by the time Lara had sorted it out.

They had been thinking of going up to the hotel for tea but didn't like to leave the houses unguarded.

'How about I phone them and ask if they could do us a takeaway?' she suggested. 'I still don't have enough food stocks to cater easily for guests.'

'And I've not bothered to buy much in. I was going to do it today but it seemed more important to get an alarm set up.'

The hotel was as obliging as ever, so she said she'd take the car in order to get the food back while he was clearing up his tools. 'You can set the table when you've finished.'

Ross was about to get out the plates when he thought he heard something next door, so he switched off the radio and listened carefully.

There it was again. He *had* heard something! It could have been a small animal or that prowler returning. Only, if he switched the lights on at the back to get a better look, he'd warn the fellow.

He ran up the stairs and peered out of the back bedroom window. There was enough light to see the silhouette of a man. Oh hell, the prowler had come back and was breaking into Lara's house.

Ross hesitated, not sure what to do. He'd never been

good at fighting and doubted he'd be able to capture the burglar on his own.

Then he saw that the man was having difficulty getting in through the kitchen window. That settled it. With a bit of luck, the new alarm would do its job and he could catch the man half in, half out.

Ross ran downstairs and carefully unlocked the patio doors of his own house. At that moment the alarm went off next door. It made a hell of a noise and the burglar let out a loud yell.

He ran along to Lara's as the man was trying to wriggle back out of the window. But it looked like he'd caught one sleeve on some jagged glass. No, not just his sleeve, the fleshy part of his forearm.

By the time Ross got to him, blood was pouring out of the cut. Ugh. It looked like black oil in the semi-darkness.

He grabbed the man, who began to struggle. The arm was slippery with blood and it was hard to keep hold.

Then someone grabbed the man's other arm and he found himself sharing the task of capturing the intruder with Cindy.

And still the alarm was screeching loudly into the night.

Suddenly other people were yelling too. The hotel's security man pounded along the back patios and grabbed the intruder, who didn't seem to be offering much resistance now.

'I've got him. Stay still, you!'

The second security man, who was rather plump, puffed along to join them and Cindy stepped back.

Then she saw the blood on Ross's hands in the light from the houses. 'Where are you hurt, Ross?'

'What?' He looked down to see that he was covered in blood. It was everywhere. 'No, it's his blood not mine. He must have lost a lot.'

Even as he spoke the man sagged, looking as if he was about to faint.

'We don't want him bleeding to death. I've done some first aid.' She tore her fancy silk scarf from round her neck and used it to put a tourniquet on the burglar's arm.

The fellow didn't attempt to resist, but he groaned and whimpered a lot.

By that time Lara had driven back from the hotel and come running through her house to join them. 'What happened?'

'Ross caught an intruder,' Cindy said.

He gave a shaky laugh. 'The intruder caught himself on the glass and if Cindy hadn't joined me, I'd not have been able to hold on to him. Then these gentlemen took over.'

'Thank goodness. And you're all right?'

'Yes, love. I'm fine.'

An hour or more had passed by the time one set of police had taken the burglar away for medical attention and another set had taken preliminary statements from Lara, Cindy, Ross and the security men.

Then a handyman came from the hotel to fix a piece of wood across the broken window.

By the time the last of the various outsiders had left, the food was cold and had congealed into an unattractive mess.

Ross looked at himself in disgust. There was something revolting about being covered in another person's blood. 'I need to shower and change.'

'Put the bloodstained clothes to soak in cold water in the bath or you'll not get the stains out,' Cindy said at once.

'While he does that, why don't you join me for a drink, Cindy,' Lara said.

'Good idea.' She winked as Ross went next door to his own house. 'I'll leave you two in peace once he comes back.'

Lara could feel herself flushing. 'There's no need for that.'

'Oh, I think there is. I've noticed the way he looks at you, and you at him.'

'Is it that obvious?'

'Yep. And why not? You're both free of entanglements, aren't you? Go for it, honey. Life's too short to waste a minute.'

By the time Ross had showered and come down to join them, Cindy was pouring Lara a second glass of wine and the two women were chuckling about something.

'Here are some potato crisps to keep you going till I can be bothered to reheat the food.' Lara tossed him a small packet.

'I'll go once I've finished my drink,' Cindy said.

That made both women giggle.

Ross took a welcome sip of the glass of wine Lara passed him. 'You look surprisingly relaxed for someone who's just helped catch a burglar, Cindy. He didn't hurt you?'

'No. Who'd have thought it, eh, me helping to catch a criminal? And you're quite the hero of the hour.'

'He'd have got away but for you, Cindy. I couldn't have held him on my own.'

'I'll drink to my two heroes, then!' Lara raised her glass.

After their neighbour had finished her wine, Ross escorted her home and came back to find Lara smiling lazily at him.

He grinned at her. 'I'd say you're nicely relaxed now.'

'I can't deny it. I'm a cheap drunk.'

She looked so flushed and pretty, he bent down to kiss her. Before he knew it, she had stood up and moved into his arms. The world blurred around them in the most enjoyable way and suddenly she began pulling him towards the stairs.

'It's time,' she said as they kissed their way into her bedroom.

'I agree with that. As long as you don't regret it in the morning. You're not exactly sober.'

'No. But we've been working towards this for a while, don't you think?'

He held back for a moment, needing to say it first, not wanting this to seem merely a physical encounter. 'I love you, Lara. I haven't dared say it before.'

She stopped and her look said it before she spoke the words back to him. 'I love you too, Ross.' Then she laughed. 'I swore I'd never love anyone again.'

'So did I.'

'Just goes to show how little attention fate pays to what we say or do.'

'Thank goodness.'

After that they didn't speak for a long time.

In the morning, they lay in bed chatting for a while. 'Can you put up with a guy who has ME?' he asked suddenly.

'I'd be happier about it if you'd try other approaches to getting better. I know your specialist put you off them but I got the name of her doctor from my friend. She recovered, though it was a slow process.'

'But—'

'Surely it can't hurt to *try* some of the more sensible alternatives? This isn't the lunatic fringe; it's a group of doctors with different views about how to treat it.'

He looked at her. 'I hardly dare believe anyone can help.'

'It isn't guaranteed, but if you do nothing, then you're guaranteed *not* to get much better.'

'Very well.'

She stopped with the mug halfway to her mouth. 'You mean that?'

'Yes.'

'Can I ask why? Last time you told me in no uncertain terms that you weren't going down any other paths.'

'It's because of you. I was going to look around for further help without telling you, see what I could find out, but if your friend has already tried this approach, we can start there.'

She dumped the mug hastily on the bedside table, then flung her arms round him.

He held her close. 'The ME just didn't seem to matter after the Nonie Jayne fiasco. I felt such an idiot for falling for her. I was depressed and angry at myself. Meeting you seems to have woken up the old me.'

'You must have started getting better already to think like that.'

He stared at her in a frozen moment of surprise. 'You know, I never thought of that.'

'Think of it now and cling on to hope. You're still on the right side of the grass, after all.'

He smiled at her small joke. 'You're so good for me. Nonie Jayne was very bad for me. I don't think she was a bad person, but we made chalk and cheese look like twins! I wonder where she is now?'

'Do you care?'

'Not about her, no, not at all, but about what she's doing, yes. I'm hoping desperately that she's not going to appeal against the finalisation of our finances so that I can get my decree absolute. Surely I'd have heard by now if she'd done that?'

'I should think so. Now, stop talking about your ex and let's grab something to eat.'

After breakfast Lara said suddenly, 'I'll have hardly any money, you know, but I can get a job.'

'No need. I suggest that when they've finished filming we move back into my family home and start culling the ornaments there. It's one thing to save family treasures, quite another to overload yourself with them.' He pulled her closer. 'The money doesn't matter at all, Lara.'

'I'm still annoyed to have been cheated but you're right. The money isn't the important thing in my life now; you are.'

She laughed and danced round the room, waving her arms about. 'I feel freed, somehow.'

'Good.' He looked out of the window. 'Oh, oh! Your ex has just drawn up outside.'

She groaned. 'Not again. Ross, can we tell him about us?'

'That we're engaged, you mean?'

'You're sure it's that formal.'

'Hell yes! You're not wriggling out of it now.'

'I don't want to.'

She went to answer the door and Ross came to stand behind her.

Guy looked from one to the other. 'I was going to suggest we take Minnie for a walk this afternoon but I think I'm interrupting something.'

'You can play with Minnie on your own today. And yes, you are interrupting rather an important moment. You see, Ross has just proposed to me.'

'Oh. Congratulations.' He gave her a rueful smile. 'I'd better warn you, then, that I've signed on to have a house built here at Penny Lake, but I'll try not to get under your feet.'

'Goodness. I thought you were settled in that huge flat.'

'It was a lonely place to live.'

'Well, I'm sure you'll find it friendly here. Cindy seems to be managing the neighbourhood social life and I guarantee that she won't leave you to sit your own all the time. We shan't be living here long-term, anyway. Ross has a house a few miles away.'

'I see. Well, I'm sure you'll be happy. You already look . . . together.'

'Yes. I think we will.'

She leant against Ross and they watched Guy walk away. 'He looks lonely. I feel sorry for him.'

'Well, ask Cindy to find him a wife. She'll sort out his love life if anyone can. I think that woman could sort anything out.'

Lara gurgled with sudden laughter. 'He won't know what's hit him. He's more used to calling the shots, but she's like a steamroller, isn't she, gentle but inexorable?'

* * *

The following day, Lara and Ross got up late, then lingered over a full English breakfast at the hotel before deciding to get back to work.

As they were walking out, a luxury car drew up and Ross clutched Lara's arm in shock. 'It's my ex. What the hell does she want now?'

'I think we're about to find out.'

The car door was flung open and an elderly man got out, beckoning to them imperatively. 'Ms Perryman, have you got a minute?'

The man turned to help Nonie Jayne out of the car and to Ross's astonishment she linked her arm in the stranger's, clinging tightly and looking on edge. He didn't think he'd ever seen her look so nervous. How strange.

'I'm Edward Charsley. I have some news for Ms Perryman. It's good news, don't worry.'

'Oh?'

'Look, do you think we could share a coffee in the hotel so that we can talk about it in comfort? Nonie Jayne and I have just driven down from London and we've some other calls to make today.'

Ross was scowling at his ex. 'If you're here with a new lawyer, I don't see why he needs to speak to Ms Perryman. And I'm *not* paying you anything else.'

'I'm not asking for anything else, Ross. I've moved on. Edward isn't my lawyer.'

'Ah. Found another old fool to marry. Well, good luck to you both.'

Lara put her hand over his mouth and before he could jerk away, she said firmly, 'Let's go inside and find out what's going on. You're jumping to conclusions, Ross.'

Edward had his arm round Nonie Jayne. 'He certainly is. I don't consider myself a fool and I'm glad to see you're a woman of sense, Ms Perryman. Shall we?' He gestured to the hotel.

Lara grabbed Ross's hand and tugged. 'Come on, you. Let's find out what's going on before we dive into action.'

He muttered something under his breath but went along with her.

When they were seated at a corner table in the bar, Edward took charge. 'Nonie Jayne owes you an apology, Ross. She was greedy about money, but I don't think she'll be bothering you again, so can we let the matter drop? She's here today only as my companion. And my business is with Ms Perryman, not you – though from the looks of you two, it's probably as well you're here with her to hear what I have to say.'

Lara kept hold of Ross's hand. 'You seem to have summed up the situation nicely. Call me Lara, please.'

'Lara it is. And I'm Edward.'

The waiter came up to take their order and when he'd left them, Edward said abruptly, 'I'm here with news of John Crichton. He was a friend of mine and I was very sorry when he stole the money from you and other people, Lara.'

'So was I.'

'He's dead now, a heart attack. But before he died, he found out he'd been duped by Sandra and arranged for most of the money he'd stolen to be returned.'

Lara stared at him open-mouthed. 'Returned?'

'Yes.'

'How much of it?'

'Nearly all. Probably about ninety per cent.'

She tugged a handkerchief out and blew her nose but couldn't stop tears of utter relief flowing for a moment or two.

Ross put his arm round her and everyone waited till she'd calmed down again.

'I'm sorry. I don't usually – give way to my emotions.'

'Well, it's rather an important piece of news, isn't it? I'm afraid you won't get the money for a while. The police will have to ensure that it's all dealt with properly. If you need help till then, I can lend you some.'

She shook her head. 'I'm fine.'

'That's good.' He explained how John Crichton had been set up and exploited in his loneliness and how his second wife was now 'helping' the police.

Lara looked at him in puzzlement. 'Why did you come to tell me in person?'

'John asked me to. He wanted me to check that people were coping and help them if necessary until the legalities were sorted out. He also wanted me to tender his apologies. He was very sorry in the end for what he'd done.'

'Thank you for coming. Is there anything else we need to take care of?'

'Not as long as you're going to be all right.'

'Oh, I will be. But I think I'd like to be on my own for a while to get used to the changes this will bring.'

Ross stood up and scowled at his ex. 'Best of luck with Nonie Jayne, Edward. You'll need it.' He followed Lara out, running to catch her up.

When she didn't speak, he didn't either, just walked beside her.

At the houses he stopped. 'Want company or not?'

'Yes, please. Just to be together. I thought I was used to all the changes but now it's changed again.'

'Good changes this time, though.'

She smiled at him. 'Yes, but you know what? You're the best change of all, Ross, so much more important than the money.'

ANNA JACOBS is the author of over eighty novels and is addicted to storytelling. She grew up in Lancashire, emigrated to Australia in the 1970s and writes stories set in both countries. She loves to return to England regularly to visit her family and soak up the history. She has two grown-up daughters and a grandson, and lives with her husband in a spacious home near the Swan Valley, the earliest wine-growing area in Western Australia. Her house is crammed with thousands of books.

annajacobs.com